Thirty minutes and two glasses of champagne later, Riley didn't fear being up in the hot-air balloon quite so much.

She smirked when Asher caught her eye as she reached for the champagne bottle. "This is really unexpected," she said as she wiggled the bottle.

"Don't forget the strawberries," he urged.

"Is this the way you persuade all those big names you sign?" She swirled a strawberry through the whipped cream while posing the question.

Asher's expression was serious as he toyed with the frayed edge of the tunic she wore. "I only break out the champagne and strawberries for the woman I'm trying to persuade."

"Hmph." She savored the fruit and cream on her tongue. "Trust me, you've already persuaded me. Many times."

"Have I?"

Before she could respond, he was kissing her deeply. "Wait," she began to say before Asher's tongue entered her mouth. "Asher…"

He wasn't ready to break their kiss just yet. The straw basket set beneath the colorful, voluminous balloon was almost as big as a small room, and offered plenty of privacy for a couple wishing to steal a sweet kiss amid paradise.

Books by AlTonya Washington

Kimani Romance

A Lover's Pretense
A Lover's Mask
Pride and Consequence
Rival's Desire
Hudsons Crossing

Kimani Arabesque

Remember Love
Guarded Love
Finding Love Again
Love Scheme
A Lover's Dream

ALTONYA WASHINGTON

has been a romance novelist for six years. She writes contemporary and historical romance and has been an avid reader of both genres since age thirteen. She loves to incorporate romantic suspense in her work, and enjoys criminal fiction in novels, movies and TV. In 2008, AlTonya released her fifteenth title. In addition to writing, she works as a senior library assistant. She also teaches a romance-writing course in Charlotte, North Carolina, where she lives with her longtime love Derric and their eight-year-old son.

HUDSONS
Crossing

ALTONYA
WASHINGTON

KIMANI
ROMANCE

To My Sister Wanda,
Welcome to the Mommy Club!

 KIMANI PRESS™

ISBN-13: 978-0-373-86106-0
ISBN-10:   0-373-86106-4

HUDSONS CROSSING

Copyright © 2009 by AlTonya Washington

www.kimanipress.com

Printed in U.S.A.

Dear Reader,

I hope you enjoyed the dramatic, passionate and long-distance romance between Asher and Riley. The situation between this couple is one I can heartily appreciate as I've dealt with it during the course of my fifteen-year relationship with my longtime love Derric. *Hudsons Crossing* is about understanding, change, a new baby…but it's also about compromise, which, next to communication, is an element that can make or break any union.

Thanks for taking time to read about the Hudsons' triumph through their changes.

As always, I welcome your comments. Please e-mail me at altonyawashington@yahoo.com, join my Yahoo Web group, LoveAlTonya, to remain updated on all my projects and visit my Web site at www.lovealtonya.com.

Blessings,

Al

Chapter 1

The New Chronicle buzzed with conversation and creative energy, as it often did as 5 p.m. crept closer. On the eleventh floor of the respected publication, the noise level was almost deafening. As usual, the final draft of the *Stamper Column* was the cause of the uproar.

Of course, Riley Stamper would have the environment no other way. She thrived on the creative havoc that churned each day at that time. Though the column bore her name, she depended on the input from each of her staff to make it happen.

Today however, Riley's smoky-brown gaze was narrowing in doubt as she read the "opinion" of one of her junior reporters.

"She's the publisher's niece Doreen. We put that in this particular write-up, and we better have hard proof, instead of gossip someone overheard in a club."

"Riley?"

"Track down who said it. Find out where they got their info, and let's talk more about it," Riley finished instructing the rookie reporter.

"Riley?"

"Yeah, Case?" Riley finished jotting down a thought before looking up at her assistant. "What's up?"

Casey Royer twisted the engagement ring she'd been wearing for two months and did a poor job of hiding her unease. "You've got a call."

Riley's attention had already strayed. "Case, take a message. You know I don't handle calls during—"

"It's Asher Hudson's office."

The creative havoc in the conference room simmered down to a hum.

Riley leaned back in the chair she occupied dead center of the table. "Asher Hudson's office? Phoenix?"

"Mmm…" Casey's brows rose a notch as her mouth tilted upward into a smile. "Apparently, they're one of those 'millions of satisfied readers' we keep on hearing about."

"I'll take it in my office." She stood, walked down the hallway and picked up the receiver.

"Mr. Hudson?"

"Uh, no, Ms. Stamper. I'm Claudette Silver, Mr. Hudson's assistant."

"Ah, Ms. Silver." Riley let some of the coldness ease out of her voice. "I suppose this is about our article?"

The smile came through the line as though it were words. "Mr. Hudson would very much like to speak with you about it."

Riley kicked off her pumps. "Well, he's proven that he knows how to reach me by phone."

This time the smile came through in the form of a full-bodied laugh. "He prefers to speak with you in person, and he'd prefer to speak with you in Phoenix."

Riley waited a beat before responding. She wasn't about to let Asher Hudson or his trusty assistant know that she was slowly yet steadily becoming unnerved.

"I don't think I'll be in the area any time soon, Ms. Silver."

"Mr. Hudson understands what an imposition this is on your time and your job."

Riley smiled and nodded. She could take a month off and still meet the deadline for her daily column with ease. Her backlog of stories was enormous, and she'd swear, sometimes the articles wrote themselves.

"Is this really necessary, Ms. Silver? Mr. Hudson can rest assured that he'd have my full attention whether we're face-to-face or across a phone line."

"He doesn't doubt your sincerity or professionalism, Ms. Stamper. He's simply a man who prefers putting faces to names.

He's especially interested in putting a face to the name emblazoned across the column that almost put us out of business."

"Right…" Riley's heart sank to her toes then.

"He'd like to fly you out here as early as tomorrow morning. He's already arranged for you to stay in one of Scottsdale's finest hotels."

"Scottsdale?"

"Mr. Hudson lives in the suburb right outside Phoenix."

Riley began to massage the dull ache at the middle of her forehead. "Of course, he does."

Once more, the smile came through the line in Claudette's voice. "He won't take very much of your time. I don't believe you'll be sorry you've spoken with him."

Riley acknowledged the truth in that. She'd seen enough pictures of Asher Hudson to know that a face-to-face meeting with him would have a fair amount of delight mixed in. Still, it was what he wanted to discuss that had the soles of her feet feeling like she was prancing on a bed of needles.

"Ms. Stamper? May I tell Mr. Hudson that he can expect you?"

Riley swallowed nerves and summoned a bucketload of courage. "What time did you say the plane leaves?"

Riley sweetened her third cup of chamomile tea and figured the hot brew would send her to the toilet more quickly than it'd send her to sleep. She'd gone home shortly after her conversation with Asher Hudson's assistant. The woman had sounded pleasant enough. Riley wondered if the same could be said of her boss. Taking a sip of the tea, she took a moment to groove to the soulful stirrings of Mary J. Blige's voice drifting through the loft. Then, reluctantly, she shuffled toward the bedroom, where she'd been making a poor attempt at packing.

"What the hell do people wear in Phoenix, anyway?" she grumbled and kicked a pair of espadrilles across the floor. The phone rang, and she almost jumped out of her skin.

"This is Riley," she answered just before another ring sounded, which would trigger the answering machine.

"May I call you Riley, or do you prefer Ms. Stamper when speaking to strangers?"

The voice prompted her to sit. Though she wasn't sure the bed was the safest place. The depth of the speaker's clear baritone rumbling through her phone line could easily stir sensations best left alone.

"Hello?"

Riley cleared her throat. "Well, that would depend on the stranger."

"Ah. Well, it'll probably be Ms. Stamper then. This is Asher Hudson."

Of course, it was. Riley gave herself a pat on the back for giving a subtle come-on to the man who was luring her out to Phoenix, most likely to attack her for casting a shadow over his business.

"Mr. Hudson, your assistant said you prefer face-to-face meetings to phone calls."

"She's right, but I had hoped to contact you first myself and ask you out here."

"Your assistant did a fine job of extending the offer, I assure you."

"I don't doubt that she did. I wanted to call and talk with you, anyway."

"Oh?" She sat a bit straighter, hoping he'd save her the trip and relax his decision to keep her in the dark until they met.

"I wanted you to know that it's not my intention to bring you here to rake you over the coals."

"Really?" She studied her foot, swinging it back and forth. "What *is* your intention, Mr. Hudson?"

"It's Asher. And my intentions won't have you regretting that you got on that plane."

Indeed. She conceded the point. But if they were anywhere as provocative as his voice, his *intentions* were gonna be pretty hard to resist.

She sighed. "You're not gonna tell me, are you?"

"Not until I see you."

"Well then."

"Mmm…"

"So…I'll see you."

"Looking forward to it, Ms. Stamper."

"It's Riley."

The bass in his voice softened. "Good night, Riley."

At the sound of the dial tone, she drained her teacup and then trudged back to the kitchen for helping number four.

Phoenix, Arizona

"A woman with a popular, prize-winning column like that is no fool."

"I'm counting on it."

Claudette Silver rolled her eyes and set a tall mug of black coffee before her boss. "Do you really expect her to tell you anything?"

"No. Though there's a slim chance that I could be wrong." Asher added cream to his coffee with one hand and used the other to work the TV remote. "Don't you want to be around to see that?"

Again, Claudette rolled her eyes. "It's what I live for, but sadly, it has yet to happen. Toodles."

"What time does her flight land?"

"Noon!"

Asher grinned when his office door slammed behind Claudette. Then he reclined in his desk chair to enjoy his coffee and the view of the city he loved.

Riley steeled herself against asking the flight attendant if she had any of those tiny bottles of whiskey inside the cart she wheeled down the narrow aisle. She'd already ordered herself to calm down more than once since setting foot in the taxi that had taken her to the airport.

She reminded herself that she was a well-known and well-respected journalist in New York. Whatever the case, learned scholars and award-winning actors alike read and admired her column. She certainly wasn't going to allow herself to become unhinged because some agent—some well-known and well-respected sports agent who was well on his way to becoming a billionaire before he was thirty—beckoned her. *Right? Right.*

The captain was announcing their descent. Riley yawned to

ease the pressure on her eardrums and closed her eyes until the plane was safely on the ground.

"Ms. Stamper, Claudette Silver. Pleasure to meet you."

"Pleasure's mine," Riley said as she extended a hand toward the woman, who looked as pleasant as she had sounded on the phone.

Claudette placed her free hand atop Riley's when they shook. "May I show you to the restroom before we head in to see Mr. Hudson?"

"Oh, no, I'm fine."

"Coffee? Tea? Something stronger?"

Riley wanted to laugh. "Maybe later," she said and gave a quick toss of her bouncy shoulder-length tresses and shrugged. "No offense, Ms. Silver, but I'd just like to get this over with."

Claudette's laughter sent her own bouncy locks of dark blond swinging about her lovely, deeply tanned face. "Please call me Claudette," she said and nudged Riley's shoulder.

Riley relaxed a thousand times and urged Claudette to use her first name as well.

Claudette winked. "Let's go."

Flexing fists about the black trousers of her suit, Riley prayed the approaching storm would be fleeting.

"…I'm just not sure right now. I promise to make the time soon."

"You say that each time we talk, and then six to eight weeks go by."

"Ma…," Asher moaned. All the while he wondered how he could negotiate multimillion dollar contracts day in and day out without breaking a sweat, and yet five minutes on the phone with Cassell Hudson could have him whining like he was eight again.

Claudette walked in then with his two o'clock appointment, and Asher agreed with the very next thing his mother said.

Cassell had been intentionally sarcastic when she demanded her son visit in two weeks. Nothing could've surprised her more when he agreed.

"Don't disappoint me, Asher."

"I promise, Ma." Slowly, he stood behind his desk. "I promise I won't."

"Well then…we'll see you in two weeks."

"Incredible," he said and almost sighed, replacing the phone without looking away from the beauty at his assistant's side.

"Asher Hudson, Riley Stamper." Claudette made the introductions and easily observed the amazement in her employer's eyes.

Riley considered it a triumph that she was able to extend her hand first. She'd seen Asher Hudson only on television. She'd seen him every time he signed a new client or made a big deal, and once when he was interviewed about a convenience store robbery he'd been unfortunate enough to walk in on. The big screen simply didn't do him justice. Her jaw had almost dropped to the ground at the sight of him. Seeing him without the glass barrier of a TV screen was nothing short of heaven.

"I'll just leave you two…," Claudette called across her shoulder, knowing neither of them heard her.

"I'm sorry." Asher took her hand at last, managed to give it a hearty shake and then waved toward one of the armchairs before his desk. "I appreciate you coming out like this on such short notice and all."

Riley graced him with a wavery smile. "You were vague enough to strike my curiosity. I'm a reporter, so it doesn't take much."

Asher had reclaimed his seat and did nothing more than nod for a time. Slowly and with no regard for the intensity of his stare, he allowed his light gaze to roam over Riley. He savored the rich dark tone of her chocolate skin and her eyes, huge pools he could almost lose himself in. Even in the dark, severe pantsuit she wore, he could tell her legs were long and strong. He found himself wondering how she'd feel against his taller frame and quickly forced his attention to the reason for their meeting.

"I guess it doesn't take much investigating to figure that your write-up on my sports agency is what pushed me to contact you." Silently, he acknowledged that had he seen her first, contacting her wouldn't have had a damn thing to do with that story.

His words, however, were just the opening Riley was waiting for. She'd come prepared to defend her work. "I never publish anything,

Mr. Hudson, without thoroughly investigating it. Every comment and every source is completely researched, confirmed and reconfirmed. People may think that column writing is simply opinion, with no real journalistic basis or integrity. I promise you, I choose with the utmost care every word that winds up in my work."

Asher propped the side of his face against his palm and listened. He honestly believed he could have listened to her all day. That admission in itself scared the living hell out of him. Grimacing a bit, he shifted his athletic frame in the chair and struggled to focus on her words and not on the delicious-looking mouth they tripped from.

"I'm sorry if you were expecting an apology from me, Mr. Hudson, but I put too much professionalism in my work to ever apologize for it." After her declaration, Riley stood with as much dignity as she could muster, gave a decisive tug on the flattering blazer and turned for the door.

At last, Asher snapped out of his daydream and rushed around the side of his desk. He caught her just as her fingers grazed the door lever.

Riley turned, stumbling back on the chic wedge heels peeking out beneath the flared legs of her trousers. She gasped at the full extent of his height and the breadth of his shoulders.

"I'm sorry." He dipped his head slightly and took a step back. "You've got it all wrong. You've got *me* wrong."

Riley leaned back against the door and hoped to slow her breathing. She watched him appearing to do the same. God, he was magnificent to look at, she thought and prayed this strange meeting would soon reach its end. Never had she experienced such an overpowering and dangerous attraction to a man. Especially not to a man whose company she'd enjoyed for less than twenty minutes.

"The reason I called you here has everything to do with your story, but not in the way you think," he explained.

The mystery of the meeting had finally grown just a tad too annoying. It was effective in getting her brain to focus on more than a flawless honey-toned face, deep-set and striking light eyes, a sensuously curved mouth and that scar along the side of his cheek... She wondered what the story was on that.

"Exactly why am I here, Mr. Hudson?"

Smiling, as if she'd given him a reprieve, he straightened and pressed a hand to his chest. "You're here because you have something I want very much, and I hope you won't make it too difficult for me to get it."

Chapter 2

"My source?" Riley stood an instant after they sat on the pearl-gray suede sofa and listened to him tell her what their meeting was really about.

"Riley—"

"*Ms. Stamper* to you, you arrogant jackass, sitting up here in your palace—"

"Riley—"

"Any fool knows that no reporter worth a damn would ever give up a source."

"Some have. Some would," he quietly pointed out.

"Go to hell," she replied just as quietly.

Asher kept his seat and would've been a picture of calm had it not been for the muscle tap-dancing along his jaw. "Would you please just sit and let me tell you—"

"Hell no."

"Dammit, Riley," he said and then stood, too. After a moment of silence, he simply waved a hand toward the sofa they'd calmly shared for all of four minutes.

As the curiosity was still nagging at her something fierce, Riley obliged his unspoken request. The blazer was becoming a bit stifling, but she felt it more important to retain a firm demeanor with this man. The stifling blazer said firm with a capital *F*.

"That story you broke in your column almost ruined the reputation of my business and—"

"I told you I wouldn't apologize for—"

"I'd appreciate it if you would let me finish," he said quietly. This time it was Riley's turn to give a graceful, flourishing wave.

"Thank you," he whispered, running a hand across the waves of silk covering his head. "I was like a monster for weeks when I heard of it and then read it. Good work, by the way." He smirked when he saw the surprise break through the tight expression she was trying to maintain. "Like I said, I didn't bring you here to rake you over the coals for the story. I don't tolerate deceit and bribery to close deals in my agency, Riley. Ms. Stamper."

"So what is flying me out to the desert about then?"

Asher relaxed on the sofa and propped a loafer-shod foot on the glass table before it. "I swear I'm not trying to bribe a source out of you. I do like conducting business in person, though." He unbuttoned the lightweight tan suit coat he wore. "I also thought it might help to look directly at you when I explain why this is so important."

Deciding she wanted to be a smidge cooler as the mystery unfolded, Riley followed suit and unbuttoned her blazer as well. She went the extra mile and pulled it off her shoulders, never noting that Asher lost the ability to speak as his eyes focused on the soft swell of her breasts, visible beneath a tailored white shirt.

"Um." He sat up and massaged the bridge of his nose and tried to put effort into focusing on something else—*anything* else.

"Are you okay?" she whispered, hoping her words nudging for him continue the story were subtle enough.

"Right, um." He left the sofa to pour a much-needed drink. "I was so angry about your story because I could've prevented everything that happened."

"How?"

"Six months before your story broke, one of my junior agents came to me with allegations that Forester Haines was making promises to clients that he couldn't keep."

Riley sat straighter, recognizing the name of the agent featured in her column. Her research and a tip about corruption and bribes had pointed to Forester Haines. When she made the connection to Asher's up-and-coming organization, she recognized it all as one of those stories begging to be plucked, explored and shared.

"Anyway, I didn't listen. Figured the guy was just heated over losing out on closing deals while Forester was closing 'em left and right. The things he said…crap he told me Forester had pulled… It was so outrageous." Asher came back to the sofa and passed Riley a rum and Coke. "I wound up firing him. He begged me…stood right there." Asher pointed to the deep armchairs before his desk. "Talked about how much respect he had for the integrity of the profession. He said it soured something inside him to see someone turning it to shit."

Riley swallowed down the drink with effort. Calvin Onsteen had said almost those exact words to her when he dropped the tip in her lap.

Asher turned the stout, beaded glass in his hand. "He told me that one day I'd see, and he hoped it wouldn't be too late. In spite of it all, he still considered me one of the good guys." He laughed then and drank deeply of the hard drink. "I'm firing the son of a bitch, and he's saying he still considers me one of the good guys."

"Asher—"

He set the glass on the table and took one of her hands in his. "Listen to me. If Calvin Onsteen is your source, I only want him to know that I'm sorry. I don't have a way to contact him…I'd like to help him if I can. I understand if he doesn't want to come back here to work, though he's got a job here if he ever wants one."

Riley's mouth was dry even as she swigged the drink. The hurt and regret came through in Asher's expression and words. He was nothing like what she'd expected. Nothing like the corrupt individual she thought she was helping to bring down when that story broke. Calvin Onsteen had told her Asher was one of the good guys. She'd cast off his musings as the silly, blind adoration men held for their idols.

Asher was standing before the floor-to-ceiling windows lining his gorgeous office. "He doesn't have family, so I don't know what his finances look like or if he's found work…." He trailed away, looked down in his glass for a while and then finished off whatever was left in it.

When silence enveloped them for the better part of two minutes, Riley figured everything had been said and stood from the sofa once more.

"I'll have a car take you back to the hotel."

"Thanks." She tugged the purse strap across her shoulder.

"Riley?"

Her hand was on the door lever.

"Have dinner with me tonight?"

The weak hand fell off the lever. "I, um, I've got a plane to catch."

He smiled and turned away from the windows. "Tonight?"

"Tomorrow."

"That's not tonight." He studied the invisible designs his index finger carved on the desk.

"Asher, I—"

"It's only dinner, Riley."

He was right, and she was being completely silly. "What time?"

"Seven. There's a good restaurant down the street from your hotel. We can eat there."

She managed a nod upon realizing she'd been gawking at him for two full minutes. "Right. So…I'll see you then." She made a quick turn for the door.

"Riley?"

She bowed her head.

"Thanks for coming."

"Uh-huh…" She raced out of the office as if the devil was at her back.

Riley celebrated the fact that she'd packed for three days instead of one. Sadly, she hadn't packed anything else nearly as severe as the black pantsuit she'd felt so confident in while going toe-to-toe with Asher Hudson.

Gone toe-to-toe? Had she really done that? She pondered the strength of that statement while studying the airy wisp of a dress that would be her attire for the evening. Asher Hudson was far more than she'd expected from a physical standpoint. There was more, of course—lots more—and the strength of *that* statement was what had her behaving completely unlike herself.

The knocker sounded at the door to the suite, and Riley surveyed herself once more in the full-length mirror adorning the closet door. The dress was not appropriate in any way for dinner with a man who'd made her tingle, oh, so scandalously during a

simple phone call. There was no time to debate on that now, and
there was certainly nothing else for her to change into.

Asher considered himself quite fortunate that Riley Stamper was
a journalist and not an agent. His career would've bit the dust long
ago had he been forced to sit across from her at a negotiating table.

What had him so infatuated, and so quickly, with her? Of
course, she was exquisite, with a face and body to keep a man
coming back for more regardless of how much or how little of
herself she was willing to give.

The thing that hooked him most about Riley was her fierce
streak of loyalty and stubbornness. He could scarcely recall his
own name today when she sat across from him and defended the
integrity of her story and her profession. In his world, reporters
were nowhere near as upstanding. He'd been dumbstruck, pure
and simple.

And yet as attracted as he was to her mind, it was her beauty
that left him speechless.

Riley must have noticed the dazed look in his gaze, because
she grasped his forearm, bared by the cobalt-blue crew-neck
shirt he wore. "Are you okay?" she whispered and then swallowed when he towered over her. "Asher?" Her eyes raked the
wicked scar before snapping to his eyes.

He knew how hungry he appeared. He wanted her to see it and
do something to diminish the appeal that she radiated toward him.

Riley tried to move away, but as she was crowded between a
god and her hotel-room door, she was quite simply…trapped.

"Maybe we should go?" She was almost afraid to breathe. The
dress she was wearing flared about her legs, and the sleeves
about her wrists, but the bodice was snug and scooped. With too
much breathing and in such close proximity, her bosom was
sandwiched against his arm.

Asher closed his eyes and nodded. "Do you have something
to, um…" He waved toward her exposed skin.

"Oh." Riley tugged her wrap and bag from the coatrack.
"Ready." She blinked rapidly and looked anywhere but at the
intense expression still evident on his handsome face.

Gallantly, he stepped back from the door and urged her to precede him. Ever so lightly, his hand pressed the small of her back, guiding her toward the elevators. Riley was so in tune to his touch, she believed she could feel each individual fingertip massaging her spine.

When the elevator doors opened, a long breath of relief whooshed from her lungs. The car held three other passengers. There would be no steamy encounters in the elevator's cramped confines. But when the elevator car hit its next stop and two others joined them, the only place for Riley to stand was smack-dab against Asher Hudson.

"All right?" he whispered, barely managing a smile as she barely managed a nod. He recalled that earlier that day, he'd wondered how her lithe, curvaceous form would feel against him.

Now he knew. The sight of her in that dress was nothing compared to the way her body felt next to his. Her thick hair was drawn away from her face and left to tumble across her shoulders in a wealth of curls. When she cleared her throat and shifted her stance, the fragrance drifting from her hair and body reminded him of green apples. Biting his lip on an oath, Asher prayed the lobby was near.

"This way," he said once the torturous ride had ended and the passengers had exited the elevator car. His heart thudded like an adolescent's when she linked her fingers through his while they crossed the crowded main floor. Going a step further, Asher tugged her hand through the crook of his arm and drew her even closer.

"So was starting your firm just the obvious choice when you left the league?" Riley reached for her Scotch and soda while awaiting his answer.

"It was *one* choice." Asher silently commended the maître d'. The seating was perfect. Secluded but not completely remote, it gave them a chance for real conversation. "At first I was ready to say goodbye to it all together."

Riley smiled and broke a tortilla chip in half. "Was basketball your first love?"

"More like fifty-first." He joined in when Riley laughed. "I enjoy it more as a spectator." He shrugged. "I had a talent for it, though, and my dad was so proud."

"Ah, men and their fathers," Riley drawled in a playful yet understanding tone.

Asher wondered if his detection of her unease was accurate. Something in the way she said "fathers" had him more than a little curious.

"So then the robbery?" she prompted when the silence grew a little too charged. She saw Asher grimace and lean back from the table.

"Then the robbery." He spoke the words and appeared to be looking out over the scene from his past. "After that, I just wanted a change of jobs *and* scenery, you know?"

"And then...Phoenix," Riley said, with laughter, to lighten whatever mood had taken hold of him.

It worked, and his laughter was hearty and easily contagious. The heavy mood was effectively lifted when the server returned with their orders of enchiladas, seasoned rice and cheesy beans.

Riley was already digging in when she noticed Asher had yet to begin.

"Does Mexican sit well with you? I didn't bother to ask before."

"It sits *very* well. Don't worry."

Asher was still hesitant. This time for a different reason. Clearly, the statuesque journalist wasn't shy about eating, he thought and watched her dine with gusto. The restaurant was one of his favorites, but not a place he'd generally take a date. Especially not a first date. He supposed the lovely Ms. Stamper relaxed him more than he'd realized.

"So how difficult is it to score your very own column?" he asked after they'd gotten halfway through the meal.

"Not nearly as easy as folks think. I was a classified ad rep for the *New Chronicle* right after college." She rolled her eyes. "I'm no salesperson, but it was a foot in the door...did that for about three years. Then, one night, I happened to be on hand at a popular nightspot when an altercation broke out between two jocks."

Asher brought a hand to his forehead. "Please don't tell me they were basketball players."

She slapped her hand against his wrist. "Even better. They were football players—huge ones. Rookies to the league and all. They made a mess of the place. My table was the last one they crashed into—with *me* sitting there!"

"God." Asher was riveted by the story and held a chip poised over the salsa as he waited for more.

"I was fine, but they didn't know that. I'm ashamed to admit that I wasn't always such an upstanding journalist."

Asher felt his mouth twitch with a smile. "You don't say."

Completely out of character, Riley giggled as the memory reclaimed her. "They were both very sorry, called, wanted to make it up to me."

"And you wanted a story."

"And I got one."

Asher dipped his chip. "I guess a lot of people wanted to know what started that scuffle."

"I guess they did, but that wasn't the story I wanted."

Asher's interest in her story suddenly intensified and his sleek eyebrows rose.

"I got them to really open up to me about rookies in the league and how much pressure there is to stand out when you've stood out your entire life."

"Good angle," he acknowledged, more impressed than he realized.

Riley shrugged and savored the last of her enchilada. "The editors thought so. They published it, and then I wrote an editorial on college athletics, cowrote a piece with one of the senior writers before getting my own staff writing position."

"Impressive."

"I did that for about four years. When they lost a column to syndication, I got the nod."

Asher tilted his Heineken bottle in her direction. "And now you're *the* Riley Stamper."

She shook her head but smiled just the same. "Not yet. Nowhere near yet."

Asher finished his bottle of beer and signaled the waiter for another. "You shouldn't be so modest. You've got no idea how many people pick up that paper. How do you think I found out about that story?"

Riley debated a moment. "May I tell you something?"

"Anything."

"Being in this business—" she pushed away her plate and smirked "—you start to become a bit cynical."

"No."

She laughed. "It's true. People rarely surprise me anymore."

Asher thanked the server for the fresh bottle, then nodded for Riley to continue.

"What you said today…I wasn't expecting that."

"What? I don't strike you as a man who could ever be wrong about anything?"

Again, Riley burst into laughter. "Don't even try it. Seriously, Asher, I…I never would've expected an agent to have that sort of integrity. You're really committed to doing things the right way."

"I was sure you'd think I was full of shit." His mood sobered. "I meant every word of it, by the way."

"I believe you."

Asher sipped from the frosted bottle and wondered if she'd believe him if he said he'd never enjoyed a dinner conversation more. Hell, did *he* even believe that? What the devil was going on here? Women were passing fancies that he'd had his fair share of, but this one seated across from him… He was hesitant to say she was different. But wasn't she? He was hanging on to her every word like some schoolboy. Whenever she stopped talking to enjoy her food, he entertained himself by envisioning them in bed together. He expelled a loud sigh.

Riley blinked and looked down at her plate. "Am I boring you? I do tend to ramble sometimes."

His eyes narrowed in surprise. "No, Riley."

She kept her gaze on her plate.

Asher leaned close and brushed the back of his hand across her jaw. "No, Riley," he said when she looked up. "I've never enjoyed a dinner conversation more." There. He'd said it.

The smile she graced him with spoke volumes. She believed him.

Chapter 3

"Brooklyn?"

"Mmm... Try Staten Island."

Asher closed his eyes to mourn his incorrect guess of her birthplace. Whatever her origin, he praised its effect on her voice. He loved her husky tone and the way she sometimes dropped her *r*'s. It was no wonder he was enjoying their conversation.

"So all that hustle and bustle doesn't make you crazy?" he asked when she caught him staring.

"Oh, no, I love it." Riley laughed when he made a face. "To tell you the truth, it's *this* that would drive me crazy."

"This?" His sleek brows drew close in confusion. "What? This? Here?"

"Mmm…"

"Peace, quiet, fresh air, sunshine…"

"We've got tons of sunshine in New York, and there're plenty of rooftops. You can grab all the fresh air you can tolerate."

Asher's incredible laughter drew loads of lingering stares. Riley's was among them.

"Fresh air and sunshine… What about peace and quiet?"

Riley shrugged. "Two out of four is definitely not bad."

"Depends on which two you find more important."

This time it was Riley's laughter that burst forth. She gained just as much male attention as Asher had from the female patrons.

"That's crazy!" She used her napkin to dab tears of laughter from her eyes.

"No, crazy is living in all that foolishness."

"Nooo, crazy is living out here in the desert."

"Maybe we should change the subject."

"Good idea." Riley laughed again, thinking of how much fun she was having. "Something safe," she suggested and took a sip from her fresh drink as she pondered. "Your parents."

Asher chuckled. "That's safe?"

"Well, do they share your love of open spaces?"

"Actually, they're back East."

Her brown eyes sparkled. "New York?"

"Connecticut."

"Hmm… That works then. For you, I mean. Connecticut's…well… Let's just say it's not Staten Island."

Asher only smiled and brushed the back of his hand against his scar.

"So I guess they don't have too hard a time getting you to visit?"

"I go back when I can."

A thoughtful look shadowed Riley's lovely face. "That doesn't sound very good."

He spread his hands. "It is what it is. So what about *your* parents?" He was eager to move the conversation away from his reasons for not visiting home more often.

Riley's thoughtful expression deepened. "My mom's in Manhattan."

"And your dad?" Asher inquired, though he got the impression she'd not be forthcoming on that front.

Riley didn't appear perturbed. "My mom raised me. He didn't stick around."

"I'm sorry, Riley." He cursed himself for prying when he glimpsed the sorrow she tried to hide.

She shrugged. "It's okay. Really. My mom did a phenomenal job on her own, I'd say."

Asher allowed her to see the emotion in his eyes. "I fully agree. Here's to moms," he said to lighten the mood. "Mine played the single role lots of times. My dad's work kept him away a lot."

"What did he do?"

"He was a bank president before he retired."

"Well, well, is this a spoiled brat I have before me?"

"Ha! Brat, yes. Spoiled, no. My mom was havin' none of that."

Riley raised her glass in toast. "Here's to moms!" She laughed when he clicked his bottle to her drink.

Asher waved toward someone across the dining room, and Riley looked across her shoulder. Her eyes widened at the sight of the man approaching their table.

"Riley Stamper. The other half of Hud-Mason. Talib Mason." Asher made the introductions while clapping his partner's back.

Riley was about to stand, but Talib urged her to sit in a voice that was pure seduction.

"It's a pleasure, Ms. Stamper."

"Uh, thank you." Riley shook herself back to her senses and ordered her eyes off the man's mouth.

Asher rolled his eyes, spotting the look of intrigue on Riley's exquisite face. His best friend's British accent never failed to draw and hold attention.

Of course, it was more than the voice with Talib. His handsome vanilla-toned face was bright, and he sported a dimpled grin. He took a seat close to Riley.

"It's Riley Stamper of the *Stamper Column,* isn't it?" Talib nodded. "I'm happy we had the chance to meet."

"And voice your displeasure over the story on your firm," Riley guessed.

"What'd you do?" Talib whispered, his dark eyes narrowing toward his partner.

Asher raised his hand defensively. "I'm innocent. The lady's far too incredible to rake over the coals for anything."

Riley bit her lip on the smile about to break free. Asher kept his gaze focused. Talib looked from Riley to Asher and smothered a groan.

"Ms. Stamper—"

"Riley. Please."

Talib smiled and smothered her hand in his. "Riley. It was most certainly a pleasure." He stood. "Can I see you, man?" He didn't wait for Asher's response.

"Will you be okay for a minute?" Asher asked and waited for her nod before leaving the table.

* * *

"What are you doing?" Talib asked when he and Asher stood in a quiet corner off the kitchen.

Asher looked toward the dining room. "You called me back here for this?"

"Come on, Ashe. Riley Stamper?"

"Did you take a good look at her, Tal?"

"Sure I did. She's bloody gorgeous, but she's Riley Stamper, and she lives in New York."

"So?"

"Ah! I see. This coming from the man whose own mother can't get him to come East for a visit."

"As a matter of fact, I'm going out there in a couple of weeks."

"Mmm, and was this before or after you met our lovely Ms. Stamper?"

Asher pounded a fist against the side of his jean-clad leg. "Get off my back, Tal."

Talib shoved both hands into his trouser pockets and smiled. "Just trying to help, mate."

Asher understood his friend's concern, which had to do with a lot more than how he felt about New York. "Thanks, Tal, but I'm not you, and *she's* not Misha."

With those words, Asher went back to the dining room.

"Wow! I didn't know Phoenix had so many lights."

"Funny."

Riley chuckled while looking down on the view from the rooftop of Hud-Mason. "You know, when you *don't* rake someone over the coals, you really do it right."

Asher studied his hands, which were dangling over the side of the iron railing encircling the rooftop. "I had to give you a good experience. Can't have you going back to New York with ill feelings toward Phoenix."

"Mmm, ill feelings." Riley turned around and braced her elbows on the railing. "Like the ones *you* have toward New York?"

He shrugged. "I'll leave it to you to change my opinion when I visit."

Riley cleared her throat on the sudden burst of emotion his words summoned. The possibility of seeing him again did things to her heart that it was far too soon to acknowledge. "Count on it," she said, hoping to add a playful mood to the suddenly tension-filled atmosphere.

The breathy quality of her voice, however, did nothing to ease the tension. Asher didn't see the point in wasting more time. Scarcely a second had passed before his mouth was fused to hers.

Surprise and need forced a gasp from Riley's throat, which allowed Asher the entrance he sought. They both moaned when his tongue enticed hers into leisurely play. The huskiness of her moan rivaled the lightness of the whimper she uttered when she kissed him back seconds later.

The tentative air of uncertainty in their kiss lasted only a moment. Quite soon the kiss turned into a lusty exploration.

"Asher," Riley breathed during the kiss. Eagerly, she wound her arms about his neck. She took advantage of the chance to test the softness of his hair and shivered at the satiny feel of the waves covering his head.

Flexing his arms about her waist, Asher acknowledged that he'd been right. She felt perfect against him. Every time she took a breath, her full bosom was crushed against his chest. Smoothly, he massaged her back with one hand while trailing the other to test the weight of her breasts.

Riley moaned shamelessly and thrust her tongue more wantonly against his. In the faint recesses of her mind, she heard the soft-spoken but ever-present voice of reason demanding to know just what the hell she thought she was doing. Of course, she wanted to kick the voice into silence, but she couldn't ignore the validity of its question. *Just a little more,* she bartered, arching herself a bit into Asher's athletic frame.

With the heels she wore, he had only about a half a foot on her. It was more than enough for them to savor the incredible feel of their bodies against each other. Riley wanted to close her eyes and give in to whatever he wanted when she felt the impressive extent of his need nudging the part of her that most craved it.

Riley!

She decided to listen to the voice this time. Coolly, she stroked Asher's jaw with the back of her hand and grew sidetracked while she marveled at the feel of his skin. Gently, she eased out of the kiss.

"Wait…" she said even as she graced his lips with another quick peck.

Asher let his head fall to her shoulder and thanked God she had the willpower to stop him. Clearly, he'd been unable to stop and thoroughly uninterested in doing so.

"Let's get you back to your hotel." He kissed her earlobe after speaking the words.

Silently, they left the roof.

"Idiot," Riley called herself when she closed the door on Asher's back.

Of course, it was the right thing to do. Hell, she'd just met the man. This was only their first date. She took a moment to massage her temples and get her bearings. This was far from a first date. They'd never see each other again. His life was in Phoenix; hers, in New York. If that wasn't an effective second date killer, she didn't know what was.

Besides, it was more than obvious that Asher Hudson had no problems getting women to fall all over themselves for the promise of a night in his bed. She didn't intend to let herself be one of them.

Already clicking open the locks to his Pathfinder SUV, Asher was having a similar pep talk with himself. Leaving was the admirable—the gentlemanly—thing to do. Hell, he hardly knew her. They'd met only that day, and they had a business relationship, for goodness sake!

Poised to open the driver's side door, Asher changed his mind and leaned against his ride. Staring up at the hotel, he wondered what she'd think if he knocked on her door right then. *Idiot,* he said to himself, knowing full well what she'd think. Asher Hudson was a conceited pig, used to snapping his fingers and having women eager to fulfill his every desire. *That* was what she'd think.

Smirking humorlessly, Asher admitted that wasn't far from the truth. Intense relationships had never held any appeal for him. Sex, however, was only a phone call or a look away. He guessed that did make him as spoiled and arrogant as she most likely thought he was.

What did it matter, anyway? He was in Phoenix, and she was in New York. He'd probably never see her again unless it was on the pages of that paper she wrote for. The thought fueled his regret and his rage simultaneously, and he decided it was past time for him to get out of there.

When he settled behind the wheel, however, all those best intentions fled from his mind. She'd forgotten her wrap. Through the rearview mirror, he saw it carelessly draped there on the backseat.

Considering it fate, Asher grabbed the garment and headed back toward the hotel.

Craving chocolate and not wanting to own up to why, Riley dialed room service and ordered up devil's food pudding with whipped topping. She hoped the simple treat would soothe her hormones and put her mind to rest. When the knocker sounded, she sprinted to the front of the suite while tightening the belt on her robe. Whipping open the door, she saw nothing on the other side that would *soothe* her hormones.

Asher clutched her wrap, ready to recite an explanation for his return.

He never had the chance.

To hell with etiquette, Riley thought as she curved her fingers into the neckline of his crew-neck shirt and drew him across the threshold. *First date, second date be damned.* She wanted this man. She wanted him now, and she was going to have him.

The wrap fell to the floor and was crushed beneath the soles of Asher's shoes when he moved to gather her close. His mouth crashed down on hers this time. His tongue ravished hers, while his hand roamed the short terry robe she wore. Expertly, he made quick work of the tight belt, and he cursed his approval upon the discovery that she was nude beneath.

Riley took the opportunity to inhale much-needed air when he pushed her against the door. He held her there, and his fabulous stare devoured her. She felt no unease. Instead, she felt beautiful, desired. Biting her lip, she waited until he'd had his fill. That, however, was far from happening. He was almost desperate with the need to have her bare in his arms. Soon, the robe was gone, held in his fist at the small of her back while he plied her with another kiss.

She arched into him for the second time that night, her heart racing with the knowledge of what was to come. What she *hoped* was to come. He was still fully dressed, and his shirt felt wondrously decadent against her skin. She rubbed against him, craving more of the friction. The whimpers she voiced while her tongue played with his held just the right amount of sweetness and naughtiness. Again, Asher backed her into the door and tugged one of her thighs high around his hip.

Boldly, her fingers curved about his leather belt, and she proceeded to relieve him of it. Asher lost strength in his legs but continued to enjoy the kiss even as he braced a hand next to Riley, on the wall, in order to support himself.

They froze like two teenagers caught at the worst possible time when the door knocker rattled against the door.

"Room service," Riley whispered against his neck.

Smirking, Asher pulled the robe in front of her and held it there. Nudging Riley to the side and out of sight, he answered the door. Riley, meanwhile, fought to gain her bearings, then accepted that her bearings were long gone. Nothing to do but accept what she'd wanted from almost the moment she'd met the man who was presently settling the bill for her treat.

Once the well-tipped waiter had gone, Asher set the tray on the desk and simultaneously pulled away Riley's robe.

"Anybody else will have to wait," he growled seconds before his tongue reclaimed her mouth.

Riley moaned and mimicked the languid thrusting against her tongue. She lost her fingers in his gorgeous hair and felt moisture glide down her thigh when he cupped her bottom and let his fingers brush the place he was most determined to explore.

"Please." She shifted her thighs and nudged his hand, desperate for whatever he'd give her.

Asher didn't need to be coaxed. While inhaling the green apple fragrance from her neck, his hand curved around in front of her waist. Seconds later his fingers were inside her body and being drenched by her need.

Riley could've screamed her delight but chose to savor it in partial silence. Erotically slow, she rode the finger he pleasured her with. She wanted to laugh when his index and ring finger joined the manipulation. His free hand tapped her bottom, and she hoisted herself against him and breathlessly delivered directions to the bedroom.

Asher barely made it inside before the need to sample her dark chocolate enticements overwhelmed him. Pressing her against the wall, he cupped her hips and suckled the firm nipples that beckoned to his lips. He alternated pleasuring one and then the other, craving the feel of the rigid peaks next to his tongue.

Riley moved to relieve him of his jeans. Her hands weakened when he treated her to the dual delight of suckling her nipples while his fingers pleasured her moist warmth. In an effortless display of power, he held her high against him while kissing his way down her body and carrying her to the bed.

Writhing against the cashmere-like feel of the pearl-gray comforter, Riley watched him fixedly as he disrobed. Impossibly, she grew more heated as he stripped to reveal more of his well-defined physique. Riley kept her smoky stare trained on his face and produced a smile of naughty invitation while kicking back the comforter. He eased beneath the linens to join her, and they both moaned at the friction between their bodies.

"Mmm...oh, no...," she moaned.

"What?" Asher raised his head at her moan.

Riley chewed her lip. "I don't, um...have any..."

He winced and reached for his jeans where they'd dropped near the bed. Riley smiled when he withdrew at least three condoms from his pocket.

Asher put protection in place but took the time to drop sizzling, wet kisses down her body. Soon Riley could stand no more of his sensuous teasing. Hands hooking about his upper back, she drew him flush against her.

"Riley," he called and shuddered when she took him in her hand and guided his power into her softness.

The cry she lilted was shaky and giddy at once. Her entire body was alternately cold and hot. Her limbs trembled with satisfaction with what was and in anticipation of what was to come.

Asher surprised himself when sounds of his pleasure touched his ears. They were sounds of excitement and pleasure, yes, but there was also the potent feeling of awakening. Perhaps it was just the reality of new sex, he reasoned. In the depths of his mind, however, he couldn't quite accept that explanation as the whole of it. Rather than dissect it all just then, he focused on the release of her body to his.

Weakened by his erotic invasion, Riley let her hands rest above her head. Her hips moved with a will of their own, it seemed. He felt incredible inside her. She wondered how much of it had to do with the state of her sex life before this moment and how much of it had to do with how he'd reached in and brought fire to something long cooled inside her.

Chapter 4

Riley woke the next morning instantly alert and instantly reminiscent of the previous evening. How could she be anything but reminiscent of the previous evening? The things they'd done. Never had she been so brazen with a man so soon after meeting him. More surprisingly...no man had ever evoked such a response from her.

Now, in the reality of the morning, however, she had to face the facts. She was alone in her bed. Correction. She was alone in a *hotel-room* bed, and he was gone. She couldn't blame him. He'd only taken what she'd offered. Correction. She'd demanded, and he'd allowed himself to be taken.

Glancing at the bedside clock, she gauged that she had about four or five hours before she needed to head to the airport. Whipping back the covers, she decided to order coffee and toast from room service and then hop in the shower. She walked naked to the living room area and shrieked when she found him wheeling in a cart filled with breakfast.

Asher's gorgeous stare brightened devilishly. "The waiter'll be sorry he missed you."

"What are you... You're here?" she gasped, propping a hand on her bare hip.

"And you sound surprised." His voice was as sweet as the way he surveyed her.

Awkwardly, Riley folded her arms over her chest and shrugged. "I just figured..."

"That I'd hit and run?"

She let him see her guilty smile. "It would've been fine. I've got that plane to catch in a few hours, anyway."

Asher helped himself to juice and took a seat in one of the chairs nearest the cart. "So you just expected me to leave without even waking you to say goodbye before you flew back?"

"Well, I…" Riley noticed him tilting his head to take stock of her appearance. She speed walked from the living room area, with Asher's laughter floating behind her.

"You didn't answer my question." He leaned against the bedroom doorway, sipping juice and watching her hunt for a robe.

"Really, Asher, it's no big deal."

"No big deal?" He set the juice on the dresser and folded his arms across his bare chest. "You just told me you expected that I'd tiptoe out while you were asleep, after we just spent the night having sex on every square inch of this place."

Riley gave up the search for her robe and headed to the bathroom for a towel. "I'm sure you've done it before," she called over her shoulder. He was filling the bathroom doorway by the time she was covering herself with a towel.

"You really think I'd do that?"

Riley tried to step around him, but he wouldn't budge. "Dammit, Asher. I'm sorry, okay? What's the big deal?"

"Ah, I see. Make light of it so it won't hurt so much when you realize I took what I wanted and left without a word."

She rolled her eyes and stumbled back when he moved forward to force her into the bathroom. "Again, I ask what's the big deal?"

"The big deal is that once again, you've misjudged me. Now you've got to do something with all that pissed-off-ness you've built up." He stopped moving when he had her trapped against the counter. "Acting cold and indifferent, like you have no idea why I'm here."

"I don't." She managed the words, though her heart was blocking her throat.

The easy, humorous look he wore was suddenly firm and dangerous. "Cut it, Riley. You know what last night was about."

"Good sex." Her reply was bold, but inside, she was a mass of nerves. Yes, once again, she'd misjudged him, and she was too stubborn to admit it.

Asher knew that, and he was beyond caring. For the moment,

anyway. Once again, she'd stoked his anger with that cool, untouchable way of hers, which he'd detected in the brief time he'd known her. He wanted to unleash the hellion she'd been the night before just once before she left him.

"Don't," she snapped when he tugged at the towel she clutched to her chest.

He obliged, only to use a different route to get to what he wanted. Riley beat her fists against his broad chest when his hands slid beneath the towel to clutch her derriere.

"Tell me I'm right, and I'll stop," he bargained while gnawing at the soft flesh at the crook of her shoulders.

Riley pressed her lips together and refused.

"Mmm-hmm…" Asher spread her thighs and stepped between. He captured a fistful of her hair to hold her still for his kiss.

Riley weakened at once, cursing herself when she kissed him back. She felt him freeing himself from the jeans that sagged at his lean hips and made one last valiant attempt to resist. She failed, of course, and found herself groping for him as he worked to undo his button fly.

"Riley," he muttered into her neck. Her bottom filled his palms perfectly when he positioned her to take him.

She let her head fall back to the mirror and raked her nails across the scar he bore, then lower, until they were grazing his taut ass. Overheated all too soon, she wrenched away the towel and drew his head to her chest, desperate to have him take a nipple into his mouth.

Asher released her bottom to clutch the rim of the sink supporting her. He increased the force of his thrusts, rotating and stroking her, with a powerful rush of possessiveness in his movements.

Riley shuddered and called his name when she felt him coming inside her. The warm spewing of his desire had her wanting him all over again. Spent, Asher took a few moments to slow his breathing and then took her back to bed for more.

Riley jerked herself awake later and knew that she was alone this time. She celebrated the fact. There were still over two hours before she needed to leave for the airport, but she leaped from the bed and into the shower. She wouldn't take a chance on him coming back, no matter how much she wanted him to. Standing under the hot water, Riley prayed that she'd leave behind whatever had gotten into her in Phoenix. She guessed she was safe because it was Asher Hudson who had gotten into her....

Manhattan, New York

"I just don't know what got into me." Riley sipped the tangy mixed drink she'd pretty much been nursing since arriving at the cocktail lounge inside the Cache Media skyscraper, which was the home of the *New Chronicle*. "I've never done anything so stupid."

Misha Bales signaled the bartender to freshen her vodka and juice. "I'd say Asher Hudson is what got into you," she drawled, pleased by the pun until she noticed Riley's scathing look. "What?"

Riley swatted angrily at a stray curl that had fallen from her ponytail. "Would you please be serious here."

"I'm sorry." Misha almost laughed as she apologized. "It's just that it's rare that I get to be in this position. You're such a goody-goody." She flinched, expecting to be hit again. "You've just never done anything this reckless," she added when Riley dropped her head to the bar top. "Did you guys, um… Did you use protection?"

"Russ! Another one over here!" Riley ordered.

"Riley!"

"We did…except for that last time."

Misha closed her eyes. "Oh my…"

"I was just caught so quickly off guard," Riley admitted to her best friend. "He wasn't what I'd expected. When he asked me out to dinner, I didn't see the harm in it. I even met his partner, Talib Mason, and then he took me to the roof—"

"Talib? Talib Mason?" Misha's slanting dark stare was riveted on Riley's face.

"Yeah… That's his partner…Misha?"

Misha groaned and began to massage a sudden ache in her shoulders.

"You know him?" Riley asked.

"You could say that."

Concerned by the uncharacteristic despair on Misha's honey-toned face, Riley clutched her hand. "What is it?"

"Nothing."

"Misha…"

She waved her hand. "Don't. I'm over it." She drank deeply of the vodka. "It was before I got the editing job at the *New Chronicle*…a nonstop drama fest that's over and done with."

Riley fidgeted with the lace cuff of Misha's blouse. "How long did it last?"

"'Bout a year."

"Oh, honey…"

"Honestly, Riley, I'm over it. He was a jackass. Let's hope his partner isn't going to follow along those lines." She smiled. "From what you've told me, he sounds like a nice guy."

"Yeah…" Riley reverted back to her dilemma. "A nice guy who resides in Phoenix."

Once she and Misha parted ways, Riley headed back up to her office where she'd been working late on ideas for upcoming column topics. Whenever she conducted, one of those solo brain-storming sessions, the ideas usually spilled forth in much the same way they did when she worked with her staff. Tonight, however, she couldn't seem to focus.

It was no mystery as to the reason. Asher Hudson was on her mind, as he'd been since she left Phoenix two weeks prior. She'd cursed herself a million times at least for even wasting the energy to think about him.

He hadn't called. But then, neither had she. She supposed it was a bit unfair to curse the man for taking what she'd wanted to give. It was a simple enough matter. One that should've been easy to put behind her. So why did her eyes well with tears when the idea of not seeing or speaking to him again came to mind?

Chapter 5

While Riley was frustrating herself over her fleeting acquaintance with Asher Hudson, Asher was arriving at JFK Airport and frustrating himself with the question, why the devil was he in New York?

He was not in New York to pursue the delicious Riley Stamper, Asher reminded himself. He was there to see his mother. Cassell Hudson had called every few days to *remind* her son of his promise to visit.

Now he was there and debating whether to call his mother or the woman he was falling in lust with. He wouldn't allow himself to dwell on the possibility that it was anything more than that.

In lust. Yes, that was far more believable. Then why wasn't he buying it? The cellular vibrated in his khaki pocket just then, and he celebrated the interruption. Checking the faceplate, he smiled.

"Hey, Ma."

"Damn light," Riley muttered upon discovering the hall lights were out on her floor. Since she had the loft apartment, she couldn't count on an astute neighbor to bring the matter to the attention of the landlords. She made a mental note to handle it and knew that was about as likely as the maintenance folk having a vision about a lightbulb needing to be replaced on the top floor.

Thankful for the moonlight drifting through the slim windows just below the ceiling, she used the illumination to hunt for her key ring. She glimpsed the key she needed and uttered a triumphant cheer seconds before she saw that she wasn't alone in the hall.

Asher hissed an oath when she screamed, and he realized what he must've looked like waiting in the shadows of a deserted corridor.

Riley was calling herself all sorts of names for dropping her

Mace spray in her bag, instead of slipping it into her purse like any sane person.

"Riley?"

"You get back!" She gave pause, wondering how the attacker knew her name.

"Riley, it's me."

Realization dawned. "Son of a bitch!" She let her bag swing.

Asher ducked the blow easily and moved in close. "Honey, it's me."

"I know!" She tried to wrench free of his hold. "What the hell are you doing here? You scared the living crap out of me."

He grimaced and stepped back. "Thought I'd surprise you."

"You succeeded."

"Can we please go inside and stop arguing in this dark hallway? Where the hell's your light?"

"Why don't you report the oversight to maintenance on your way out?" The pointed request was ignored, and she tried to shut the door on him. "What are you doing here?" She hurried through the loft, switching on lamps until the place glowed golden.

Asher strolled in, appreciating the warmth of the elegant yet comfortable dwelling. "Since you weren't going to be the bigger person, I decided to contact you first."

"And in person, too. Boy, you and phones must not get along at all."

Asher rolled his eyes and headed for her kitchen. "I promised my mother I'd visit."

"How sweet. Why don't you go and raid *her* refrigerator, then?" Riley watched, amazed as he helped himself to a bottle of juice.

Asher's expression was somber. "Calvin Onsteen called me, Riley."

She blinked and then gave a quick toss of her head. "Calvin Onsteen?"

"Don't even try it. You remember who he is."

"Ah, yes." She set her bag on one of the high-backed stools circling the breakfast nook. "The junior agent whose life you ruined."

Asher bowed his head to accept the dig and the fact that she wasn't going to own up to contacting her source. "We had a good conversation. He's living up in Boston, using his law degree to set up a private practice. He sounds good." He sent her a sideways glance when she tried to appear nonchalant. "I only wanted to thank whoever asked him to call. The talk did both of us a world of good."

"I'm glad." Honesty radiated from her words. "So—" she smoothed her hands across the marble-like countertop "—is that it?"

"They're a couple more things." He set aside the juice and leaned against the opposite side of the counter. "I wanted to apologize."

Riley only shook her head.

"That morning in your hotel room…" He reached for her hand and brushed his thumb across her knuckles. "I shouldn't have…done that without a condom."

Riley blinked and tried to tug her hand back. He wouldn't let her. "It's all right, Asher."

"No. No, it's not. I should've been more careful with you." He stared intently at her hand. "I just…just didn't stop to think about anything other than what I wanted. I'm tested every year." He sighed and moved back. "You shouldn't have anything to worry about…."

She nodded. "Same here, and I'm on the pill."

Asher dipped his head when he felt his jaw clench. He didn't want her to see his reaction to that little tidbit. He didn't know how he felt about her being sexually active. That was a lie. He knew how he felt about it. If she wasn't using birth control with him and him alone, then he hated it.

Riley bumped the toe of one of her black square-toed shoes against the side of the counter and waited. When he seemed content drawing invisible designs on her countertop with his fingertip, she cleared her throat and stood.

"If that's all, Ashe—"

"It's not. I want to keep seeing you, Riley." He nodded once, as though he'd satisfied himself by admitting that aloud.

Riley leaned against the counter. "How, Asher? In our dreams? Because that's the best we'll do between Phoenix and NYC."

"I know it'll be rough."

"Rough." She reached for the bottle of juice he'd set aside and took a sip. She didn't see the smile Asher gave when she drank from his drink. "No, Asher, first, it'll probably be pretty cool, a bicoastal relationship so to speak." She tipped the bottle in a mock toast. "Then it'll become a pain in the ass, and we'll wind up hating each other."

Asher shook his head. "You're very cynical, aren't you?"

Riley spread her hands. "Life of a reporter."

"More like a woman who's afraid to take a chance."

Riley bristled while accepting the blow. "It won't work."

He muttered another curse, and then, with swift steps, he closed the distance between them. His kiss was thorough and searching, and he forced her tongue to duel with his.

She continued her campaign against anything more serious. "You only *think* you want this."

He was beginning to adore her stubbornness. "*Know* I do," he argued.

When he leaned close again, Riley prepared for another kiss. His mouth brushed her forehead, though, and with that gesture, he left her.

"What is going on with you?" Cassell Hudson whispered the words in awe once she'd topped off her son's coffee.

"Ma, I really do plan on visiting more. I just—"

"No, no, love, not that. I mean, you're different," she said and smiled. "Phoenix must be agreeing with you. You look almost giddy."

Asher could have choked on his coffee. "An educated woman like yourself can come up with a better word, I know."

"Oh, shush. Besides, it fits you perfectly." Cassell set the glass carafe back in the coffeemaker and turned. "I would say, you look like you're in love, but…"

"What?" Asher was riveted by his mother's words.

Cassell blinked. "Well, are you?"

Asher laughed suddenly to dismiss the annoying emotion swelling in his chest. "Not even close, Ma. Seeing someone new, is all."

"You are." Cassell sighed the words and reclaimed her seat at the small breakfast table they shared in her kitchen. "Well, who is she? When will we get to meet—"

"Hold it, Ma." Asher stood and went to stare out over his parent's dew-drenched backyard. "Before you get excited, you may as well know that I've known her only for about three weeks. This could all be over like that." He snapped his fingers, even as the words produced bile in his throat.

"Do you believe that?" Cassell added cream to her coffee.

"I don't know." Asher bowed his head. "I don't know if I'm comin' or goin' with her." He leaned against the French doors guarding the patio entrance. "I *do* know that it's too soon to bring her here. I'd terrify her if I said I wanted her to meet my parents."

Cassell's laughter was like a little girl's giggle. "Oh, sweetie, I promise you that won't change. Your father and I grew up together, and I was still scared out of my wits when he said he wanted to tell his parents how he felt about me. You take this slowly, all right? Time can be the best tester of all."

"I agree with that, Ma." He reached for his mug. "I fully agree with that."

"I guess I've got you to thank for my hall lights being magically fixed when I got home from work the other night."

Asher kept his attention focused on cutting his salad. "It's too dangerous to be groping around in the dark."

"Mmm, yeah, you never know when an agent may be lurking in the shadows."

He graced her with a wink. "We can be dangerous guys."

"Tell me about it."

"Well, well! Asher Hudson and the lovely Ms. Riley Stamper. Out on a date? Is this business or pleasure?"

Riley groaned inwardly and watched as the reporter scribbled away furiously on his pad. "It's bus—"

"Pleasure," Asher commented.

Mortified, Riley could only glare at him while he fixed her *colleague* with a smug smile.

"And I'd like to keep it that way," he added.

The reporter nodded. "Yessir." He made a final notation and then bid them good-night.

"What are you doing?" she asked through clenched teeth.

Asher was once again focused on his salad. "If you just tell them what they want to know, they leave you alone."

"Dammit, by morning the whole town will be buzzing about us."

"You think?" Asher took a moment to consider her point. "You really think we're *that* newsworthy?"

Riley fanned her face with one hand and plucked her snug peach top away from her chest with the other. "You're an idiot."

"No, I just don't care what the press does or doesn't think."

"Then why couldn't you tell them we were out discussing a story?"

Asher shrugged and scanned the crowded dining area of the bar and grill. "It didn't occur to me to lie."

Riley's mouth fell open and remained that way for several seconds. With great effort, she finished her dinner and kept her conversation to a minimum.

"I just think it's better if we keep this quiet, that's all." Riley had decided to withhold further comment on their budding relationship until they were in the privacy of her loft.

Asher didn't mind letting his annoyance show then, either. "Better for whom, Riley?"

She pulled her head out of the refrigerator. "Huh?"

"Who are we trying to protect here? Our privacy or something, *someone,* else?"

She rolled her eyes and dipped back into the refrigerator. "Don't be stupid."

Asher, however, had been dying to learn more about her social life. It was near impossible for him to believe that as lovely as she was, some other man hadn't already stolen her heart.

Riley found the dip she was looking for and set it onto the counter while slamming the refrigerator door shut with her foot. She saw that Asher was still waiting for an answer.

"I don't believe this," she muttered. "Are you jealous?"

He leaned across the counter and raked her face with his light eyes. "Should I be?"

She gasped, realizing then how serious he was. "There's only the column, Asher." She kept her tone firm but quiet.

"Hard to believe that."

"Why?"

"Do you ever look in the mirror?"

Her cheeks burned at the compliment. "I swear it. There's no one for you to be concerned about."

"Then why the birth control pills?"

"A girl's gotta protect herself." She lost her taste for the dip and set it back inside the fridge. When she turned, Asher was glaring again. "Dammit, I never said I was a hermit! And what about you? Mr. Gorgeous Beyond Belief Superagent! Don't tell me there isn't a bevy of brain-dead beauties lining up to fill your bed every night."

Asher rolled his eyes.

Riley took that as his response. "Right. I'm going to bed. The door will lock behind you when you leave."

Seething, he watched her round the corner and disappear out of sight. He beat a path to the front door but stopped halfway there. Leaving wasn't an option for him, and that meant that he was definitely losing his mind.

Riley had already snuggled down in bed by the time he got there. Disrobing, he slid beneath the sheets and pulled her back against him.

Cherishing the spooning embrace, Riley still felt the need to voice one last point before sleep hit. "Asher—"

"Shut up."

She did and then fell quickly and deeply asleep.

Asher woke to the feeling of a newspaper smacking against his cheek.

"What'd I tell you?" Riley opened her copy of the *First Beacon* and pointed to something on the page labeled Entertainment. "Looks like we made the morning edition of smut."

Asher wiped sleep from his eyes and rested back on his elbows to watch her rant.

"Well? Are you gonna say anything?"

Asher yawned and thought about it. "Guess we are as important as you thought."

Riley rolled her eyes and prepared to stomp away from the bed.

"Hey, hey…" He caught her wrist and pulled her down next to him. "Why are you so upset about this? Are you *that* ashamed of being linked romantically to the man you tried to *stamp* out?"

"Funny." She couldn't help but smile. "Things like this turn messy, and then, with us living so far apart…I can see the stories now. What *I'm* doing behind your back, what *you're* doing behind mine…"

Asher made her straddle his lap. "I don't intend to lose you over some unsubstantiated crap in a paper. Look at me." He waited for her eyes to meet his. "I want a relationship with you far too much to ruin it, but you've got to want it, too."

"It's gonna be messy." She raked her nails through his hair.

He smiled. "Many things worth having can get that way."

"I want this." Her hand trailed across his shoulder, and she marveled at the power resting beneath his sleek skin.

Asher cupped her neck in his palm and drew her into his kiss.

Chapter 6

Over the next several weeks, Asher and Riley spent a tremendous amount of time together. Not easy, considering the distance existing between them. Still, they managed. Neither could deny the powerful tug of attraction, which rose to new levels no matter how far apart they were. As a result, they were both eager to remain visible in each other's lives.

Riley ran roughshod over her frequent-flier miles as she accepted each and every one of Asher's requests that she visit. It had yet to occur to her to ask why he rarely made trips to New York. She didn't care, or at least, she didn't allow herself to. Spending time in Scottsdale and Phoenix was a dream, and Asher treated her like she was smack-dab in the middle of a fantasy.

He did, however, make a few trips to the Big Apple. Each time, Riley strived to pack as much excitement into the visit as possible. Difficult, considering Asher seemed interested only in spending time alone with her. He was, of course, a good sport when meeting her friends and colleagues. With regard to her female friends and colleagues especially, he accepted the way they ogled and swooned with a humble ease, which endeared him more to Riley.

Still, Riley had stalled on arranging a meeting between Asher and her dearest friend, Misha Bales. In light of Misha's troubled relationship with Asher's best friend and partner, Talib Mason, Riley predicted Asher's potent charm might not stand a chance.

Indeed, Misha's guard was definitely up when she saw Asher Hudson. The worn saying "Birds of a feather flock together" stuck in her mind, and she looked for similarities, mannerisms that resembled those of her horrid ex, Talib Mason. They wore their looks and confidence with ease. That was clear. Still, like Talib's, Asher's confidence didn't appear to be accentuated by smug arrogance, which flashed like a beacon with some men. If anything, his arrogance was playful and adorable. Misha stiffened inwardly. After all that Talib had put her through, she could still dwell on everything she loved about him.

It didn't take much for Misha to observe that her best friend was headed toward that same path of love and adoration. Riley was smitten. That was a certainty, Misha thought while watching Riley and Asher stroll through the dining room of the Caribbean soul food eatery. Misha cocked a brow. Truth be told, Mr. Asher Hudson appeared equally smitten. He didn't let go of Riley once, not even when she had to merge in front of him when they approached two dining tables set too close together to leave a wide enough aisle in between.

Misha wouldn't let her premature approval rule her. She knew how loyal a man could be to his friend. She was sure Riley had spoken of her and sure that Asher was aware of what had gone down between her and Talib.

Something noxious roiled in her gut. No doubt, Talib had made her look like a backstabbing slut. Misha pushed back her chair and prepared to stand. She was about to find out how approving Asher Hudson was of his new girlfriend being close friends with a woman like her.

Asher tilted his head and nudged Riley. "Is that her?" he asked, noting the slender beauty across the room.

Smiling, Riley gave a small nod. "Mmm-hmm."

"Talib never introduced me before." He slanted Riley a devilish look. "I see why," he teased and grunted when she poked an elbow in his ribs.

Misha extended her hand and was already shaking Asher's hand firmly when Riley began the introductions.

"I'm a little nervous," Asher admitted, his earlier ease having quickly vanished.

Misha blinked. "Nervous?" She watched the powerful agent bite his lip in what had to be an uncharacteristic gesture.

"Meeting you tonight." Asher cleared his throat twice before continuing. "And hopefully, Riley's mother, when she thinks the time is right...I pray you'll both approve of me."

"Approval?" Misha was even more dumbfounded, and she blinked this time.

Asher nodded as though he'd said nothing out of the ordinary. "You're her best friend, and I swear I think she'd dump me if you didn't think I was good enough."

Misha would have laughed, but just then she looked at Riley. She stood there, clutching Asher's arm and biting her lip, as he'd done earlier. The apprehension in Riley's eyes gave Misha pause, and her heart melted. Slowly, she looked back toward Asher and smiled.

"No, I don't think you'll have any trouble gaining my approval." Misha joined in when he laughed. She winked at Riley and saw the apprehension turn to happiness.

"So? What do you think?"

Riley and Misha had time alone after Asher saw someone he recognized and excused himself from the table to say hello. A bit of the apprehension returned to Riley's eyes when she asked her friend to share her true impression.

"Honey, who wouldn't approve or be in awe of a man like that?" Misha asked.

Riley's expression relayed her agreement. "Still, that's really only about looks and appeal. Don't you have any thoughts about him as a person?"

Misha squeezed Riley's hand. "Sweets, that's a lot more than looks and appeal. Still...I don't know him well enough. Talib never introduced me when we were...together. But, Riley, in the brief time I've been in his presence, I can tell the guy is very much over the moon for you." She shrugged. "I can see he's making you happy, and right now that's enough to secure him a very high place in my book. What?" Her eyes narrowed in concern when she saw Riley look down at the table.

"It's only been a few months...." Riley focused on the invisible swirls her nails drew on the tablecloth. "I've let myself go *over the moon* for him, too. I don't know if I'm coming or going."

Misha looked across the dining room, at Asher. "It's amazing how the right man can do that to a woman."

Riley shuddered and smoothed her hands along the snug cotton sleeves of her navy wrap dress. "It's only been a *few* months, Misha. How the hell can I be sure if he's the right man or not? I've never even believed I wanted to look for the right man."

"Honey, why are you doing this to yourself?" Misha laughed.

"I just feel so juvenile," Riley hissed and dragged all ten fingers through her tresses. "Swooning over a man I barely know."

"Yes, well, I think that's why they call this the 'getting-to-know-you' stage."

Riley smirked. "Right. And I've already slept with him, and I think I'm falling in love with him...."

Again, Misha squeezed Riley's hand and pushed her drink closer. "Stop stressing over this."

Magically, the order worked. Riley visibly relaxed, closed her eyes and smiled. "You're right." She took a sip of the smooth vodka. "Maybe it's not even love. Maybe it's just really great sex talking."

"Ha!" Misha took a swig of her martini and smiled as well. "It's amazing how really great sex can do that to a woman."

Laughter flowed between the two friends.

Virginia Stamper's expressive gaze was as wide as a kid's in a candy store when Riley led her from the aircraft that had just transported them from New York to Phoenix. Virginia's eyes grew wider still when they focused on the man who approached them on the tarmac. She watched him squeeze her daughter tight while nuzzling her neck and trailing his fingers through the flirty new cut she sported.

"Mrs. Stamper, it's a pleasure," Asher said once Riley finished the introductions.

The lovely retired RN was uncharacteristically captivated and took a smidgen longer than necessary to respond. "It's a pleasure to meet you as well."

The breathy tone in her mother's usually firm voice had Riley smirking. Asher didn't seem to notice that he'd thoroughly charmed the woman, even as he smothered both her hands in one of his.

"I hope you had a good flight," hc said.

Virginia glanced behind her. "Wonderful. I've never been on a private jet before."

Asher winced. "I hope it wasn't too much. Riley said it'd make a good impression."

Virginia patted his arm when he released her hands. "There was no need for that. I've been impressed by you for months now. Riley can't say enough incredible things."

"Really?" he asked.

In spite of the fact that he'd been seeing Riley for nearly five months, Asher seemed stunned by the news. The little-boy uncertainty on his face and the way he spoke the word charmed Virginia far more than she realized.

"Bags are loaded, Mr. H. We can head out whenever you're ready."

"Thanks, Joel." Asher shook hands with his driver and then waved toward Virginia. "Would it be all right for Joel to take you to the car while I speak with Riley for a minute, Mrs. Stamper?"

Virginia was already accepting the arm Joel offered. "It's perfectly fine," she said and launched into a conversation with the twentysomething chauffeur as they walked off.

Riley's expectant stare turned curious when Asher's easy expression appeared to sharpen.

"When did you do this?" He trailed his fingers across the flattering yet shorter hairstyle she now wore.

Reflexively, Riley's hand rose to her hair. "About a month ago. Don't you like it?"

The hairstyle, with its haphazard array of clipped and flipped locks, accentuated the oval shape of her face. It emphasized her expressive eyes and full mouth. Asher was bereft of words to describe how lovely she was to him.

"I love it." His voice was made rougher by the onset of emotion. "Just makes me realize how little of you I get to see." A muscle flexed quickly along his jaw. "Sometimes the reality of how far apart we are hits me right between the eyes, you know?"

Riley tugged at the hem of his brown crew-neck shirt in an effort to bring him closer. "*You're* the one with the private jet, Mr. Hudson. What?" She moved back a little when something flickered in his light eyes. "What? Did I say something?"

He blinked. "No, why?"

She shook her head, but her gaze remained focused. "I always see that look when I mention you traveling to New York. I even see it when you're there."

"You reporters," he teased and drew her into a sweet kiss. "All alike, but I'm about to burst your bubble, Ms. Stamper."

Riley stood on the toes of her coral peek-a-boo pumps. "Is that right?"

"I'll be smilin' in NYC by the end of the next week."

"Ha! Right, and I'm gonna run naked across your parents' front lawn."

Asher smiled, appearing pleased by that vision in his head. "That's somethin' I'd love to see, but it might not go over too well when you meet 'em for the first time."

"Them? Who?" Riley blurted when she found her voice. "Your parents?"

Smug and pleased, Asher leaned down to kiss her temple, and then he launched into a lighthearted conversation about all his plans for Riley and her mom as he led the way to the car.

"I had no idea you were serious. Don't you think this is a bit soon? Won't *they* think it's a bit soon?"

Asher shrugged and kept his gaze focused on the circle his thumb was making on her wrist. "I figured since I met your mom, this was the right time."

"Well, now we know." Riley made a move to drag her fingers through her hair but had to settle for fidgeting with a glossy clipped lock. "Five months is the right time to meet the family."

Asher pressed a kiss to her wrist. "Nervous, Ms. Stamper?"

Before Riley could answer, she heard a woman's voice cry out Asher's name. She and Asher stood to greet the handsome couple approaching them in the quiet upstate bistro where they were meeting for dinner. Seconds later, she was being introduced to Jones and Cassell Hudson.

"I'm sure meeting me is very sudden for you both." Riley decided to bite the bullet once the elder Hudsons had lavished compliments on her, telling her how lovely she was.

"Nonsense," Cassell scoffed while they took their places at the table. "I'm eager to meet anyone who can get my son to visit her more than once every other year."

"Especially when she's as beautiful as you are and we see our son so smitten," Jones added.

"So how long will it be until you ask her to marry you, Asher?" Cassell inquired while coolly reaching for the drink menu.

Riley would have choked had she been eating. Genuine laughter scrambled up her throat as she looked to Asher for encouragement. The choking sensation overwhelmed her again when she saw nothing but seriousness in his eyes.

"Asher, why didn't you correct them?"

"About?"

"Marriage, Asher," she ranted while they stood in the corridor outside her loft.

Asher, however, was too interested in unbuttoning Riley's coat to give much explanation. "I just made my mother's whole year," he said when she slapped his shoulder. "Any kid worth a damn lives for that."

"Even if it's not true?"

Asher's jaw clenched. "Isn't it?" With effort, he managed to keep his voice soft.

For what had to be the tenth time that night, Riley felt the need to laugh. "Have you lost your mind? You hardly know me."

"I know enough."

Riley bristled, trying to dismiss the tingle when his fingers grazed her breasts. "There's more to this than physical attraction."

"Damn right, but it's the part I'm having the most fun with just now." With those words, he held her against the wall next to her door and nuzzled her neck.

"What am I doing?" Riley sighed.

"You're falling in love with me," he growled close to her ear.

"And what are *you* doing?"

"Falling right back."

He kissed her deeply then, and she didn't even notice when he took her key and urged her past the doorway to the loft.

Chapter 7

Riley added more lemon to her tea and savored the warmth coursing through her body. Frosted air rushing from the vents made the treat utterly enjoyable even at the height of summer.

She'd told herself she was out of her mind visiting Phoenix in July but accepted that the time of year was of no consequence. Besides, somehow she and Asher had braved the storminess their unorthodox relationship had created. They'd become a media sensation almost overnight. Once word got out about the relationship between the columnist and the sports agent, Riley and Asher's celebrity status had rocketed to new heights.

The media apparently loved them. An article on the Stamper/Hudson romance was a sure bet for high sales. Everyone marveled at their long-distance relationship, which had survived almost a year, with love and passion intact.

Riley couldn't imagine her life without him in it. She found herself thanking God daily that Asher had bulldozed his way into her life and forced her to grab on to what she wanted without concern for the unexpected.

They were having a wonderful visit, but there was no surprise there. If she wasn't in Phoenix, he was in New York. Mini-vacations with the man she loved had done wonders for her body and soul.

The present visit was a perfect example. They'd been thoroughly enjoying one another and making lots of love. It'd been one wonderful experience after another. Still, Riley had to acknowledge that there was something different this time. His desire for her hadn't cooled a bit, she mused, studying the tangled covers of the king-size bed across the spacious room. However, he was in a strange mood, and she couldn't figure out the best way to coax him out of it.

She'd gotten up a bit earlier that morning and decided to eat alone to ponder that very thing. Part of her wondered if her insecurities were rearing their ugly heads. Was she overreacting? She was finishing up her light breakfast when he found her in the sunroom.

"What's wrong?" were his first words to her.

Riley shrugged. "Just wanted to get an early start."

"What for?"

"I was hungry."

Asher cast a skeptical look at the half-eaten toast and the corner of a beef sausage patty on her tiny plate. "Obviously."

Deciding to bite the bullet, Riley pushed back from the table. "I'm trying to figure out how to do something."

"Mmm…" Asher's attention was focused on fastening his shirt cuffs.

"Wondering how to ask about this mood of yours."

She had his attention then. Asher finished with the cuffs and frowned her way.

"Mood?"

"Mmm…"

"Why do you believe I'm in a mood?"

She detected that dangerous tone in his voice and could tell she'd grazed a nerve. *Good.* She'd get him to be honest with her far more quickly if he was angry rather than calm.

"Just a feeling. You've seemed kind of distant." She cleared her throat when he came to tower over her.

"Distant?" He toyed with the clipped locks of her hair, loving the way the new hairstyle flattered her lovely face. "Distant," he repeated, trailing a lone finger across her collarbone. "And how many times have we been together since you got here? I've lost count." He sighed, bringing a hand to his jaw, as though he were trying to recall.

Riley pursed her lips at his sarcasm.

He leaned close, dipping his head to hers. "Sorry, but I can't remember. All I can lock in on is that this is the first day I've put on clothes since you've been here."

"All right. Look—" she jerked away from him "—it's clear you're in a mood, so don't even try to act like I'm imagining things here."

"Dammit, maybe I'm tired of having to plot schedules and meetings to see you." He finally lost his temper. "Maybe I'm tired of having to book a flight to see my girlfriend." He raked a hand over his neck and turned away. "Hell, maybe I'm tired of you being my girlfriend," he muttered.

Riley heard him as clear as if he'd said the words through a bullhorn. The chime of his cellular phone caused a break in the conversation.

Devastated, Riley shuffled to the rear of the sunroom and stared unseeingly at the beautiful expanse at the rear of the estate. She blinked tears away and put anger in their place. She had seen it coming, after all. It'd been fun while it lasted, and she certainly couldn't blame him because she'd gone and let herself fall in love with him while he'd been planning to end things. Is that what had been happening during all the time they'd spent together? When had it stopped being about fun and lust and become true emotion?

She had a nagging feeling that she was misjudging him yet again, but she wouldn't let herself dwell on the fact that his feelings could be even the tiniest bit similar to hers. Especially when she could be wrong. Especially when she was probably *very* wrong.

"Baby, I gotta go," Asher said as he shut the phone and shoved it in his trouser pocket. As though nothing had happened between them, he pulled her against him and pressed a lingering kiss to the crook of her neck.

Jerkily, Riley turned to watch him sprint for the door. Her mouth fell open when he had the nerve to send her a wink before he disappeared.

"And he left, just like that?"

"Just like that."

"And there's no way you misunderstood what he said?" Misha asked.

Riley flexed her fingers around the phone receiver. "I heard him, Misha."

"Honey, it's been almost a year. The man is obsessed with you. I think he loves you."

"That's what I thought—what I hoped."

"Riley…" Misha could hear despair in her voice. "Honey, why do you do this to yourself?"

Riley closed her eyes in hopes of warding off the demons of insecurity that had plagued her since childhood. This time, however, it was much worse. This time the insecurity was causing her to ruin things with the man she was falling in love with.

"Riley—"

"No, Misha. I need to get back, anyway. I can imagine what my desk looks like."

Misha sucked her teeth. "Vic and the crew have it all under control."

Riley tossed a few more articles into the suitcase lying open on the bed. "I need to get out of here, honestly. All this heat's starting to fry my brain."

"You're hurting."

"As long as I stay here." Riley held the phone in the crook of her neck and quickly tossed more items into the suitcase. "I'm sure my crew left me enough work to dig into."

"Well, Bastian won the sports writers award this year. You know how many years he's been drooling over it." Misha was referring to Bastian Grovers, one of the *New Chronicle*'s senior writers. "Maybe you could cover his acceptance and give yourself a change of pace."

Riley was satisfied. "Sounds like a plan."

"The time away should help you see how rash you're being."

The connection ended before Riley could argue with her best friend.

"What the hell?" Asher whispered when his Pathfinder rounded the curve in the driveway. He spotted one of his limos parked before the front door, trunk open and suitcases waiting to be loaded. "Riley…" He sighed.

After parking the SUV haphazardly on the grass, he hopped out and met Riley as she was coming down the front steps.

"What are you doing?" he asked, out of breath and wearing a look of fearful disbelief.

She fidgeted with the gold chain at her neck. "There's a story. I need to—"

"Don't lie to me."

"It's the truth."

"Not all of it."

She blinked, unable to hide the guilt in her eyes. She was beginning to see why he was so good at his job. "It's enough."

He caught her arm when she tried to pass. "Why are you doing this?"

"I'm in your way here."

Asher almost laughed, while casting a fleeting glance toward his home. "You're gonna have to do a lot better than that."

She tried to wrench away from him. "You know what I mean."

"'Fraid I don't."

"'Maybe I'm tired of you being my girlfriend.' Sound familiar?"

His light eyes confessed all as memories of their conversation earlier that day filtered through his brain. He ran a hand across his neck. "I've never been so misjudged by anyone in my life—even when I've deserved it."

He'd released her arm, but Riley didn't bolt. "You're trying to tell me I'm wrong?"

"Very," he said on a weary laugh. "I don't want you to leave." He never wanted her to leave.

She'd prepared herself to hear anything but that.

"I love you," he whispered.

Correction. She'd prepared herself to hear anything but *that*.

"You don't know what you're saying." Her brown eyes were saucer wide as she stood before him and shook her head.

Her complete confidence in his ignorance stoked his frustration like a poker to a dying flame. Riley could see it in his eyes but steeled herself against believing that his feelings had truly turned down the road hers had taken long ago.

Asher took a moment to calm himself. "What's going on here, Riley? The truth."

"I'm just waiting for the bubble to burst and for you to tell me that this is over."

"Is that what you want?"

She was suddenly cold beneath the light cotton fabric of the petal-pink blouse she wore. "It could be for the best. We've been at this longer than either of us expected. You said it yourself that you were tired of booking flights to see your girlfriend."

"That was an expression, Riley, dammit." He felt the extreme urge to shake her then. "Hell, Riley, when I want to see you, I can hop on my own damn plane. I don't want you to go. But I won't force you."

She managed to move past him at last. "I'll call when I get back."

"Riley, please—"

"I promise I'll call." She pressed her hand to his chest, relishing the warmth and power there.

"So, it's that easy for you to walk away from me?" he snapped.

Riley curled her fingers into the front of his shirt. "It's not easy for me at all."

"Be honest, Riley. It's you who doesn't want this."

"No! No. Asher, I love you."

"Prove it."

"What?"

"Marry me."

Riley was blinking so rapidly, it was a wonder one of the long lashes didn't wind up in her eye. "You said you were tired of me being your girlfriend." She sounded lost.

He shook his head at her bewilderment. "Because I want you for my wife."

"But…why?"

"You mean, aside from the fact that I love you?"

"You don't know what you're saying… You can't."

His jaw clenched. "I do."

"I can't."

"Why?"

"Asher, we wouldn't even be living under the same roof."

"And?"

Her heart lurched. "You're crazy."

He smiled, looking down at the ground. That was quite possibly true, but during the time they'd been seeing each other, she had banished more than a few of his ghosts. Part of him prayed that as his wife, she would silence the rest. He believed that she loved him, but in the end, the decision would have to be hers. She would have to come to him as he'd come to her.

"You know, Riley, you're probably right... Having a wife I hardly see is sure to be ten times worse than having a girlfriend I don't see."

Stunned, Riley let him escort her to the limo. "But—"

"Call me soon, okay?" he asked softly, brushing the back of his hand across her jaw while she looked up at him in dumbfounded amazement.

"Asher—"

"No, Riley, you're right. Took me a while to finally admit that, I guess." He shrugged and favored her with a crooked grin. "I've never been one to admit when somethin' was a lost cause." Asher nodded to the driver, who'd finished loading Riley's things in the trunk.

Riley felt her heart sinking with every word he uttered.

He leaned inside the limo and kissed her cheek. "Take care of yourself, all right?"

Riley just blinked. Asher closed the door and knocked on the roof of the car to instruct the chauffer to drive on.

Riley was halfway to the airport when her shock subsided and tears filled her eyes.

Chapter 8

The annual New York Sports Writers and Editors Association banquet was held on a rainy Saturday evening. Luckily for Riley and Misha, the blinding rainstorm began an hour after the event began. Consequently, the duo was able to preserve their dazzling hairstyles and party in style on the top floor of the five-star Shallot's Tavern.

"Then he just told me to go."

"Just like that?"

"Mmm-hmm…"

Misha smiled and accepted a fresh drink from the bartender. "Disappointed you, huh?"

Riley stopped toying with the lock of her hair and let her hand fall to her shoulder. "Disappointed?"

"Mmm-hmm."

"Not disappointed. Surprised."

Misha sipped and savored her potent margarita. "Surprised, huh?"

"Yes, Misha, surprised," Riley groaned, losing her taste for the beer she'd requested. "One minute he's proposing, and the next he's bidding me a safe return to New York."

"Yeah…" Misha dangled her pump-shod foot. "I guess you were surprised and…devastated when the man you love called your bluff and told you to go."

Misha was right, and she sauntered off before Riley could tell her so. No matter, because moments later one of the evening's honorees was offering to buy her a drink.

* * *

"So I guess I can assume you already have the spot picked out for your award?" Riley was asking as she and Bastian twirled around the crowded dance floor.

He was already nodding. "Polished, with a big spotlight over the top."

Riley laughed. "Congratulations. Seriously, Bastian, I know how long you've wanted this."

"Just make sure this story of yours makes me look better than I already do."

Riley scrunched her face into a skeptical expression. "You know, my column's known for wiping the floor with folks."

"Ever thought of changing your pace?"

While she playfully contemplated the suggestion, the smile Bastian wore grew brighter, and moments later he released Riley's hand and slipped his hand from around her waist.

"Congratulations, man," a male voice said.

Everything flew from Riley's head as she stared up at Asher. Dressed in a beautifully tailored tuxedo, he was even more dashing than usual. She was rooted to her spot while he and Bastian carried on a light conversation. She was still in an absent state of mind when Bastian placed her hand in Asher's.

"Sorry about this," Asher said after Bastian left them alone to dance.

Riley snapped to at last. "It's not a problem, really."

His smirk was a mix of humor and something…almost dangerous. "Maybe not a problem for you, but I don't think Grovers would agree."

"Bastian? We didn't come together, Asher."

"I wasn't prying."

She was already shaking her head, suddenly feeling desperate to explain. "It's not like that between—"

"I wanted to apologize." There was humor in his expression, and something else…something dangerous.

His words stopped her explanation. "Apologize?"

Asher lost his train of thought when his fingers trailed down her spine, and he was captivated by the satin texture of her skin. "It occurred to me that I'd probably been wasting your time."

Riley was growing more confused by the moment. "Wasted my time?"

"Almost a year."

"Asher—"

"Maybe a part of me was ready to move on to something you weren't ready for." He shrugged and focused on the pulse beating at the base of her throat. "You probably tried to tell me that lots of times, and I just didn't listen. For that, I apologize."

She understood completely then, but it didn't stop her heart from sinking. "You weren't wasting my time, Asher."

"I appreciate you saying that."

She blinked in disbelief. "You think that? Honestly?"

He stepped out of their dance and squeezed her hands. "A year is a long time to waste with someone, don't you think?"

Tears of frustration filled her eyes. "I didn't waste my time."

He smiled, obviously not buying her words. "I only wanted to tell you that. Thanks for listening."

"Asher?" She watched helplessly as he walked away.

"Thanks." Misha accepted a fresh drink from the bartender and was turning to head back to her table when she froze.

Her ex, Talib Mason, was making his way to the bar himself. Misha felt like a deer caught in headlights—desperate to flee but too terrified to move. She mused that he might not even recognize her. It'd been close to three years, and she was sure he hadn't been a hermit all that time.

Slowly, she walked toward him, hoping to pass unnoticed on the way back to the *New Chronicle*'s table. She was almost halfway there when he stopped, stood straighter and appeared to stiffen.

So much for not recognizing me, Misha thought. He saw her, all right, and it was clear from the look on his gorgeous face that his disgust with her was still alive.

"Talib!"

Misha gave a start then and realized it was Riley who had

called him. Talib hesitated a moment before turning in Riley's direction. Misha took advantage of the distraction to bolt.

Riley noticed Misha rushing off but had no time to worry about her friend. She rushed toward Talib, catching hold of his jacket sleeve as she closed the distance between them.

"I need to find Asher. Will you tell me where he's staying while you guys are in town?"

"You really love him, don't you?" Talib remarked, smiling at Riley's harried appearance and the fear in her eyes as she nodded at his question. His friend had been dying a little each day over the fact that she didn't want the sort of relationship he did. Talib was pleased to see that Asher was about to be very pleasantly surprised.

"Please, Talib," she said on a sob of desperation and then laughed her relief when he recited the hotel name and room number.

Asher left the banquet, at which Hud-Mason had been named Agency of the Year. He didn't usually make efforts to attend award banquets, especially not in states outside of Arizona. He had gone to New York on the chance of seeing Riley.

His mother had said time was the best tester of all. He'd decided to give Riley the time she needed, but staying away from her was not an easy thing to do. All he'd wanted to do earlier was pull her close and kiss her until she agreed with anything he said. But this had to be her decision. Not the decision she felt he wanted her to make. Now, he could only hope that the possibility of losing what they had was just as unthinkable for her as it was for him.

After leaving the banquet, he drove around for a while. It was still raining heavily. Eventually, he tired of the messy road conditions and traffic and headed for his hotel.

Nothing could have surprised him more when he stepped off the elevator, searching his tux for the key card to his room, then finding Riley huddled on the floor outside his door.

"Jesus…," he whispered, dropping to his knees next to where she sat, curled up and appearing to shiver as she dozed. Muttering a curse, he stood, opened the door and then pulled her into his arms and carried her into the room.

Riley squeezed her eyes shut tight at least two times before she realized Asher's image was no hallucination.

"Hey," he whispered, smiling as he brushed his fingers across her brow.

"Asher?"

"Mmm-hmm…"

"You weren't here, and I…" She shivered again, smiling when he drew his tuxedo jacket more snugly around her bare arms. "Security recognized me…let me up. I didn't want to go back out in the rain and decided to wait here."

"I know." He pressed a possessive kiss to her temple and sighed.

"I love you," she blurted, grasping a fistful of his shirt. "I love you. I never wanted to leave. I just…I'm scared. This is all so soon, so fast. Marriage is a big step. I don't know if it's for me, and I don't want to ruin us."

His heart was in his throat. "You don't have to be afraid of me."

She grimaced. "Not you. It's…past stuff that creeps in. I…I never know when it's gonna crop up. I do know that I love you. I want you with me."

He certainly knew all about *past stuff* and only murmured soothing words against her temple.

"Will you ask me to marry you again?"

His heart began to beat in his throat then. "I don't want to pressure you."

"I love you, and I don't want to lose you, either."

He closed his eyes to mutter a thankful prayer.

Riley inched close to seek out his lips, and they shared a sweet kiss.

One week later, Asher had managed the impossible. He had coaxed changes in schedules and arranged to have his parents, Virginia Stamper and Misha flown out to Scottsdale to bear witness as he and Riley became Mr. and Mrs. Asher Hudson. The elder Hudsons and Virginia Stamper became fast friends. The group spent their time sightseeing and sharing stories of their children. Misha, meanwhile, took advantage of the impromptu vacation to absorb the sun and enjoy the various man-made indulgences available on Asher's estate. Everyone delighted in the happy time, with the exception of the bride. Riley found that she was too preoccupied to do much else than ponder what was in store for her in the future.

Virginia pushed at her daughter's shoulder in hopes of waking her when breakfast was sent to the bedroom suite courtesy of Asher's kitchen staff. Riley had slept there with her the previous evening, as opposed to returning to her own room…or Asher's. Virginia was more than a little curious about what had her daughter so on edge the eve of her wedding.

Giving up on applying nudges to Riley's shoulder, Virginia poured a cup of the fragrant coffee and sweetened it with cream. Trailing the cup beneath Riley's nose, Virginia waited and smiled brightly when her lashes fluttered.

"Only a few more hours until you're Mrs. Riley Hudson."

With effort, Riley produced a smile. "I'm keeping my last name. Professional reasons." She pushed herself from bed.

"Professional reasons." Virginia nodded. "Are those the only ones?"

Riley was on her way to the food cart when she heard the question. Her face wore a strange expression, and a response was not forthcoming.

"Do you love him, Riley?"

"Very much."

"But?"

Riley balled her fists in the hem of her sleep shirt. "I feel so weird saying it."

"Honey, why?"

Riley turned and began lifting the covers from the food. "People see each other for years before they feel that way, don't they?"

"Not necessarily."

"And even then, things can go haywire without you ever seeing it coming." Riley went on as though she hadn't heard her mother.

"Have you talked to him, honey?"

Riley bit her lip. "He wants it so, and so do I. I just…"

"Any particular reason why *he's* pushing for it?" Virginia tucked her gown beneath her as she sat on the bed.

Riley noticed her mother staring at her tummy, and she laughed. "It's not that, trust me. I'm definitely *not* pregnant. He told me that he was tired of me being his girlfriend."

"Well, what's wrong with that?"

"Nothing, but maybe that's why I'm more nervous than I should be. We're so far apart from each other, and our being married isn't gonna change that." Riley joined her mother on the bed. "I don't want to disappoint him, but I don't want to lose him, either."

"Oh, honey." Virginia cupped Riley's face. "I'm sorry I don't have any answers."

Riley smiled while blinking tears from her lashes. "That's okay. Right now, all I need is a shoulder."

Sighing, Virginia pulled her daughter into a hug.

Misha smiled, satisfied that she looked the part of a proper maid of honor. The dress was simple yet elegant, tailored yet uniquely suited to enhance her slender build and subtle curves. Glancing at the dresser clock, she decided it was time to get a move on and headed for the door.

When she whipped it open and found Talib Mason on the other side, she almost stumbled back on the silver pumps she wore. He barely smiled, and Misha was too on edge to notice the softness in his eyes, relaying what he wouldn't say.

"I'm supposed to escort you. Best man," he explained.

"Right." Misha blinked herself back to reality. "I, um…just need to get the flower thing."

Talib leaned on the doorjamb and watched Misha place the floral headpiece atop her head.

Misha was surprised she was able to focus on a thing with his gaze steered her way. He was as extraordinary as she remembered. *Riley, you owe me big-time!* she thought.

Talib had the same thought in his head regarding Asher. He'd been thrilled to be best man, but that thrill had vanished quickly when he was informed that one of his duties would be to escort the maid of honor, Misha Bales. He hadn't talked to her in almost three years, and dammit, he could still remember the way her perfume lingered on his sheets after he'd had her there.

"We better get going," he said, suddenly feeling himself tense and tighten from memory.

Misha gave a start and hurried to the door. She hesitated when he offered his arm, but took it and refused to moan over the feel of his bicep's iron thickness when she took hold.

Later that evening, under a sky tinged orange by the setting sun, an exquisite ceremony took place. Virginia and Cassell sat teary eyed while watching Jones escort his soon-to-be daughter-in-law down the aisle. Misha took her place while Talib clapped his best friend's shoulder.

The minister introduced them as Mr. and Mrs. Asher Hudson shortly after. The couple shared their first kiss as man and wife while the small crowd in attendance cheered their approval. Of course, Asher and Riley were too preoccupied just then to notice.

Chapter 9

Riley savored the feel of her husband's lean, chiseled frame behind her. She bit her lip and winced in pain and pleasure at the sensation on her skin when he smoothed his hands across her hips and then around the lush curve of her thighs.

"Asher…" she moaned, biting her lip again when his fingers grazed the sensitive flesh of her sex. "Baby…I ache," she told him, even as dull stabs of desire began to run through her ravished flesh.

Asher Hudson hid his handsome honey-toned face in his wife's chic mop of clipped hair. He inhaled the fresh green-apple aroma that always clung to it.

"Not for long," he promised, raising one hand to cup a dark chocolate breast, which fit perfectly in his palm. All the while he continued to manipulate the satiny petals of her womanhood.

"Just an hour, Asher, please…?"

"No, I haven't had you in a month."

Clearly, he intended to make up for that sad fact. It was hard to believe they'd been married little over six months. They'd been making love steadily from the moment one of his cars took them from the airport to his home in Scottsdale. *Home,* however, was a poor choice of words. The place was the size of a small town. Riley believed her aching body was living proof of that. They'd enjoyed each other in every corner of the dwelling.

Asher seemed quite determined to make love to his wife every minute of their time together.

"Asher, please." Riley figured if she sounded pathetic enough, he'd give in to her.

"I plan to," he whispered next to her ear and grinned when he felt her slippery need coating his fingertips.

"Shut up," Riley moaned while arching against the gentle thrusts inside her body.

Asher complied and buried his face in her hair again. He continued to thrust his fingers inside her body, the sound of her satisfied cries, presently muffled by the pillows, fueling his ego. Still treating her to the heavenly finger play, he nibbled her shoulders and back. His tongue traced the length and dip of her spine.

"Now please," Riley begged then, but she could tell from his chuckle that he wanted to play a little longer.

He nibbled the firm, healthy rise of her buttocks before his lips and tongue feasted on the highly sensitive area between. Riley arched and moaned his name with such vigor, Asher was robbed of whatever restraint he had. Seconds later, he was replacing his mouth with the part of his body she was presently demanding.

Every part of him weakened when he was inside her, yet the desire to have her overruled the weakness. He couldn't stand much more of this. He needed more of her; he needed…all of her. Dismissing the stirrings of a frustrating train of thought, he focused solely on the moment at hand. Riley was an eager participant and threatened to make him come much too soon. Gripping her hips, he eased her off his erection in hopes of extending what had to be their tenth love session of the evening.

Deciding to take control, Riley turned the tables and shoved Asher on his back. Roughly, she straddled his powerful frame and then settled herself upon his impressive length in a torturously slow manner.

"A nap next, yes?" she bargained.

Asher was already thrusting up into her. "Whatever you want," he groaned.

The lower level of the house was almost saturated by the sound of needy cries and moans. Asher gripped Riley's hips again but had no thoughts of pulling her off. He gasped his love for her while filling her with his seed….

* * *

Riley smiled and snuggled a bit deeper into the luxurious Egyptian cotton linens grazing her skin. Her smoky gaze was filled with contentment while she studied the incredible tropical-like view of the rear of the estate from her cherished position in the king-size bed.

The sun beamed down, and that was most often something Riley could've done without. But here…here it was like paradise. Of course, she knew that had everything to do with her present company. Waiting for the day of this trip out to Phoenix had almost driven her crazy with anticipation. That wasn't surprising. Whenever the opportunity to be together in the same time zone presented itself, she and Asher always jumped at the chance.

Turning to her side, she watched him then. His face relaxed in sleep, Asher appeared to be as content as she was. She knew, however, that beneath that easy exterior beat the heart of a man who wouldn't rest until she was a permanent resident of Scottsdale. She couldn't blame him. After all, who wouldn't want to live in such exquisite surroundings?

Stretching languidly, she took a slow scan of the bedroom. Huge bay windows lined the rear wall. Set before the windows was a luxurious overstuffed sky-blue sofa flanked by two deep armchairs. A glass coffee table topped off the setting and held a tray with fresh coffee and Danish, courtesy of the morning staff.

Riley frowned a bit, wondering when the workers had had the chance to arrange the setting. She'd never figure it out, of course, since everything in Asher Hudson's world always seemed to be a wish away. Riley didn't know if the power her husband wielded impressed her or set her on edge.

All thoughts fled her mind when she felt herself being tugged across the mammoth canopied bed. Her smile reemerged as she trailed her fingers along Asher's forearm, which was presently locked about her waist. She shivered when his mouth grazed the dip between her shoulder blades.

"Still aching?" he murmured.

Riley shivered again. "Does it matter?"

"Of course. I'd consider it my duty to make it go away."

"Mmm..." She snuggled deeper into the embrace. "I'm sure leaving it alone is all that's required."

His arms flexed about her waist. "I'm afraid leaving it alone doesn't work for me."

"I see, and what *does* work for you?" she breathed and a moment later found herself being subjected to an exquisite oral treat.

"Well, I guess you were right," Riley acknowledged later, upon realizing she felt no trace of discomfort once he was inside her.

Asher rested his head in the crook of her neck and thrust slowly, savoring the way she trembled below him. They made love across every square inch of the bed. When they collapsed a long while later, Riley begged him to feed her before subjecting her to more torture.

Asher kept her pressed back against his chest as persuasive fingers fondled the puckering flesh guarding her femininity.

"That feel like torture to you?"

"Asher..."

Chuckling, he reached for the bedside phone and ordered breakfast from his cook downstairs. While they waited, he subjected her to deep kisses and more fondling.

"So what can I do for you today?" Asher inquired while they breakfasted on three-cheese omelets, steak strips and buttermilk biscuits.

Riley's teacup froze in midair. "Don't you have work to do?"

"Tons."

"Well?"

"Well...you're here."

"So?"

"So work is a nonissue when you're here."

Riley was even more surprised, especially since Asher had already told her he wanted her to stay at least a week. "I can't believe you'd consider shrugging off work for that long."

"I wouldn't *consider* shrugging off work." He chewed contentedly on a corner of the steak. "I'd *actually* shrug it off."

Riley set aside her teacup and leaned back. "You're serious?"

"Painfully. Do you know how much work I'll have to catch up on when you leave?"

"Well, why don't you just—"

"Riley? It's done." He winced and added a small shrug. "Almost."

"Almost?"

"There's a thing."

"A thing?"

"Tomorrow night."

Riley exchanged her tea for orange juice and sipped. A knowing expression came over her face. "Hmm…is this *thing* tomorrow night a party?"

The guilt in his bright stare forced a curse past her lips.

"Shh…" He leaned across the table and squeezed her hand in his. "It was the one thing I couldn't get out of. I promise we won't be there long. All you've gotta do is hold on to me and look absentminded and beautiful."

Riley shrugged. "I can certainly handle the absentminded part."

Asher simply observed his wife, watching as a look of disgust crossed her lovely dark face. She detested parties. Damn, he loved her. In a world where self-absorbed phonies and opportunists were abundant, she'd always been like a breath of fresh air. Her only concern was the time they shared alone together. For Riley Stamper, a splashy party with "the beautiful people" was about as exciting as watching paint dry.

"What?" Riley noted the intensity in his stare.

"You know tomorrow night's party isn't the only thing I have in store for you."

"Uh-oh…" Riley's lashes fluttered as she brought a hand to her forehead. "Don't tell me. It's a brunch with a thousand of your closest friends?"

Asher's hearty, contagious laughter filled the bedroom. "You know, that's not a bad idea." His laughter mounted at the wilting look she sent his way. "How'd you like to see another view of Arizona?"

Riley's head tilted as curiosity bloomed in her eyes. "What've you got in mind?"

Asher, however, was bent on secrecy. "I guarantee it'll take your breath away."

She had no doubt, since every minute with her husband did precisely that.

Asher read her expression easily. "Stop it. You need to eat."

"Can't you give me a little hint?" She forked a portion of cheesy omelet. "Just a *little* info about it?"

"A *little* info. Let's see…" Asher stroked the strong curve of his jaw and debated. "Ah! You'll need to get dressed."

"You're a crazy man," Riley breathed two hours later, as she stood with Asher on the rear lawn and stared openmouthed at the hot air balloon waiting to give her "another view of Arizona." "Have you lost your mind?"

She dragged her gaze away from the vibrant hot pinks, sky blues, greens and purples bursting to life on the balloon. Her heart somersaulted at the crooked grin he flashed her way.

"Don't even try to get out of it. You work at altitudes higher than this thing will go." He pointed toward the sky.

Riley grunted. "There's always more beneath my feet than…hot air, though."

"Live a little."

"That's what I'd like to do."

Asher was still laughing outrageously as he turned to greet the balloon captain, Elliott Wells. They spent several moments catching up while Riley took a closer, skeptical look at their transportation.

"Have you done this before?" she asked when he finished his conversation with Elliott and returned to her side.

"It's a good selling point for potential clients looking to be traded out here." He hooked a thumb through a belt loop on his jeans and glanced up at the balloon. "After an aerial view of Arizona, most can't believe they'd ever chosen to live anyplace else."

Riley smiled and bowed her head. It wasn't hard to figure out what the adventure was about. Still, she decided not to call Asher on it and swallowed her unease in order to play along.

* * *

Thirty minutes and two glasses of champagne later, Riley didn't fear for her life quite so much. She smirked when Asher caught her eye as she reached for the champagne bottle. "This is really unexpected." She wiggled the bottle.

"Don't forget the strawberries," he urged.

"Is this the way you persuade all those big names you sign?" She swirled a strawberry through the whipped cream.

Asher's expression was serious as he toyed with the frayed edge of the dashiki she wore. "I only break out the champagne and strawberries for the woman I'm trying to persuade."

"Humph." She savored the fruit and cream on her tongue. "Trust me, you've already persuaded me. Many times."

"Have I?"

Before she could respond, he was kissing her deeply. "Wait," she said against his tongue, which was thrusting into her mouth. "Asher…"

He wasn't in the mood for resistance. The straw basket set beneath the colorful, voluminous balloon was as big as a small room almost and offered a modicum of privacy for a couple wishing to steal a sweet kiss amid paradise.

The kiss they shared, however, was far from sweet. It was torrid, lusty, in its desperation. Riley needed him at once but steeled herself against begging.

"This isn't fair," she moaned.

"You're not enjoying it?" he whispered into her mouth.

"You know it's beautiful… All I want is to be with you at home."

"What can we do at home that we can't do here?" His fingers grew bold, cupping her breast and fondling a firming nipple.

Riley bit her lip on the cry his touch elicited. "This isn't the place. Come on. Stop now."

"You're right." He stopped suddenly and didn't tell his wife that he'd glimpsed the disappointment on her face. "This isn't the place." He dropped a kiss on her forehead. "I intend to correct all that." He shook his head, dismissing the question he was about to utter, and turned her in his arms.

They embraced while staring out at the beauty before their eyes.

"So how do we get back?" Riley asked as they stood watching the balloon lift off from the clearing and leave them alone in the woods.

Asher grinned. "You in a hurry?"

"No." She was massaging her arms and looking anything but calm. "Just a little nervous about being in, um…"

"So much open space?"

She waved him off. "I'd just like to know how we're supposed to get out of here, that's all."

Asher tugged her along, not stopping until they approached a tree. He held her against the trunk and leaned close to nuzzle her ear. "I'd be more interested in what we're gonna *do* while we're here."

Riley's gaze was naughtiness and innocence combined. "What've you got in mind?"

"This first." His mouth slid around the curve of her jaw, and he kissed her.

The kiss was even lustier than before. Yet in spite of being alone, Asher had no intentions of taking her there. Riley had other ideas and did what she could to entice him to have her then and there. Asher obliged her for a time, losing himself in the light, clean fragrance clinging to her skin and the softness of her breasts filling his hands. When her fingers traveled past his waist to fidget with the buttons securing the fly of his sagging jeans, Asher almost lost himself in his desire for her.

Forcing strength into his legs, he hoisted her against him. Still kissing her, he carried her deeper into the woods and toward his next surprise.

Riley was so involved in their kiss that it took some time for her to notice the spectacular sight past his shoulders. When he broke the kiss and lightly bumped his forehead against hers, Riley's lashes fluttered. She looked beyond him, at what appeared to be…

"Asher…is that… Is that a tent?"

Still holding her, he turned to look at the structure in the distance.

"What is this?" she breathed when he started walking toward it.

"This is what we're gonna *do* while we're here." He joined in when she laughed. "Better yet, it's *where* we're gonna do it."

"Well, can I look around first?"

"Sure." He approved but began tugging her out of the dashiki while she oohed and aahed over the tent, which looked more like a mini hotel suite.

"This is lovely," she breathed, absently raising her arms in order for him to relieve her of the lightweight garment.

"Yes, it is," Asher said and sighed his agreement when she was bared to his gaze.

Riley's interest in her surroundings was quelled for a time when he pulled her back next to him. Making love had her full attention.

Afterward, they shared an incredible supper of grilled salmon steaks, Texas toast and salad beneath late evening skies outside the tent.

"You can live like this every minute you're here, you know?" said Asher.

His cool, informative tone had Riley smiling. Carefully, she placed her fork on the table and decided it was time to lay the real cards on the table. Leaning across the small square table, she brushed the back of her hand against his cheek.

"What's going on?"

Asher kept his gaze on his plate. "I just miss you, is all."

She smiled and raised her brows in a teasing manner. "Is it all this great weather and sensual temptation?"

Asher turned deadly serious and gripped the hand she'd brushed across his cheek. "I miss you. There isn't another woman who can do for me what you do. You should already know that. You really wanna know why it's so easy to shrug off work when you're here? Because I can hardly think of anything else when you're around me."

Riley tried to keep things light. "And you really want me around, distracting you twenty-four-seven?"

He stood and began to clear the table. "If that's all I could get, I'd take it."

"Asher…"

"Let's dance."

Thankful he'd changed the subject, she smiled and placed her fingers against his palm. Riley was immediately entranced by the endless sky and the glittering stars, which were more dazzling than the brightest city lights.

"So incredible…" she declared while looking up.

Asher agreed completely, though his eyes were focused solely on her.

Chapter 10

"**A**sher Demond Hudson, no way are you gonna get me to believe I'd get this kind of treatment every day if I were here." Riley gasped as she gazed down on the exquisite camp retreat they'd shared the evening before.

Now, instead of a hot air balloon carrying them toward the horizon, it was stylish black helicopter, with Asher at the controls.

"Was this thing down there all night?" She waved her hand.

"Got there early this morning."

"No way was I sleeping *that* hard."

Asher leaned his head back against the seat and smiled. "I swear you were, and by the way, you're welcome." When she pinched his arm, he cried, "Ow!"

"Arrogant swine," she accused amid her laughter.

"I agree with your comment." He rotated his arm to ease the ache her pinch had caused. "Just remember, this arrogant swine has your life in his hands."

Riley eyed the flight panel warily. "I'm trying not to think about it."

"I know you've ridden in a chopper before, Stamper."

"Course, I have. But never have I ridden in one where I had intimate knowledge of the pilot," she said, speaking over the interference from the headset she wore to communicate with Asher.

"Ah." Asher's fingers flexed around the stick. "So I'm your first?"

"Humph. I guess you are."

"Good. Keep it that way."

She fixed him with a heavily sugared look. "After last night, that won't be a problem. Incredible in every way."

"Shut up. I'm trying to concentrate," he said after they'd laughed for a good minute.

Riley's eyes twinkled mischievously. "Am I upsetting your concentration, Mr. Pilot?"

"You have no idea…."

Laughter filled the cockpit once more.

Riley asked about Asher's best friend and business partner, Talib Mason, while they lounged in massive amounts of cool shade, compliments of the lofty palm trees that sprinkled the rear of the estate and sheltered the pool area.

"Seems to be doing fine." Asher took a swig of his Heineken. "He was sorry he couldn't be in town to see you this time around."

Riley watched him thoughtfully. "Why'd you say that he *seems* to be doing fine?"

"Come on." Asher fixed her with a knowing look. "Would it surprise you to know that he's still suffering over her?"

Riley nodded, not surprised at all. "She's still suffering for him."

"So how is she?" Asher inquired about his wife's best friend and editor, Misha Bales.

"All that brash, sassy, hard-nosed editor and woman of the world stuff has everybody fooled."

"Everybody except you," Asher noted, watching his wife help herself to a taste of the Red Stripe beer she'd been nursing.

"They're just both so stubborn," she declared, thinking of their friends then.

Asher agreed, with a grunt, and then looked over at Riley. Seconds later, the two of them were dissolving into peals of laughter. Silently, they accepted that for them to call anyone else stubborn was truly a case of the pot calling the kettle black.

"So…what's next?" Riley asked after they'd enjoyed the shade in silence for a while.

Asher drank deeply of his beer. "I'm not sure all my feats are working on you."

"They damn well are, since I'm only falling more in love with you," she swore.

Asher rolled the stout green bottle between his palms. "But not in love enough to stay?" He spoke casually enough so that it seemed he didn't want a response.

Riley, however, had had enough and set her bottle on the wooden table between them. "Asher, exactly what would you have me do here? You know I can't leave New York."

His gaze was cool as it traveled the length of her legs and arms, which were bare thanks to the daring bikini she wore. "Someone holding a gun to your head?"

"I could ask you the same," she muttered.

Asher's beer bottle froze in midair. He raised his brows, as though he were considering her question, and then continued with his drink.

Moments later, a perky housemaid came outside to inform them that lunch would be ready in one hour.

Asher pushed off the chaise lounge. "Think I'll go up and take a shower."

When he was gone, Riley let her head fall back against the chaise lounge and let loose a long groan.

Asher stood beneath the spray of water and just let the hot beads stream across his face, neck and shoulders. Not even a cold shower would have eased his anger.

Subtlety had never been his strong suit, especially not when it came to Riley. He'd wanted her from the moment they met. At first, it was simply because of her looks—the dark chocolate face; the big expressive brown eyes; the mouth; the body. He grimaced, feeling his own body react to her image in his head.

Then he'd come to love her to insanity. She was a loving, giving and strong companion. She'd become stronger and more loving and giving as his wife. Asher had never felt more complete, and little did his wife know that her treasured existence in his life was what allowed him to do his job so well.

Sadly, he didn't feel that street went both ways. Sometimes he figured she'd prosper just fine without him in her life. He shook his head to dismiss the thought. He knew she loved him as obsessively as he loved her. Then there was her job. The column she'd transformed from a popular but lighthearted editorial into one of the most respected journalistic efforts in New York City. Business people and college students alike enjoyed their coffee and bagel over the *Stumper Column* each morning. They shared their own ideas about her topic of the day. She had her picture on the side of a bus, for goodness sake!

She deserved to hold on to that, he thought. She deserved to *want* to hold on to that. Again, he shook the annoying thoughts from his mind and chose to focus on his shower. He'd just finished lathering up when the glass doors parted.

His jaw dropped, as did his eyes when they drifted from Riley's lovely face to her lovely bare body.

"I don't want to fight," she whispered, tugging her bottom lip between her teeth when he grabbed her waist and pulled her into the shower.

They were kissing instantly, but Riley backed away and continued to lather him with the soap resting in its holder.

Asher leaned back against the tiles and watched her take the utmost care in bathing him, rinsing him.

Riley paid special attention to the breathtaking array of muscles lining his abdomen and looked on in awe as her nails brushed the carved beauty. She moved on to pay homage to his arousal, erect and ready, and smiled a bit when his groan filled the steamy shower.

Shortly, however, he could take no more and drew Riley to her feet. He trailed kisses along her jaw, neck and shoulders as he posed her to receive him. Her laughter was a clear indication of the pleasure overtaking her when she felt him inside. The laughter, though, was short-lived, as the pleasure forced wanton moans from the back of her throat.

Not surprisingly, the couple decided to spend lunchtime in the shower.

After lunch Asher and Riley drove into Phoenix where Hud-Mason was located. The sports agency Asher had started with

Talib had become world renowned within just three years. Now, at the onset of their tenth year, the partners were celebrating success after success. It was rumored that the gorgeous duo could charm an athlete away from his or her present representation as easily as they could charm a woman away from her desire to say no.

Riley thought how fitting that accolade was as she waltzed into her husband's stunning corner office. She recalled the day when she'd been summoned there, terrified, until that terror merged into desire once she met the man in charge. Without a doubt, she'd been totally charmed by Asher Hudson's coolly arrogant, provocative demeanor.

She took a seat behind the large, almost intimidating desk and watched him speak with the junior agent who'd asked for a moment of his time when they stepped out of the elevator. Folding her arms across the wine-colored capped-sleeve top she wore, Riley relaxed in the silver-gray suede chair behind the desk and simply observed. She admired everything, from the hang of his sagging denims to the tilt of his head. He spoke with both authority and comradery.

"Now, please tell me why you wanted to drive all the way out here," he said once the mini meeting had ended and he'd shut the door.

"Can't a wife see where her husband works?"

"You've already seen it—many times."

"Not for a while, though. Besides, I like watching you work," she purred.

He grinned, and for a second, Riley thought he was embarrassed. The effect endeared him to her even more.

Asher rounded the desk, with every intention of kissing her. knock at the door halted his pursuit.

"You might get your wish," he groaned and called out for the ⸱ker to enter.

⸱ey, Ashe. Brandon told me you just got in." Claudette Silver ⸱ in, harried and breathless, referring to the junior agent ⸱opped Asher at his office door. "Hey, girl!" She forgot ⸱ boss as she hurried over to greet his wife with hugs ⸱lk.

"Got some stuff for you to sign," Claudette told Asher once Riley had crossed the room to the bar for a bottle of juice. "Have you told her about the trip yet?"

Asher shook his head while signing the requisitions his assistant pushed at him. "I'm gonna try surprising her. What do you think of my chances?"

Claudette uttered a decisive humph and tucked a lock of her dark blond hair behind an ear. "They're about as good as my chances of picking up a rich, sexy man at this party of yours tonight."

"Well, there's gonna be tons of 'em there, so you never know."

Folding her arms across the prim honey-brown suit jacket she wore, Claudette winked. "Remember I also said sexy."

"Right." Asher grimaced then and tried to appear hopeful. "You might get lucky. Just be there, beautiful and bright eyed, tonight."

Claudette rolled her eyes toward Riley. "He this pushy about parties with you?"

"Every chance he gets," Riley confirmed while stepping into Asher's embrace. He slipped an arm about her waist and took a sip of her juice.

"Oh well…" Claudette acquiesced to defeat and gave Riley another hug before she left the office.

"Seriously now, do you promise this'll be the only party while I'm here?" Riley asked once she was alone with her husband.

"That's hard to say." He sighed and instantly had to beg for mercy when she began to tickle him. "Hold on! Hold on now. What do I get if I promise it's the only one?" He held her arms to her sides.

Riley's brows didn't rise, though clearly she was considering the question. "I can think of quite a few things, actually." She tapped a nail on her lips and debated. "I suppose I could *ration* them out while I determine if you'll keep your word."

Asher's eyes narrowed playfully. He set aside the bottle juice, then backed her toward his desk. "When does this *rationing* start exactly?"

Riley held the front of her blouse together in a gesture of demureness. "Why, Mr. Hudson, surely you're not sugges

"I'm doing more than *suggesting,* Miss Stamper."

With that, his hand disappeared inside her blouse

* * *

The party had been going strong for almost an hour and a half when Riley finally connected with her husband. She was quite pleased that she'd been enjoying herself so thoroughly. Asher worked with a great team of people, and they treated her with an ease that told her they viewed her as more than just the boss's wife. She was strolling toward the splendid buffet tables situated in a far corner of the rear lawn when Asher caught her waist.

"Will you dance with me?" He nuzzled her ear while making the request.

Riley couldn't help but smile as the way he had posed the question made it sound as though they were still dating and there was still that vague uncertainty between them. Placing her hand in his, she accepted.

In silence, they swayed to a jazzy yet sultry rendering of "Betcha By Golly Wow!" performed by the neo-soul artists hired for the party.

"Asher?"

"Hmm…"

His response vibrated through her, and she shivered. "Um, would you mind telling me what this party is for?"

"We just signed a few new clients." His fingers strummed the area of bare skin visible between the low-cut bodice of her dress and the chic slit skirt that flowed past her ankles. "It's just a get-together for my people. We tend to celebrate with either a party, drinks or dinner when we close a big deal."

"Mmm…" Riley's contentment soared. The sultry setting, the music and the faint hum of conversation in the air was the perfect recipe for relaxation. "Shouldn't Talib be here? He's a part of it all, right?"

"Not back from his trip yet." Asher stepped back as thoughts of his friend began to weigh heavily on him. "Besides, it's like pulling teeth, getting him to socialize outside the office."

"Humph. I can definitely understand that, considering where parties rank on my to-do lists."

Asher grimaced. "It's not the same where Talib's concerned, though."

"Because of Misha."

He shook his head. "Don't mention any of this to her, all right? I'd hate for her to know he's pining for her and to think there's a chance for them."

"Oh, I can promise you, Misha's got no notions of a reunion with your boy." Riley peppered the statement with a flip shrug. "She never really went into all that happened between them but I know she's not up to opening herself up to tension again." Riley wound her arms about Asher's neck. "And speaking of tension, I feel none of that here. Thank you for a great vacation." She brushed her lips against his cheek. "It's gonna be so hard to leave when the time comes."

Riley continued to sway to the music, never noticing the muscles dancing a jig of rage along Asher's jaw.

Chapter 11

Two weeks later...

Riley called out to Asher, then clapped a hand over her mouth when she opened his study door and saw that he was on the phone. She was about to back out of the doorway, but Asher waved her forward.

"Cooper? Coop? Listen, we'll have to finish this later. My wife's here. Yeah...yeah, we'll talk tomorrow."

"You didn't have to do that," Riley gently scolded and gave an airy wave toward the phone. Asher was already leaving his desk and crossing the room. "What I had to ask could, um—" The rest of her sentence ended on a moan when his mouth came down on hers.

Quickly, Riley dissolved into a mass of need, her body going pliant against the brick wall of his chest. She'd always considered herself a strong woman. Against this man...she felt strong yet drunk with desire in the same breath. Her body overruled her mind when his image emerged in her head. It had been that way from the moment he summoned her to his office the day after he broke the story of corruption in the ranks of his now multi-million-dollar sports agency.

Snapping back to the present, Riley discovered she was half and half out of her bra. Asher was working her nipples into peaks while his lips suckled the diamond studs adorning her s. She called his name in an attempt to urge him to wait, oice came out as a weak gasp, and she sounded more an firm.

For just a few moments, she let herself float in this provocative state he'd created. His mouth glided down the column of her neck, and then he was suckling the firm peaks of her bosom, which filled his hands.

Riley cleared her throat then. "Asher… The car's late… again."

"I'm sorry." He sounded far from sincere.

"Asher, I have a plane to catch."

"Tomorrow."

"You've told me that three times already." Agitation began to squelch Riley's desire.

Asher's desire began to merge with agitation as well. "What's your hurry?"

"I have work."

"And I haven't seen you in a month."

"You knew I couldn't stay."

"You're my wife."

"And you know my obligations. They've been the same since the day we met."

Asher left her side then. Riley could see the muscle flexing wickedly along his jaw.

"What about your obligation to me Ri?"

Ri. He only called her that when he was truly pissed with her. She rolled her eyes and set about fixing her clothes. "It's my job."

"It's a column, and you can write it from anywhere."

Riley's hands stilled on her sleeve, and she watched him, as if stunned. "You know it's more than that. My *column* is a lot more than opinions spilling out of my head. They're facts, they're flushed out, confirmed, researched, and for you to make light of it—"

"Riley, everything else *is* light when it's weighed again our marriage."

"So I guess that includes *your* job, too?" she challer watching him, defiance in her smoky stare. "Does it, A Hmm? Scrapping for dollars for overindulged, overp overgrown kids?"

His gaze narrowed more dangerously. "That's wha

of my work?" His voice grated while he smoothed the back of his hand across the wicked scar on his cheek.

Riley sensed that things were going down an ugly road, but it was clearly not a new road. The subject was always lurking there, in the corridor of their marriage, and it had been forged during their courtship.

"Asher, you know I really don't want to do this." She gave a quick smile. "I only want to go."

"I don't want you to go," was his simple reply as he turned back toward his desk.

"I, um…I could always call a cab," she threatened, ignoring the lurching of her heart.

Asher grinned but kept his eyes focused on a page he held. "It'd get no farther than the gate," he warned.

Blinking, Riley dismissed her unease and walked over to the large oak desk he stood behind. "Are you hinting that you'd keep me here against my will?"

He turned to her so suddenly, she didn't have time to react. "Against your will?" He raged softly, easing his hand past the slit in her skirt. "So being there is more important than being here with me, is that it?"

Riley's lashes fluttered as an instant need surged through her. Admirably, her thoughts remained on track. "This isn't about that."

"The hell it's not. I want you where I am."

"Then come to New York. You can run your business there as easily as I could work here. Maybe more so." Her lips thinned when he rolled his eyes. "Why should *I* be the one to move, Asher?"

"Because it's not that easy for me to just pick up and move headquarters."

"Bullshit. You just don't want to."

He had the nerve to wink at her. "That too," he confirmed.

"Hypocrite."

"If you like."

"I should've known it would come to this."

Asher moved his hand and muttered a curse. "What, Ri? Wanting my wife at my side?"

"Dammit, I *am* at your side. Our lives have always been unorthodox, but I've always been by your side whenever I could."

He smirked. "Whenever you could, huh?" Slowly, his dark gaze raked the length of her body. "I want more than that," he said.

Riley raised her chin. "But not enough to come where I am."

"This is stupid, Ri."

"Yeah, hypocrisy's a bitch."

He massaged the bridge of his nose. "I didn't ask you out here to argue."

Riley sneered. "No…you *asked me out here* to celebrate our marriage, right? Right, Asher?" Folding her arms over her chest, she fixed him with a knowing smile. "Or did you ask me to come out here to force me to stay with you?"

"*Force* you? You're my wife, and I'd have to *force* you?"

It broke her heart to know she was causing the pain in his eyes. Now that they were on the ever-present road, however, there was no getting off until they reached the end.

"I warned you this would happen, remember? I warned you…." She was more or less speaking to herself. "But *you* were the one who wanted to get married." Her sigh was followed by a gasp when she realized what she'd said.

Asher's head snapped up, and the hurt on his face was replaced by a look of stunned disbelief.

Riley was also in a state of disbelief. They were still standing close to one another, yet she refused to meet his gaze when he dipped his head to look at her.

"You know, I've never forced a woman to do anything against her will," he said and looked away when she dragged her eyes to his face. "I'm not about to start now. I can't stop you. I won't. You want to leave me. You…don't want to be married, then go." He said this in spite of the fact that he could scarcely hear above the pulse thundering in his ears. "A car'll be waiting when you walk out the front door." He turned away then, sickened by the lie he'd spoken. He'd never let her leave him. He'd foolishly underestimated her will to maintain the fierce independence that seemed to rule her.

"Go, Ri, I mean it," he said when he saw that she was still

watching him. "But if you choose to stay, you'll do it here in Phoenix."

Riley shook her head dazedly. "An ultimatum?" She spoke the word as though it were foreign to her ears. She opened her mouth, closed it and then tried to speak again. "I can't believe you'd make me choose between—"

"It's a simple enough choice."

"Because *you're* not the one who has to make it!"

Asher stifled his next words in his throat. He wouldn't beg her. He wouldn't tell her that the distance was killing him or that he was going out of his mind with worry when she was in New York. Issuing the ultimatum had been a caveman move, but that he could tolerate. That had its own rewards.

Right about then, Riley was thinking of *rewarding* the man she loved with a quick jab to the gut. An ultimatum? Damn him. If she hadn't heard it with her own ears, she never would've believed he'd uttered such nonsense. Yet there he was, issuing the order as plain as day. Moreover, he'd done it in that unyielding, coolly confident manner that made him the most sought-after and successful agent in the country.

She would've given him anything he wanted if only he hadn't asked her to abandon the one thing that made her who she was. The one thing that gave her an identity. Her independence was the thing that would still be there regardless of what happened in love. Something inside wouldn't let her risk losing that.

Asher brushed the back of his hand across the scar along his left cheek. He could see the defiance in her eyes—the lovely brown orbs that had the power to make him do anything she desired. He wouldn't give in to her on this. On this one thing, he wouldn't yield. She'd come around to his way of thinking soon enough; of that he was confident.

Just then, however, he knew he couldn't stomach hearing whatever she was about to say. Instead, he clenched his jaw tight. Slipping a hand inside his charcoal slacks, he coldly appraised the length of her body.

"Be gone by the time I get back," he said. Without a look back, he left the study and slammed his way out of the house.

* * *

"Casey? Is Vic anywhere around? I want to talk to him about this piece for next week's run," Riley called out in the direction of the open door leading to her assistant's office area.

Seconds later, Casey was sticking her head in Riley's door. "Vic took some vacation time. He left just before you got back from Phoenix."

"Oh," Riley replied, more subdued. "Thanks, Case."

It'd been two weeks since the ill-fated trip to see her husband. She'd already picked up the phone six times, intending to call and agree to his terms. *Terms? Ha! His ultimatum.* She always reminded herself of that and promptly slammed the phone down.

Twisting her cushioned slate-green desk chair to and fro, Riley wondered if he was suffering as much as she was. She wouldn't let herself believe that was possible. After all, he wasn't being asked to give up anything.

Except his wife, a voice chided.

Groaning, Riley stood and fluffed the hem of her flared mocha skirt. She made her way to the brass bar cart in the corner and was about to pour a drink when a knock sounded on the door and Misha waltzed inside.

"Pour me one, too," Misha asked.

"It's only ginger ale," Riley warned.

Misha shrugged. "Spike it."

Grinning, Riley added a bit of vodka to Misha's glass and took her drink neat.

"So what brings you by?" Riley asked when she was seated back behind her desk.

"The most important type of business—gossip," Misha shared, with a wicked chuckle, narrowing her tilted dark eyes.

Riley was studying her drink. "I should've guessed."

"Word has it that our top fact-checker is spending his vacation time trying out for a spot on a certain New Jersey basketball team."

"Vic?"

"And the lady takes home the six-piece luggage set!" Misha bellowed in her best game show host voice.

Riley clicked her nails against the beaded exterior of her glass. "How in hell do you come by all this stuff?"

Misha recrossed her long legs and winked. "It's not what you know. It's who you sleep with."

"Slut."

Repositioning her pencil-slim frame on the chair, Misha gave an airy wave. "I prefer the term *man's lady,*" she teased.

Riley didn't bother telling her friend that the phrase had nowhere near the same connotation.

"Actually, I came by this news during a simple dinner. One of my dinner partners asked how you were doing. More accurately, she wanted to know how that 'fine-assed Asher Hudson' was doing, and then she went on to say that she wondered if he'd grace NYC with his presence since one of his new acquisitions was on the way to landing a prime spot on a certain franchise roster."

Riley was sitting straight up in her seat by then. "Vic? A client of Asher's?"

Misha raked a hand through her healthy shoulder-length tresses and smirked. "I don't get why you're surprised. It wouldn't take much more than Vic mentioning he was on your staff to do the deed." She popped a chunk of ice into her mouth and crunched. "Asher Hudson may be the most shrewd agent in the business, but he's like an eager-to-please little boy when it comes to you."

Riley looked away, downing the rest of her ginger ale as she stood and began to pace her office while Misha rambled on. An eager-to-please little boy was a far cry from the unyielding man she'd left a couple of weeks earlier. God, what if he had to come to New York on business? How would she handle it? How would they handle seeing each other after the drama that had exploded between them?

Maybe she wouldn't have to suffer it. He was as stubborn he was. He probably wouldn't even grace her with his ce. Riley managed a smile at the thought and ignored the cries that said the dramatics of the situation were just g.

Three weeks later…

Talib Mason scratched his whisker-roughened cheek and regarded his partner with a cool grin. "Isn't there some law against using business funds for pleasure trips?"

Asher didn't bother to look away from the PDA he was tinkering with. "Whatever do you mean?" he murmured.

Talib's grin simply broadened. "Come off it. Your business for Victor Lyne? Hell, that won't take up nearly as much time as business with your lovely wife."

Gracing his friend with a narrowed gaze, Asher shrugged. "One of the perks of being the boss."

"Well, it's good to see you smile, anyway," Talib noted, rubbing his fingers through the full mass of waves on his head. "You've been like the walking dead for the past six weeks."

Asher stood then and cursed Riley below his breath. "Why the hell does she have to fight me so? Why can't she just… submit, just once give in?" He turned when Talib's deep, British-laced accent filled the air.

"Would you love her nearly as much as you do if she gave in to you on something that means so much to her?"

Asher's expression relayed a quiet confidence. "I can change her mind."

"And you really think that's the best way to go at this?"

Asher waved off Talib's concerns.

"Maybe you should—"

"What? Wait for her to come around?"

"I was going to say compromise."

"I'm heading to New York. That's compromise enough."

This time it was Talib's turn to wave off Asher.

"All right then, how's this for a compromise? By the time I'm done with her, she'll go anywhere I ask."

Easing a hand into his trouser pocket, Talib stood as though in awe. "Seduction? You really think you could seduce a woman like that into following you back here?"

Asher smirked. "She's my wife."

"She's a hard-as-nails journalist, and she's no fool."

"And *I*, my friend, am very persuasive."

Talib laughed then. "Tell me you're not foolish enough to believe this could work."

Asher walked past Talib and clapped a hand on his back. "If it doesn't work, I'll think of something else. But you can bet your ass, I'll have a helluva time trying." Growing serious then, he crossed his arms over the front of the sandalwood crew-neck shirt he wore. "I'm not sure she believes I love her enough, Tal. I don't think she quite believes me when I say she's mine and I'm hers—forever." Closing his eyes against the dazzling Phoenix landscape past the office windows, he turned back to Talib. "Giving her an ultimatum was the last thing I should've done. But I would've said anything to get her to stay."

"Why would you let things go that far?" Talib took a seat on the edge of the desk.

"Her living in New York scares the hell out of me." He slapped his hands on the windowsill. "It scares me more since we got married."

"Understandable. So tell her then."

"I would." Asher turned back to the view. "Then she'll want to know why, and I'm not ready to tell her that story."

"Ash—"

"I don't need her feelin' sorry for me because I froze up, did nothing…"

"I think she'll probably feel proud when she learns what really happened there."

"Humph. Right."

Talib stopped himself from saying more and silently prayed that his two stubborn friends could somehow cross the bridge that was beginning to separate them.

"This better be damn good at one a.m.," Misha slurred, tugging at the scarf that covered her head while she leaned her front door.

brushed past Misha and walked into her posh Manhat-
"Am I interrupting anything?" she whispered.
nately not."

"Good. I've made a mess of things. Such a mess of things," Riley chanted, pulling her sweater more tightly around her frame.

Misha yawned. "I take it this is about Asher?"

"Yes and no."

"Hmm…mysterious. Will this be a lengthy confession? Should I put on coffee?" Misha was already turning for her kitchen.

Riley blinked absently. "I don't know if I should." She settled on the edge of an armchair.

"Lord, you're talkin' crazy. Here." Misha pulled Riley from the chair she'd chosen and led her to the one next to a floor vent, where soothing heat rushed out to warm the room. "September's already chilly as hell. We're in store for one cold winter."

Riley barely listened to Misha's rambling. Instead, she smoothed her hands across the cotton sweats she sported and continued to ponder her dilemma.

Misha stooped before her friend and wrapped her hands around the arms of the chair. "Talk to me," she urged, shaking her head when Riley only closed her eyes. "Tell you what, let me go and get that coffee started first. Maybe it'll loosen that tongue of yours."

"Misha, wait. I, um, I don't know if I should…"

"Sweetie, it's only coffee."

"I just don't know if it's good for…"

"For what?" Misha clutched the backs of Riley's knees. "Honey, you're scaring me."

In response, Riley reached inside her sweater and pulled something from an inside pocket.

Misha's dark gaze widened when she focused on the white plastic stick Riley handed her. Her arched brows lifted higher when she took note of the telltale plus sign in one of the clear ovals of the pregnancy test.

"Oh," Misha breathed before pressing her free hand to Rile∙ nonexistent waist. "Guess Asher was determined to leave a∙ pression this time."

"Guess so…I, um…have to admit I was a bit forgetf∙ some things while I was out there with him, namely, ∙ control pills." Riley covered her face with her hands an∙ to shiver anew.

Misha was laughing then as she pulled her friend into a tight squeeze. "Oh, congratulations, girl! This is the most incredible news! The most blessed news."

Riley burst into tears then, and Misha joined in with tears of joy and laughter.

"So what did Asher say when you told him?" Misha folded her legs beneath her and watched with expectant eyes. When Riley simply shook her head, Misha's expression turned from expectant to disbelieving.

"You haven't told him?"

"I didn't, um…I didn't tell you all about my trip to see him in Phoenix." Riley settled on the floor, next to Misha, and absorbed more of the flowing heat. "We didn't part on good terms. He gave me an ultimatum."

Misha tilted her head. "Ultimatum?"

"Either stay in Phoenix with him or forget our marriage." Riley did an admirable job of staving off more tears as she spoke.

"No way," Misha breathed, now bracing her hands behind her as she settled back.

Feeling stronger, Riley stood to pace the room as she recounted the conversation with her husband.

Silence filled the living room for a long time after Riley shared the story. Misha experienced an uncharacteristic moment of uncertainty about what to say. Wincing in frustration, she tugged the scarf from her head and raked a hand through her wrapped tresses.

"Sweetie, I'm sure he'll be thrilled when you tell him."

"Misha, this is about more than that."

"Oh, honey, when he hears about the baby, whatever problems you left in Phoenix will—"

"No, Misha, no. Are your forgetting that we aren't like other couples?" Suddenly feeling overheated, Riley whipped the sweater from her back. "We don't live under the same roof. Hell, we don't even live in the same time zone." Closing her eyes, she inhaled deeply before cupping her hands over her belly. "The baby in our future doesn't change the fact that we're at a stalemate." She shrugged. "Neither of us is willing to compromise."

"Do you love him?"

Riley blinked. "What?"

"Asher. Do you love him?"

"Yes."

"More than the column?"

Riley hesitated and then shook her apprehension off. "Yes."

Misha's gaze narrowed in a telling manner. "But?"

Riley wouldn't pretend and reclaimed her place in the armchair. "The column, my career... It's always been there, and it never changes."

"Ah." Misha flexed her toes toward the vent. "So you love it because it doesn't change, and yet that's exactly what you want Asher to do."

"I don't."

"Don't you?" Misha gave her a saucy wink. "Honey, you're forgetting that I've been there since the two of you got together. Asher's wanted you—*all* of you—since then. He's never made a secret of it, and you stayed with him, loved him and married him, anyway."

"I *do* love him."

"I know, and you also thought that you could change him." Misha sat crossed-legged in the middle of the floor. "Men like Asher Hudson don't change. You want 'em, you gotta take 'em as they are."

The words frustrated Riley more and more. She felt the overheated sensation course through her once more. "Dammit, Misha, Asher knows how to compromise. It's what he does for a living."

Misha didn't bother to tell her friend that the fact that Asher Hudson *didn't* compromise was probably why he was so successful.

"Maybe I could…persuade him to come around to my way of thinking. Who knows?"

"Oh, honey, is it really so hard to be the bigger person here? No pun intended." Misha cast a humorous glance toward Riley's tummy. "You're about to have a baby with the man you love. It's surprising how many women are never able to boast about that." Satisfied that she'd provided the more thorough argument, Misha stood. "In the end, isn't it about what's best for my little nephew? What kind of life will he have being with two parents who can't even decide where to live?"

Riley reached for her sweater and began to fidget with the frayed sleeves.

For a second time, Misha tilted her head. "My God... Are you thinking of not telling him?"

"I haven't decided yet." Riley had the decency to admit it.

"Coffee for me. Herbal tea for you." Misha decided to leave and prepare the beverages, instead of telling the mother-to-be that she was being an idiot. Before she left the room, however, she turned, with a last bit of advice.

"Don't play with this man, hon. Especially not when he's your husband."

"A baby's not a reason to stay together," Riley continued, watching Misha, with hurt and defiance filling her eyes. "I know that better than anyone. It's hell on the parents, but that makes it three times as hard on the kid."

"So what?" Misha challenged. "You really think you could even get away with not telling him this?"

"He's in Phoenix."

"And you just figure you won't see him for the next nine months?"

"We're practically on two different coasts. I think it could be arranged."

Misha propped a hand on the waistband of her gold sleep pants. "And what if he comes here for Vic?"

"That's just a rumor."

"Mmm-hmm... And when the baby comes?"

Riley's cool vanished somewhat. "Then I guess we'll be having this conversation again."

"The test was accurate, love. You're pregnant."

Riley gave a refreshing sigh and nodded over the confirmation.

Dr. Lettia Breene cocked her head. "Have you told Asher yet, hon?"

Riley laughed. "That's the question of the week."

Lettia smiled and slipped a pen into the front pocket of her crisp white coat. "I know how…unorthodox your situation is. I know it makes things more difficult, but you need to be aware that keeping your stress level low is of the highest importance." Turning back to her desk, Lettia leaned over the front and scribbled a prescription for prenatal vitamins. "Contact me with any side effects you may experience after taking these." Lettia passed Riley the prescription. "These things affect each woman differently, and we may need to make some adjustments." Lettia's firm expression softened into one of sweet delight as she pulled Riley into a hug.

"Congratulations, girl." She pressed a kiss to Riley's cheek. "Stop by the front desk, and my assistant will give you the next appointment date." She gave Riley a quick shake. "Next time we meet, I expect to see that worry gone from your eyes."

Outside her doctor's office, Riley leaned against her Mustang and groaned. Telling Asher about the baby would relieve the lion share of her stress. And where would that leave things? He'd never relent on trying to get her to move to Phoenix then. Shaking off the unease, Riley reached into the pocket of the lightweight lavender jacket she wore. She was in search of her phone when the chimes sounded to signal her next appointment. As she was already late, her thoughts shifted away from Asher and back to business as she rushed off.

Bastian Grovers smiled knowingly when he looked up from checking his PDA and saw his lunch date arriving at the Shell.

"Damn," Riley moaned spotting the empty tea glass and used linen napkin on the table. "And I had my heart set on the shrimp Alfredo." She closed her eyes in regret when Bastian patted his stomach.

"And, boy, was it good," he proclaimed. "I ordered after trying your cell for the fifth time."

"Please forgive me." Riley thought back to her doctor's appointment. "It couldn't be helped."

"No worries. I managed to handle a bit of paperwork I'd been putting off as well." Bastian set aside his work and focused on Riley more closely. "Are you okay? You look tired—around the eyes."

It felt good to drop the facade. "I could use a nap, but I wanted to be here for our talk." Riley took one final refreshing sigh. "So do I have time to hear the condensed version of what you wanted to discuss?"

"Walk me to my car while we talk?" he bartered.

"So how much farther before I find out what's on your mind?"

Bastian grinned and nudged Riley's shoulder with his own. "I need a favor, Riley."

She slowed her steps and squeezed his arm. "You okay?"

Clearing his throat, Bastian forced a more calming expression to his face. "It's a professional favor."

"Professional, huh? Now what could a lowly columnist do for a high-powered sports editor like yourself?"

"Forget it." Bastian was rolling his eyes as he grimaced. "You could give my entire team a run for its money. You have on several occasions, as I recall."

"So what's this about, then? You don't look too eager to tell me." Riley tilted her head for a closer look at his face.

Bastian's grimace sparked the faint dimple in his cheek. "It's about Victor Lyne."

Riley closed her eyes in realization. "Well, well, my little researcher's name is getting around town like a rocket these days."

"You mean someone else already asked you for the story?" Bastian seemed to groan.

"Huh?" Riley didn't mind letting her bewilderment show. "Would it be too much to ask you to start from the beginning?"

Bastian stopped walking and pressed a hand to the front of his champagne suit coat. "I want the exclusive on the newest addition to the New Jersey franchise."

"That's still speculation." Riley shrugged and looked down. "Besides, I haven't seen or spoken to Vic since I got back from Phoenix."

"I was sure Asher would've mentioned it, seeing as how he's Vic's rep."

Bastian spoke in an absent tone, and Riley didn't bother with a response. Silently, she acknowledged her surprise—and suspicion.

"Bottom line, Riley, is that we want to officially break the story about his signing."

"Um, Bastian—" Riley tucked a clipped lock of hair behind her ear "—you do recall that Vic works just one floor down from you?" They'd reached Bastian's SUV, and Riley leaned against the back.

Bastian moved close. "I'm asking you because we're tight, and I know your…interest in sports matters. You may be thinking of running the scoop."

"It never crossed my mind." Riley brought her hands together in a loud clap. "But it's not even about that. It's up to Vic to share the story—if there *is* one—with whomever he chooses."

"So what *do* you think?"

Riley tugged on the lapel of his suit. "I think I have no interest in running an exposé on my fact finder's moonlighting. You've got my blessing."

Bastian clenched a fist in triumph and then pulled Riley into a tight hug and planted a lengthy kiss on her mouth.

Riley laughed. "You may want to learn to control those emotions when you ask for stories. Everyone doesn't know you as well as I do."

Bastian kissed her again. "Where are you parked? I'll walk you."

"No need." Riley pointed to her Mustang, parked a short distance from where they stood.

"Far enough," Bastian noted, taking Riley's arm and escorting her over. His smile was sun bright as he watched Riley settle into her car and drive away.

Riley had contemplated going home for a nap to reward herself for the good deed she'd done for Bastian Grovers. Instead, she headed back to the office, where she found an unexpected guest.

"Well, well! If it isn't the man of the hour!" Riley grinned when Victor Lyne jumped from his seat and smiled bashfully.

"Sorry for hangin' around in here, Riley."

"Please, you know my office better than I do." Riley took a seat behind her desk. "So, um, how was your vacation?"

Victor chewed his bottom lip and leaned forward to grab the

stress ball of rubber bands from the desk. He tossed the ball back and forth yet offered no conversation.

Searching for a way to spark a discussion, Riley nodded toward the stress ball. "You've got great hands," she sang, a pointed melody.

Vic looked up, with yet another bashful look on his rugged face. "Guess you heard."

Riley tossed her lavender jacket on a nearby chair. "New York is, in many ways, like a small town. Word travels very fast."

"Everything happened fast." Vic seemed to groan while covering his face in his hands.

"People tend to move fast when it comes to acquiring someone who could be the next Jordan."

Vic laughed at his boss's summation. "I'm nowhere near that."

Riley shrugged. "Some folks continue to hope." She left her desk, tugging at the tight sleeves of her navy top. "Drink?"

"OJ."

Riley decided to have one as well.

"I really came by to apologize," Vic said while her back was turned.

"Apologize?" Riley's surprise was clear, yet she retrieved the drinks with ease.

"Asher's my agent, and he got me that tryout in Jersey."

"And?" Riley challenged while handing Vic his juice. "You know, you don't have to apologize for wanting to sign with a man who many consider the best agent in the business."

"No, you don't get it." Vic grimaced, as though he'd lost his taste for the juice. "I'm talking about the *way* I got him." He sighed when Riley fixed him with a blank stare. "Understandably, your name carried a lot of weight with the man. I happened to take advantage of that when I met him during all-star weekend in Vegas. Dropped your name, he told me to come see him, and…"

"The rest is history." Riley raised her juice glass in toast.

"I'm really sorry I—"

Riley waved her hand. "I once got a tip on a story from a man who went to first grade with my mom—*first* grade." She chuckled while thinking about it. "I reminded him of it, and he recalled that she was the girl who used to pour water into his galoshes." She laughed along with Vic. "Point is, you use *all* your contacts—no matter how minute."

"Thanks, Riley." Vic's dark features relaxed. "Knowing you're cool with this'll make it all easier when Asher comes and starts setting everything in motion."

"Oh." Riley focused on her glass. "When's he coming out again?" she inquired, as if she'd simply forgotten.

Vic didn't catch on to the act. "Should be any day now. I had no idea so much negotiating went into a contract."

Riley swallowed around the lump rising in her throat. "Yeah, it's a real demanding job."

"Asher said he'd be here for at least three months."

Riley downed the rest of the juice in one gulp.

Chapter 12

Riley rushed into her loft apartment, kicked the door shut and dropped the grocery bag on the first chair she approached. Leaning against the back of the hunter green and maroon sofa, she closed her eyes and wondered if she was winded from the seemingly brief walk from the corner market to her Manhattan loft. Perhaps it was because the little bundle was zapping her energy. Maybe it was because the little bundle's father was waging war on her nerves and her independence.

Riley shook her head and refused to think about it. All she wanted was to fall into bed and shut out the world. Pushing off the sofa, she shed her dress and under things on her way through the comfortable yet elegant digs. In the bedroom, she slinked into an emerald satin robe.

She set off for the kitchen, knowing sleep would be a long time coming without a fragrant mug of herbal tea. In the time it took for the water to simmer in the chrome kettle, Riley was again pondering her call to Asher. Not telling him about the baby now would agitate things more than they already were. *Telling* him now would only intensify his demands that she leave New York, thereby making it impossible for her to relieve her stress, which her doctor suggested she rid herself of.

Maybe several hours of sleep would help her to get a better handle on things. Satisfied that the idea was the best she had, Riley prepared the tea to take back to the bedroom. She was turning from the stove when she saw Asher leaning against the kitchen entryway. The mug almost slipped from her weak hand.

"Business," he explained.

She leaned against the counter for support. "I heard."

"So much for surprising you." Asher pushed off the entryway and strolled slowly toward his wife.

Riley could scarcely hear over the pulse throbbing in her ears. "Believe me, I'm surprised."

He was standing right before her then. "You always make a habit of leaving the paper three hours early?"

She stood blinking up into his probing light brown stare for almost half a minute before words came. "I, um… It's been a long day."

"I can tell," he muttered, brushing his thumb along the corner of her eye and not caring for the weariness plaguing her gaze.

Riley felt her temples vibrate in anticipation of a lecture. "Asher—"

"Later," he urged and took possession of her mouth seconds later.

Riley's response was eager and immediate. Her lips weren't the only energized part of her body as she met the force of his kiss. Of course, this was all to be expected. Her reaction to Asher was always eager and…immediate.

They kissed for the better part of three minutes before another layer was added to the pleasure.

Riley didn't realize he'd unraveled the silken belt at her waist until she felt his fingertips strumming a tune along her hips and buttocks. This was all it took for her need for him to crest to a perfect pitch of arousal. Shamelessly, she rubbed against his lean, athletic frame. She wasn't the least bit agitated when Asher murmured a little mmm hmm as if he knew all too well the response his touch would generate.

She could've cared less, of course. After all, she'd been craving his touch for over six weeks. She wanted whatever he'd give her. Riley moved to undo his trousers and whined when he stopped her.

"Asher you don't have to—" she began when he started to kiss his way down her body, but her words caught on a throaty moan.

Asher was on his knees before her. His powerful hands gripped her bottom while simultaneously spreading her thighs to drive his tongue inside her.

The slow, moist lunges had Riley raking her hands across Asher's head and gripping fistfuls of the worsted fabric of his olive-green suit coat.

"Yes…yes, Asher, that's it…." The welcoming words as he invaded her with rotating thrusts brought her closer to the ripe thrill of orgasm.

Riley practically sobbed his name when his hold tightened about her dark thighs to prevent her from moving as he cherished the extra-sensitive patch of flesh above her sex. The maddening nibbles made her want to melt onto his tongue as it soothed the place his lips and teeth had ravished.

Easily, he drew both her long legs across his shoulders and supported her with an impressive show of strength. Once again, he took her with his tongue. The relentless yet all-too-delicious stabs made her climax *all too soon*.

Riley was all but spent as she gripped the edge of the counter, yet her gaze was focused as she watched him rise to his feet. She kept looking for some sign that he'd noticed some change in her body, such as the narrowing of his eyes.

There was no such sign, and Riley put her most innocent look in place when he stood, towering over her.

"Don't even try it," he ordered, seeing right through the innocent display. "Sleep. No arguments."

Riley couldn't stifle the relieved sigh that fluttered past her lips. Happy to be bullied by him, she nuzzled her face into his neck when he carried her from the kitchen.

She dozed off during the brief trip from the kitchen to the bedroom yet stirred when she felt him settling her in the middle of the bed. She conked out again before he closed the bedroom door.

"Can't be," Riley breathed when she stared at the gold-encased bedside clock, which read 9:32 p.m. Sleep had worked its very real magic, and she woke refreshed and feeling as though she could get a sizable chunk of work out of the way.

Of course, there was eating that needed to be done, and Riley's appetite now screamed to be satisfied. Her nostrils flared in response to the delicious aromas slipping into the room. She didn't have long to wonder about them, thankfully. The door opened, and there was Asher, carrying in a tray practically over-flowing with food.

Keeping her smile soft, Riley leaned back on her elbows and watched him. Who would believe the high-powered sports agent Asher Hudson would perform such humble tasks as bringing his wife dinner in bed, which *he* had prepared?

"What?" Asher queried when he noticed her smile.

Riley only shrugged. "I'm just not used to this." She snuggled deeper under the covers, loving the feel of the crisp gold sheets against her bare skin.

Asher bit back the words that scrambled up his throat. He wanted to tell her she could have *this* every day if she'd come back with him.

"Quite a stash of food you got in there," he observed instead. "Lotta healthy stuff. I thought you were the junk-food junkie of our dazzling duo."

Riley sat up in bed. "Do you have something against a person trying to eat well?"

Asher unfolded a napkin and placed it on her lap. "Not a thing." Silently, he admitted that advising her on her eating habits made him feel as if she, with her strong and independent self, might just need him.

"So what's up with this health kick?" Asher passed Riley a deep ceramic plate loaded with a helping of the fragrant chicken fettuccine.

Riley accepted the teasing with ease. "Maybe I've just been craving all the cooking you'd do when you got to town on…business."

His playful wince added an adorable element to his expression. "Sorry for not telling you sooner," he said.

"How long has all this been in the works?" Riley reached for the Parmesan cheese.

Asher claimed his spot on the other side of the bed. "Met Vic about eight months after he went to work for you. I knew about him way before that, though. I followed his college career." He shrugged. "I told him I was surprised, but that I understood why he didn't want to pursue the pros further."

Riley savored another bite of the flavorful chicken and creamy noodles. "And why would you understand that? Most agents can never understand money being a deterrent."

"Not about the money for Vic." Asher took a swallow from the Heineken beer bottle he'd set on the nightstand. "He'd seen too many of his boys caught up in ugly lifestyles that brought 'em down quick. Apparently, it scared him to think he could wind up like that."

"Humph." Riley's warm eyes twinkled with mischief. "Most agents would say, 'Ah, you're better than that, kid. No way would you be that stupid. Now let's go make a trillion.'"

Asher graced his wife with a dimpled grin, which turned into something more pensive. "I could never say that. Not when I understand so well where he's coming from."

Riley saw the unease darkening his fair features and wanted to ask more. She never had the chance.

"Anyway, back to the subject at hand. Where are you hiding all the junk?"

Laughing, Riley once again prepared to defend her improved eating habits. The phone interrupted their banter, and she looked at Asher. As they normally had so little time together, phone calls in the middle of dinner usually went unanswered.

"Take it," he urged, with an encouraging smile. He took his plate, intending to grab a third helping, and appeared more than a little stunned when Riley held out her plate to request a refill as she picked up the phone.

Misha was on the other end of the line. "Look alive, girl. We're being summoned to an eight o'clock breakfast meeting with the bigwigs at the paper."

Riley halted her appraisal of the sleep pants hugging Asher's hips and focused on her editor's words. "Bigwigs?"

"Mmm…In the morning at Red Sun."

"What about?" Riley swung her legs across the side of the bed.

"Hell if I know. Everybody's lips are tighter than a banker's ass. Guess we'll just have to wait till the morning."

"Asher's here."

Misha's giggle was a mix of delight and naughtiness. "I'll let you get back to bed then."

"Wait. How'd you know I—"

"You've got Asher Hudson in your apartment. Where else would you be?"

"Good night," Riley sang. Yet when the call ended, she chewed her thumbnail and pondered.

"Bad news?" Asher had returned with helping number three and took note of her expression.

Riley shared the highlights of the call while devouring the heaping dish of fettuccine. For a time, Asher was speechless, looking on as his slim, nude wife wolfed down the food.

"Sounds mysterious. Keep me posted?" Asher watched her nod and then hooked a thumb over his shoulder as he returned to the bed. "If it won't put you out too much, I was thinkin' about working out of the study."

"No, no, it's fine," Riley said through a mouthful of noodles. She shook her head in an eager manner. Already it felt so good to have him there—to have him near. "I hardly work out of there, so I'm not sure what supplies you'll need."

Asher nodded while feasting on his third helping of fettuccine. "I'll check it out. Don't think I'll need much. I don't plan on spending much time in there, either."

"Oh?"

"Gotta keep an eye on the reps in Jersey. Make sure they don't try to screw the kid."

Riley set aside her plate. "Are you sure he's ready for this, Asher?"

"More than," he replied, without hesitation. "Besides, he's got a good head on his shoulders."

"Still." Riley scooted close and tapped her fingers on his thigh. "Good heads go surprisingly airy when dollar signs are involved. Just watch out for him, okay?"

Asher set aside his plate and turned to cup Riley's face in his wide palms. "I'll treat him like he's my very own—which he actually is."

An Important Message from the Publisher

Dear Reader,

Because you've chosen to read one of our fine novels, I'd like to say "thank you"! And, as a special way to say thank you, I'm offering to send you two more Kimani™ Romance novels and two surprise gifts – absolutely FREE! These books will keep it real with true-to-life African American characters that turn up the heat and sizzle with passion.

Please enjoy the free books and gifts with our compliments...

Linda Gill

Publisher, Kimani Press

off Seal and
Place Inside...

The way he said it, sounding every bit the overprotective father, had Riley opening her mouth to tell him the news that would forever change their lives. Instead of talking, however, she covered her mouth and bolted from the bed.

Asher left after her. His handsome face was alive with surprise and horror as he watched her vomit into the toilet. When she was done, he helped her to her feet. Once he'd cleaned her up, he carried her back to the bed.

"Are you staying?" Her voice was barely above a whisper.

"I'll be up pretty late." Asher helped her into a T-shirt. "Probably fall asleep in the study."

Riley's mouth curved into a pout. "Because I heaved up your dinner? Smell like vomit?" She almost cried.

"Shh…" Asher wanted to laugh, but he could see the despair in her eyes. "Shh… You don't smell like vomit. You smell good enough to eat." He nuzzled his nose beneath her ear and then trailed his mouth along her jaw. "You taste even better." Softly, he thrust his tongue past her parted lips.

"I'm sorry, anyway."

"No more apologies." He brushed her nose with his. "I know you enjoyed it. You just overdid it. Only so much you can fit in this little space, you know?"

With his hand resting on her tummy, Riley made an effort to speak again, but Asher stopped her.

"Rest now. No more talking, no more phones." With that said, he pulled the cord from the handset. "You have an early meeting, and you need sleep."

"Asher—"

"Trust me, love. I intend to collect on all my good deeds from today."

He plied her with another sweet kiss. Riley was moaning in seconds. The tingling arrived next, frenzied and maddening. Admirably, she cast it from her mind, knowing the desire would go unsated.

As expected, Asher ended the kiss and finished tucking Riley into bed. When she closed her eyes, he let the concern return to his face.

* * *

Red Sun was a Japanese-owned café that served breakfast specialties from around the world. Misha arrived early and focused on heading into the already crowded and lavish establishment to meet with the heads of Cache Media. She was tugging on the cuff of her gray silk blouse when she spotted an old acquaintance.

"Well, well, Red Sun *does* cater to some sophisticated tastes," she said in greeting to Talib Mason.

"Sophisticated and exquisite," Talib replied in a tone and with a look that said he wasn't referring to his appetite.

Silently, Misha ordered herself not to let her lashes flutter in response to his voice. The regal British accent only added to the man's provocative appeal. For an instant, she let herself recall the memory of hearing her name swirling in his mouth.

"So I see the rumors are true." She closed a bit of the distance between them. "I take it your presence out here has to do with one of my fact-checkers."

Talib's deep-set and slightly slanted eyes were focused solely on Misha. "Keeping tabs on me?"

She glanced down at the gray peekaboo pumps below the cuffs of her slacks. "I may've heard your name mentioned somewhere."

"Ah…" Talib stroked the sleek hair covering his jaw. "A little pillow talk?"

Ouch. Misha wouldn't let the barb sting enough to remove her cool smile. "I don't share pillow talk."

"But wouldn't that depend on whose pillow it was?"

Ouch again. A change in subjects was definitely in order.

"This restaurant has a great menu." Misha glanced around at the elegant surroundings.

Talib glanced around as well. "We got a recommendation for it. I'm just checking it out for Asher."

"Ah, so Asher's trusting you with his stomach these days?"

The grin made his rich dark eyes twinkle. "You know how he is. New place, and it's New York…"

Misha pressed her lips together. "Right. I remember…."

Talib's smile was humor mixed with curiosity then. He took a step closer, slipping a hand into the pocket of his chestnut-brown trousers. "How much have you told your friend about all that?"

Misha's healthy locks brushed her cheeks when she shook her head. "You never really told me much. Besides...I don't share pillow talk, remember?"

Humor left his gaze, yet curiosity remained. "Not even mine?"

What would he say if she told him there hadn't been any since his? Humph, he'd never believe her. She tilted her head in greeting. "Good morning, Talib."

He stepped back and nodded. "Always a pleasure, Misha."

"Pleasure's mine." She spoke too low for him to hear as she watched him leave. Moments later, she felt a chin rest on her shoulder. "Don't, okay?" she pleaded while bowing her head.

"Wasn't that Talib?" Riley asked. "My God," she breathed, marveling at the man's appearance.

"Uh-huh..." Misha agreed, allowing herself to melt just a little.

"Sure you wanna join me and a bunch of stuffy old coots for breakfast when you could follow that?"

"Please, Riley," Misha hissed. "We've been down that road, remember?"

"And you're sure it's a dead end?"

Misha turned, fanning her blouse away from her chest. "He thinks I slept with him for a story."

"And did you?"

Misha closed her eyes. "I was working with someone who didn't care for confirming certain facts before running with the story. When it all came out, it looked like I was involved...I let him believe it."

"Why?" Riley was intrigued. She'd never been able to extract much information from Misha about her relationship with the man.

Misha groaned. "Because he never would've believed I slept with him because I was in love with him. Our old coots are here." She interrupted Riley's next question and headed for the dining room.

"Sorry. Thought I saw 'em," Misha explained five minutes later, when they were seated at a square table set for five.

Riley didn't spare her editor a glance. "It's okay. I'll just take that to mean your love life is off-limits to discussion."

Misha gave a mock salute. "That's right, due to the lack of existence. Now yours, on the other hand…"

"To quote your earlier words, 'don't, okay?'"

"You're glowing, you know," Misha whispered, as if it were a hot secret. "I *would* say that's one of pregnancy's more wonderful side effects, but then I know there could be another reason for that glow…."

Riley rolled her eyes toward a menu. "Yes, there could be…."

"Coffee. Black," Misha told the waiter who'd approached. "So'd you get around to telling him about the new addition to your club?" she asked once Riley put in her order for hot herbal tea.

"I haven't told him. *Yet*. I plan to ASAP. I don't think I can look at him every day for the next three months without him knowing."

Only one of Misha's perfectly arched brows lifted. "So he *is* in town for Vic's signing? That's really a go? Talib didn't actually confirm it."

"Yeah, it's confirmed." Riley slammed down her menu. "But before you start brainstorming story angles, you should know I already promised Bastian the exclusive on breaking Vic's news. So it's completely out of our ballpark—no pun intended."

Misha responded with a secretive smirk, which Riley didn't have the chance to question. Their breakfast dates had finally arrived, and after settling down and ordering, Shepard Cade, VP of creative development, got to the point.

"We've been batting around the idea of spinning off from our very popular columns one new main publication. We'd like for the two of you to head up the works."

Riley and Misha sat in stunned silence for quite a while. After sharing a knowing smile with her associates, publisher Gloria Reynolds leaned close to the table.

"We understand that this news is quite dazzling." She cast a pointed look toward Riley. "But even dazzling news has to be weighed and discussed. Especially when one has a new marriage and a husband living halfway across the country."

Hunching against the chill biting her arms beneath her cashmere sweater, Riley noted that she now had even more to consider.

"We'd like the two of you to delegate tasks to your staff," Gloria continued. "Take time and think this over. Discuss it with your families." Another glance toward Riley. "Orly?"

Marketing VP Orlando Tims handed Misha and Riley twin packets. "We've put these together to assist in your decision. Should give you a bit more info on the new pub."

Riley and Misha tore into the packets and were already tossing out questions by the time the breakfast orders arrived. Breakfast was delicious, and the conversation was heavy.

Asher snorted and gave a weary grunt into the pillow and finally managed to crack open an eye. Glancing at the bedside clock, he saw 10 a.m. on the digital pad. Waking up to that sight was about as unfamiliar as the present view of Central Park in the distance.

He let his face drop back into the pillow and contemplated another hour. Negotiation meetings wouldn't start with the team execs until tomorrow morning. Still, he had a crap load of other work to handle....

What's wrong with me? Asher questioned the sudden bout of laziness. Of course, it was obvious. He slept so well only when Riley was around him. Though she wasn't physically there in the apartment just then, having her in the same state, city and zip code was enough.

And the fact that it was New York? Asher smoothed the back of his hand across the wicked scar on his cheek. The question was enough to pull him up from the pillows, which were softly scented with his wife's fragrance.

Maybe Talib was right; maybe he should just tell her why he wanted her out of there. Easy enough, but how could he admit that to her when he got sick just remembering it? Hell, she'd lived in New York all her life. The last thing he wanted was to scare her. But she wouldn't leave without a damn good reason. Would knowing that the actual events that transpired during a convenience store holdup still haunted him to distraction be enough?

Virginia Stamper spoke to the tiny boxes of African violets like a mother tending her children. Riley leaned against the brick ledge and watched the woman enjoying her favorite hobby.

"So if you talk sweetly enough, will they respond?"

Hands poised over an empty pot, Virginia looked across her shoulder and then rushed over to envelop her only child in a warm hug. Virginia's dark face held a resigned look when she glanced back toward her flowers.

"I'll be moving my flock inside in a few more weeks. This winter promises to be as cold as a frigid bitch."

Riley chuckled, scratching at her temple while her mother sauntered back to the flowers. "You know, Miss Ginny, you're gonna have to tamp down that language now that you're going to be a grandmother."

Virginia dropped the clay pot she'd just picked up. Whirling around, she regarded Riley with disbelief. Immediately, she rushed over to cup Riley's face for a kiss and hugged her tight.

"When? How far along are you? What is it? Stupid question, Gin. Of course, you don't know that yet." She spoke absently, running her hands over Riley's arms and shoulders.

"No word yet on whether you'll have a *grandson* or *granddaughter* to spoil, but my doctor says I'm about six weeks along," Riley shared through her laughter at her mother.

"Oh, that Asher," Virginia declared, resting one hand on the side of her lovely face. "Not only is he sexy and gorgeous as hell, but he keeps his promises."

Riley laughed again but tugged at the hem of Virginia's rust-colored smock. "What are you talking about?"

"Well, he promised to make me a grandmother within two years after the two of you got married." She patted Riley's tummy and winked. "I like a man who keeps his promises."

"He never told me the two of you talked about kids." Riley sounded captivated.

Virginia shrugged and reached for a brush and dustpan to

clean up the broken pot. "I didn't get too specific, but I heard enough to know that he wants that very much." Forgetting the pot, Virginia looked up at her daughter. "You haven't told him, have you? Why?"

Riley felt a chill beneath her blazer. "Had a meeting this morning... They offered me a new job...heading my own publication."

"Ah." Virginia's smoky eyes twinkled in acknowledgement. "Which explains the real reason you're here. A talk with the devil mother who chose career over family."

Riley shook her head, sending locks of her chic cut bouncing. "You weren't *that* bad. But that *is* why I'm here."

"You want to know if you can have both?"

"You did."

"No, love." Virginia returned to sweeping up the clay pot. "I had my career and my child. The man didn't stick around, remember?" Clearing the broken pieces, she tossed aside the brush and dustpan. "Don't base your decisions on mine, baby. I didn't really have a choice in the way things turned out."

Riley went to lean against the brick ledge. "But your career was always there."

"Because it *had* to be. Your father was a self-centered jackass. When things got rough, he did what a self-centered man does best. He ran." Bracing her hands on her thighs, Virginia pushed to her feet. "Honey, is everything all right between you and Asher? Is that why—"

"No, no, no, everything's good." Riley winced as the lie touched her ears. "But he did leave me with an ultimatum."

"Not in his vocabulary," Virginia replied.

Riley smiled. "Leave New York or leave our marriage."

Virginia considered the words but a moment before shaking her head. "He could've meant anything by that—"

"Ma—"

"And, anyway, I don't see why it's a hard choice for you to make."

"Why? Because writing a column isn't nearly as important as scoring an extra million for an already overpaid athlete?"

"Riley—"

"Or perhaps not as important as heading up your own medical ward—"

"Love, shh…shh…" Virginia rushed over, pulling her daughter into a rocking embrace.

"I feel so small when you do that, Mama."

Virginia kissed her temple. "I'm sorry, honey. I know and I'm sorry."

"Asher makes me feel lower."

"Because he's the man you love." Virginia massaged her daughter's back. "It always hurts when they don't support us the way we do them." She pulled Riley over to stand with her next to the brick railing. "When I told your father I wanted to go after my nursing degree, he just laughed and laughed… The hours were hell, but I succeeded, and then there were more hellish hours. When I actually got a decent position…" Virginia's eyes misted as the memories took hold. "Thank God for your granny Lil. You know, when I said things got tough, it wasn't just financially… It was marital, too. Eventually, the money got better and better, but *he* only got angrier and angrier. I felt more and more powerful, and that power outweighed whatever love I had for him."

Riley was shaking her head. "Mama, that's not—"

"Now just wait a minute, all right?"

Virginia placed a finger across Riley's lips. "I know that's not what's going on between you and Asher, which is why I'll tell you not to base *any* of your decisions on mine."

"I need insurance, Ma."

"Explain."

Riley closed her eyes. "I've never admitted that. Not even to Misha."

"Honey, don't you trust him?"

"I do…but…"

"Honey?"

"What?"

Virginia patted Riley's hands to stop her from wringing them. "There's no halfway with trust, love."

"He's keeping something from me."

"Something."

Riley grimaced. "It's not anything like that. I have no doubt that he loves me, but…I've just always felt there was something, something beneath the surface that he's not saying. At first, I told myself I was just imagining it."

"And?" Virginia tugged on one of the cuffs of Riley's blazer.

"Now I'm afraid to just chuck it all, to walk completely away from all that I have."

"Marriage is full of fears, love. You still have to face 'em, though."

"Well, until I can—" Riley smiled up at the sky and then down at her mother "—I'll hang on to my insurance."

"And once he tells you this secret you think he's keeping?"

Riley could barely shake her head, and then she practically melted into her mother's hug.

Chapter 13

Riley got home around 2 p.m. The loft was suspiciously dim for the middle of the day, but she didn't question it just then. Instead, she pressed her forehead against the door and replayed the conversation with her mother.

How'd things get so complicated? She felt a hunger pang, as if it were a response. Smiling, she brushed her hand across her still-flat tummy. "All right, little baby." She took a mental inventory of everything in her cabinets. Sadly, her cravings turned either to sweet and gooey or crunchy and salty.

She decided to think about it while she changed clothes. She was about to turn away from the door when his hands eased around her waist.

"Mmm…you're gonna have to go. My husband's back in town, you know?"

Asher grinned, causing his probing light brown gaze to narrow. "I'll make it fast. Promise." Slowly, he nuzzled her ear and suckled the lobe while tugging at the zip front of her blazer.

"That's not a promise I'd be proud of keeping." Riley's tease caught on a gasp when his hands found their way into her bra. She let her forehead fall to the door and moved against Asher, who was presently clothed in a navy towel. Biting her lip, Riley lost herself in the sensation of him behind her.

The pleasure was overstimulation at its best, and she was soon turning to face him. She practically climaxed while splaying her hands across the impressive slabs of muscle packing his chest and abs.

Riley's moans wavered when he kissed her. Asher held her

neck to keep her in place as his tongue delved deeper repeatedly and possessively. Riley pulled at the knot securing the towel at his waist, but he patted her hand.

"Later," he whispered.

Whimpering her protest, Riley obeyed and kissed him with increasing eagerness. Moments later she wore nothing but a pair of lacy panties. Asher's groans joined her sighs of delight as he buried his face in an abundance of fragrant cleavage.

Riley arched into the ravenous suckling and moaned his name. Asher felt his legs go weak.

He honestly didn't think he could leave her there when it was time to go. He was so starved for her, and every time he took her, he grew more insatiable. The way she chanted his name was enough to render him stiff and throbbing with need. Her hushed voice and the way she dropped her *r*'s...He'd lived off phone sex with his wife for far too long. Now he wanted her voice, her body, a touch away.

Again, Riley moved to tug away the towel.

"Later," he told her...again.

Dismissing the order, Riley folded her hand over the stiff length of flesh beneath the towel. "Now," she declared, squeezing and fondling him without mercy.

Asher smirked. "Dammit, Riley." He slammed his fist on the door and then snatched away her panties with a flick of his wrist. The towel left his waist seconds later, and they were soon enjoying each other enthusiastically against the door. He kept his grip tight about her thighs and spread her to accommodate his frame more comfortably.

He gasped into her shoulder.

When he drew back in an attempt to prolong his enjoyment, she put him back inside her and dared him to resist the pleasure that time. "Don't faint on me now," she teased when his legs weakened.

Asher managed a chuckle but didn't lose his focus. His back glistened with sweat as he took her against the door. Riley's needy groans soon resembled tortured whimpers, she was so lost in delight.

The next several moments passed in a long erotic blur.

* * *

Much later, following a tasty supper of roast turkey sandwiches and broth, part two of the cozy interlude commenced.

"I'd set it up to take you here in the tub," Asher said while his light eyes scanned the bubbles clinging to her dark skin. "I tried to make it past the front door, but you wouldn't let me."

Riley settled more snuggly into his lap. "Not a problem." She rode him slow, loving the way he bit his lip as the pleasure consumed him. "You've got all night to take me right here."

Asher leaned his head back against the mauve tiles. "I intend to do exactly that."

"I guess you'll have to save a *little* time for this business you're here to handle."

Asher let a grimace mar his handsome honey-toned face. "Don't let tomorrow barge in yet, all right?" Cupping her face, he drew her into a branding kiss. "I wish we could stay this way for a lifetime," he confided, with his forehead pressed to hers.

Riley took a deep breath and nodded. "That'd be nice, but it'd probably get pretty uncomfortable with three in here for a lifetime."

Asher only smiled, cupping her breasts while engaging her in another slow kiss. Gradually, however, the kiss lost some of its intensity.

"What did you just say?" He leaned back to frown into her face.

Shrugging, Riley simply dipped her head to lick water droplets from his chest. "I said the tub is a bit small."

"For three?" Asher prompted when she said nothing more.

"Mmm-hmm…" Riley's tone was soft and perky. She continued to lap at the water droplets sprinkling his skin.

"Riley?" Asher firmed his grip on her arms. "Three?" He gave her a tiny shake.

She winked and, with a saucy smile, tilted her head. "You know, for such a hotshot agent, you're kinda slow at times."

His face was a picture of reluctant amazement. "I'm afraid this is one you're gonna have to spell out for me."

She kissed the tip of his nose. "I have your baby inside me, Asher Hudson. Does that spell it out?" His gorgeous face was stilled by shock, and Riley thought he'd never appeared more adorable to her. Laughing then, she snapped her fingers before his face.

He caught her hand and dropped a kiss into her palm. The other hand he pressed to her flat abdomen. His eyes were trained there for a time before returning to Riley's face.

She grew concerned by his stillness. "Baby? You okay?"

"I put a baby there?" He was still in a state of disbelief.

Riley sat back a bit and smiled. "I think you had a little help." Her lashes fluttered when he stiffened again inside her. Asher tugged her into another kiss.

The sweet, gentle moment turned into something thoroughly lusty. Riley was more than ready when he took her hips and began to move inside her. When he stilled, she wanted to cry.

"Is this okay?" he was asking.

"It's very okay," she said, her response clearly reiterating her impatience to have him. "Asher, please." She took the lead, riding his erection hungrily. Desperately.

Water sloshed along the sides of the candlelit clawfoot tub. Asher desired his wife more then than in all the time he'd known her. Still, he cautioned himself against handling her too roughly.

"Don't do that," she ordered, wanting all he had to give and laughing in triumph when he answered her demand.

Afterward, they lay sprawled and naked in bed, with a chilled bowl of sweet fruit between them.

"Now I understand this health kick of yours." He laughed and bit into a slice of kiwi.

"I take offense to that." Riley searched for another small cube of pineapple. "It hurts to know that you don't think I could change my evil eating habits on my own."

Asher set aside the bowl and covered her body with his. "I'm glad to know the baby is enough to make it happen."

Riley smoothed her hands across his flawless skin. "The baby is *more* than enough." She arched into his chest and thrust her tongue into his mouth.

As they kissed, Asher reached for a tiny sliver of the ice that surrounded the chilled fruit bowl. He used it to outline her nipple.

Riley shrieked out a breathless laugh in response to the twin sensations of ice cold and passionate heat prickling her body.

Asher used the ice in a devastating fashion. He drove her near to insanity with the freezing-cold ice before warming her to a sizzle with his mouth. Riley shivered beneath the covers when his hot tongue swirled about a frosty nipple. He changed lanes then, feeding her the sweet fruit, chilling her with brief ice baths and plying her with kisses.

"Mmm…Asher… Does all this mean you're happy about the baby?"

His fierce look softened as the news reclaimed his heart. "I've never been so happy. Thank you," he said and then showed his appreciation.

Riley sobbed his name when the ice melded with her sex producing pleasure and pain. The silken petals of her womanhood puckered and tensed beneath the manipulation. Her cries of satisfaction mixed with heavy breathing when he soothed the effects of the ice with the ravenous feasting of his mouth. His tongue explored every part of her core—thrusting, rotating, stroking….

She was in the throes of a strong climax when she felt him inside her. Her arousal was turned inside out. When he gathered her close, Riley was torn between wanting to drift off into a content slumber and wanting to delve into one of the many important conversations they needed to have. Things had been left so unsettled between them. Now, for the first time ever, things felt all too right. A myth? Yes. But she'd take it. She'd relish the dream and deal with the reality later.

"So if you're cool with Vic goin' with the five-year, *five-dollar* deal, then we can have him sign the papers today and be back in Phoenix by supper time."

"Sounds good."

Talib set his chin against his palm and waited, wondering what had Asher so unfocused. They'd met for a working breakfast at Red Sun, but Talib had soon realized he was the only one with work on the brain.

Eventually, Asher's pen swirls on his pad slowed, and he frowned over at Talib. "Did you say five-dollar?"

Talib reached for another pat of butter. "I did, and if I were as clueless as you seem to be right now, we'd have Vic runnin' his ass off for peanuts."

"Sorry, man. Guess I am a little out there today."

"You mind telling me about it?" Talib couldn't hide the concern on his face as he watched Asher down a glass of juice in one gulp.

"Riley's pregnant."

Concern turned to disbelief and then to delight. Talib's handsome face beamed as brightly as the grin he sported. Standing, he offered his hand to shake and drew Asher into a tight hug. "Did you plan this?" he asked and laughed.

"Not at all."

"But you're happy as hell?"

"Damn right."

"And how's she?"

"She—she's great." Asher spoke as if it were a surprise for him to admit it.

Talib took note. "So what's up?" He reclaimed his seat at the table.

Asher followed suit. "I always figured I'd have to battle with her over havin' kids when the time came."

Talib tugged on his ear and winced. "Well, you did say it wasn't planned, mate."

"It's still a surprise to me." Asher topped off his coffee. "She doesn't seem upset by it at all. She's already settled into the idea." He flashed Talib a wink. "Even changed her eating habits."

"Get out."

"I'm serious. She acts like she really wants it."

"And that surprises you? She's about to have a baby with the man she loves." Talib raked a hand through his thick hair and shrugged. "That's every woman's dream, isn't it?"

"Not every *career* woman's dream," Asher said sourly.

"Ah…and what'd she have to say about that?"

Asher shrugged then. "She didn't say a thing. Why would she?"

Talib leaned closer to the table they shared. "What are you

thinking? What?" he said when Asher shrugged. "You think she's so thrilled about a trip to mommy land, she'll forget about career world?"

"That so hard to believe?"

"No, but this is Riley we're discussing." Talib reached for the pot of coffee then. "That career is her life."

"And this is a child." Asher leaned back and spread his hands. "I'd say that trumps career."

"Mmm… So that means *you're* letting go of the career world as well?"

"Me?"

"Child trumps career, remember?"

Asher smiled.

"What?" Talib challenged, his dark eyes sparkling wickedly. "We can't choose family over a job?"

"That's not it." Asher shook his head and focused on sweetening his coffee. "There's no way to compare our careers."

"They're both careers, mate."

"You can't compare what I do to that little column of hers."

Talib didn't join in Asher's arrogant chuckling. "A lot of people put a lot of stock in that little column of hers. Don't forget, she almost put us out of business once."

Asher's confidence dwindled a tad. "I haven't forgotten that. Doesn't mean I view our jobs as equal, though."

"Ah." Talib noticed their breakfast partners arriving and waved. "Just make sure you don't say that to her."

Asher stood to greet their approaching associates. "I'm pretty sure I'll never have to," he said softly to his partner.

"This'll be a perfect night for it Miss Cassell. We don't have anything planned…mmm-hmm…okay—all right, see you then." Riley cleared her throat and set down the phone once the connection was broken. She'd just ended a call with Cassell Hudson, Asher's mother.

Riley smiled, her thoughts returning to the call. Cassell was as excited as a girl about to have her sweet-sixteen party. She'd prepared a great evening to celebrate her son's homecoming.

Misha waited in the office doorway. She caught the last seconds of the call and winced.

"Boy, I'll bet you're not lookin' forward to that."

Riley spared a fleeting glance toward her friend. "What?"

"Please, girl, an evening with your in-laws? Yuck."

"It's not like that, Misha."

"Right, and how often do you see them, anyway?" Misha lay back on the sofa and crossed her legs at the ankles. "They live in Connecticut. Asher's in Phoenix…."

"Which is why we probably get along so well." Riley joined in when Misha laughed.

"Well, I hope you don't go vomiting all over the place."

Riley waved off the prediction. "Near or far, I've always gotten along with them. Besides, Miss Cassell can cook her butt off."

Misha kicked off her baby-blue pumps and flexed her stockinged feet. "Do they know about the baby?"

"If they don't yet, they will tonight."

"You told Asher…." Misha sat up straight on the sofa. "How'd he take it?"

Riley twisted a wayward lock around her finger and shrugged. "I think he's pretty happy, but we didn't, um…talk much about it."

"You do look pretty satisfied…." Misha's glee mingled with something smug. "I gotta hand it to you, Rile. Not many women could have their man, baby and career fall in line that way."

Like a shade drawing down against the sun, Riley's mood dimmed. "Don't crack open the champagne yet." She smoothed suddenly damp hands across the seat of her salt-and-pepper slacks. "I haven't told him about the job."

Misha nodded. "Rationing out the news, eh? Any reason why?"

"A damn good reason." Riley was pacing her office then. "The minute I tell him, he'll ask if I'm turning it down, and I'll have to tell him no."

Asher savored the view as he leaned against the doorjamb of Riley's office, hands hidden in the pockets of his olive trousers. His cool appearance belied the fact that he was seething. In spite of the fact that he'd been propositioned six times since he'd passed the hallowed doors of Cache Media, the sight of another man perched so comfortably on the side of the desk nearest his wife's chair was enough to make him envision all sorts of delicious tortures he wanted to inflict.

Until she caught sight of him in the doorway. Then her lovely face lit up, with an expression completely unlike and completely better than the one she'd held while speaking to the gentleman perched right next to her.

Indeed, Riley's heart was in her throat. Such was the case whenever she glimpsed Asher anywhere she wasn't expecting him. Thrilled to have him there, she laughed and left her chair, thus ending her discussion with Bastian Grovers.

She wasn't shy about throwing herself into Asher's arms and kissing him with an eager fire. When they hugged, Asher's observant eyes narrowed toward Bastian.

"Grovers."

"Good to see you, Ashe. Lotta talk around here about Vic. Congratulations."

Asher kept one arm linked about his wife's waist when the hug ended. "Just doing my job."

Bastian's hearty laughter filled the room. "I'll say. *Sports Beat*'s gonna do a piece on Vic. We'd like to have you give a few quotes as well."

Asher was diplomatic to a fault when it came to his clients. "I'd suggest we wait round for the contract to be signed before we start to announce it from the rafters, but you feel free to talk to Vic." He shrugged. "Can't hurt to have a *little* prepress."

Bastian nodded. "Gotcha. Thanks, man." He sized up the couple and then grinned and headed for the door.

"Finally," Riley breathed once they were alone. Standing on her toes, she provided her husband with a more thorough kiss. Asher didn't waste time accepting, as he cupped the back of her neck and took charge of the kiss. Riley was seconds from locking her office door but knew they couldn't count on the time needed to *really* enjoy one another. With a sigh, she pulled out of his loose embrace. "So what brings you by?"

"Ma said she called you about tonight. Thought we could leave from here, unless you need to go back home first."

Riley was already heading back to her desk. "Leaving from here's fine. You might be bored stiff, though. I can't leave for another twenty minutes or so."

Asher watched her shuffle through the file folders littering her desk. "Take your time," he said and went to set up shop in the tiny alcove at the rear of her lovely office.

Asher studied Riley. He was totally absorbed in watching his wife handle her job. She never lost her focus or her cool, not even when a harried young reporter rushed in, claiming to have deleted her entire documents folder. Riley took care of the crisis without ever leaving her desk and gave the worried writer a quick tutorial in case the problem should ever reoccur.

Asher whistled when she set down the phone. "Impressive."

Riley graced him with a wink and a wave. "That's why they pay me the big bucks."

Asher stifled his next remark when someone else rushed into the office, needing Riley's assistance. Inside, he was wondering if she'd ever walk away from it all. In spite of the confidence he'd shown during his discussion with Talib, Asher realized he was in no way certain of her intentions. They hadn't gotten around to talking about their living situation since she'd told him about the baby.

Moreover, they hadn't spoken of the *ultimatum* he'd issued before she left Phoenix. Things were in a somewhat sublime tailspin, and he had no clue where they'd all land.

Riley's thoughts had veered in the same direction as Asher's. Once the next crisis was averted, she returned to her desk slowly, contemplating telling him everything and judging his response.

"Something you want to say?" Asher kept his attention on his PDA. He could feel her alluring brown stare focused his way.

"Casey?" Riley buzzed her assistant and waited for a response. "Run interference for me, will you? When we leave, you can take off for the day."

"Thanks, Riley! You guys have a good night."

"Memories of your ultimatum come to mind," she said, watching him pocket the small device and stand.

"Forgive me." He said it so simply, so humbly.

Riley was floored.

"I never should've put that on the table," he said.

"Would you be saying that if the baby wasn't in the picture?" She leaned back against the desk and watched him, with challenge in her eyes.

Asher shrugged and shook his head. "I can't say. But either way, I wouldn't have meant it."

Just then the theme music from the eighties television series *The A-Team* filled the room. Asher smirked adorably while pulling his phone from the inside pocket of his suit coat.

"Hudson." His expression and voice went softer, and he smiled. "Hey, Ma."

"I can't tell you how good it feels to hear your voice and know you're only a couple of hours away."

Asher turned and strolled back across the office. "I know, Ma."

Cassell dwelled on the fact a moment longer before she got to the point of her call. "Would you two mind terribly if we went out for dinner and came back home for dessert? I've been in meetings with my charity committee all morning, and I haven't done a thing with dinner. I only made dessert."

"I don't see a problem with that." Asher eased a hand into his trouser pocket and watched Riley resume scanning the paperwork at her desk.

"We'll have to get a move on, I'm afraid. Your dad made reservations at Neale's."

Asher checked his wristwatch and grimaced. Since the elder Hudsons lived in Connecticut, that meant he and Riley would definitely have to hustle.

"We'll see you soon, Ma." Asher wrapped up the call, told his mom he loved her and then explained the accelerated plans to his wife.

With the "ultimatum" conversation tabled for the moment, Riley set aside her editing and headed for her private washroom.

"No, Asher," she warned when he marched in behind her and proceeded to relieve her of the tailored black shirt she wore. "Asher…"

"Just a second." One hand had already ventured inside her shirt; the other was making its way into her trousers.

"No. Mmm…" Persuasive fingers were inside her panties and weakening her legs….

"Hey, Riley! Congrats, girl!"

With an airy wave, Riley kept a firm grip on Asher's arm as she practically dragged him to the elevator bay. Asher assumed the well wishes were in reference to the baby, when, in actuality, they were related to his wife's new job offer.

"So have you told your mom yet?" he asked while they descended to the lobby of the *New Chronicle*.

"She's really impressed with you." Riley leaned against the opposite wall of the elevator car and smiled at Asher's confusion. "She told me about the promise you made about making her a grandmother."

Asher shrugged. "I like to keep my promises." He peppered the tease with a lazy wink.

"Well, now she's your biggest fan." Riley focused in on one of her black peekaboo pumps. "'Not only is he sexy and gorgeous as hell, but he keeps his promises,' I think she said."

Asher hugged himself. "Ms. Virginia is so good for a man's ego." He burst into laughter at the playfully sour look his wife sent him.

Waverly, Connecticut, epitomized the phrase "small-town allure." The Hudsons had moved there when Asher's father became the town's first black bank manager.

Riley had always been somewhat awed by Asher's childhood—not the norm by any standards. At least not any standards *she* was familiar with. His parents were high school sweethearts who grew up in a town much like Waverly. They were both from large, well-to-do families with staunch African Methodist backgrounds. Jones and Cassell Hudson had attended the same college, where he majored in finance and she obtained a teaching degree.

But Cassell Hudson had never utilized her degree—not in the workforce at least. Instead, she'd lavished all her considerable knowledge on her son. This had become even easier when Jones obtained the position as bank manager.

As a full-time mom, Cassell had been anything but the norm. While most toddlers were learning how to put one block on top of the other and using their fingers to pick up food, in addition to chewing on them, Asher was being taken to museums at home *and* abroad. The trips didn't end once he started public school, though. Weekends were spent visiting historical sites all over the country, and Asher had a fierce command of American history. So much so that when it came time to learn from the pitiful lone chapter on slavery and the Civil War, Asher informed his teacher that the material was grossly inaccurate.

The teacher brushed him off, of course. That is, until Cassell stepped in and, after little debate, was brought in to give a lecture to her son's fifth grade class on African American involvement before, during and after the Civil War. She was a phenomenal woman, Riley believed, so similar to her own mother yet so different in other ways.

Being a wife and mother was Cassell's life, and she thrived on it. For Riley, it was hard to swallow that a woman could so happily put her welfare and the welfare of her child in the hands of her husband—high school sweetheart or otherwise. But Cassell had, and the results were marvelous.

Asher drove into the wide horseshoe drive before his parent's home. Clearly, the neighborhood catered to a mostly older set. People who'd already raised their kids and sent them off to prosper in the world. Coral Crest was too serene, too polished, too quiet a development.

Such perfection gave Riley an eerie sense of unease. She thrived on the craziness of the city, the unexpectedness of it all. Areas such as the Hudson's suburban oasis, with everything elegantly in its place, unsettled her.

Asher shut down the rented truck's smooth engine and soaked up the quiet. Unlike his wife, he thrived on the environment. There were no hordes of people all jockeying for a place on the same square inch of concrete. Fresh air, a place to think… He cast a glance at his wife, knowing the peacefulness was enough to make her heave.

Opposites attract was a very real statement as it related to them.

"You know, she's gonna ask us to stay the night," he warned and let her see his surprise when she said she'd packed a bag and put in a few things for him as well.

The natural arch of Riley's brows rose a few inches. She smiled.

Asher smirked and pulled the keys from the ignition. "I was sure I'd have to bully you into a shopping trip for the things we'd need."

Riley's smile deepened and narrowed her eyes. "I'm always in the mood for shopping, but we're good unless you need anything."

"Sounds good," he murmured, nodding as his light eyes drifted toward her mouth. "Give it up," he ordered.

Riley scooted over the gearshift lever and eagerly obliged the order for a kiss. She was seconds from straddling his lap right there in his parents' front yard when Asher broke the kiss and left the truck. He walked around to open her door but wouldn't let her pass when she stepped down.

"Thanks for doing this." He smoothed a hand across her tummy and nudged her ear.

Riley's smile turned curious. "You say that like I would've had a problem with coming out."

"Obviously, visiting my folks isn't tops on your to-do list." He shrugged. "You're right in New York, and I'm in Phoenix. I probably speak to 'em more than you do."

"Well, baby, they are *your* parents." She scanned the land-scaped perfection past his broad shoulders. "And everyone stays so busy, you know? Your dad's still on the go with the bank, and your mom has all her volunteer projects. I've got *my* job...."

Asher looked down where his hand still covered her stomach. "With the baby coming, I guess you won't have much of an issue with that." He didn't wait for a response but pressed a quick kiss to her cheek and went to get the bag.

Riley frowned as she watched him.

Jones and Cassell Hudson were fit to be tied when their son and his wife announced the addition to the family. Asher, like

Riley, was an only child. Jones and Cassell had struggled for many years with the fact that there would be no other children due to Jones's low sperm count. The news of the baby meant more to them than anyone knew.

There was a round of drinks before the group left for the restaurant.

"I guess I'll have to tally my frequent flyer miles for all these trips to Phoenix to see my new grandbaby," said Cassell.

Riley's grip tightened on the goblet of sparkling grape juice when Asher didn't correct his mother's assumption. Thankfully, Jones was there to keep her mind off of it. His attentiveness and interest in whether she had everything she needed soothed Riley's racing thoughts. Having never really known her father, she'd always felt a closeness with Asher's dad. She'd often told her husband that his father had a soft, easy, yet firm manner with people, which probably came in handy. She was certain customers left his bank with smiles in place, even after being turned down for a loan.

"So will you be having the baby in New York?" Jones topped off her juice.

Riley studied Asher and his mother across the den. "I plan to have it here." She smiled when Jones smothered her hand in one of his. "As for the rest… We'll have to wait and see what happens."

Jones's dark, mellow stare narrowed as he focused on his son. "I expect you won't stick around long, but I *do* hope the baby'll be enough to make Ashe visit a little more." He sipped a bit more of his cognac. "I don't know if anything's got the power to do that."

"Yeah…" Riley blinked as tears filled her eyes.

"Still…this *is* a baby. Men turn to mush over their babies, you know?"

Riley considered the man's words. "Mr. Jones, what do you know about Asher's…aversion to New York?" Her dark face was aglow with curiosity. "I mean, I know some folks just don't like the place, but I just think it goes *way* deeper for him."

Jones grimaced while the alcohol burned his gullet. "Cass and I never understood it much, either. He wasn't always like this."

The man stroked the whiskers roughening his honey-toned skin. "He lived his life in the suburbs. Trips to the city were like going to the zoo, and he was happy to be there, but happier still to return home." He shook his head. "Whatever happened to make him…hate it so…happened during his second year in the league and whatever it was made the *hate* specific to New York."

"He was shot during that time. The store robbery," Riley replied, turning the goblet in her hands. "That must've played a part."

Jones only smiled. "He never told us. Who knows? Maybe it was just that. Being shot and the devastation of it were probably enough to make him hate it."

The explanation was simple enough and quite understandable, Riley thought. She couldn't zero in on why she didn't believe it.

Chapter 14

The drive from Connecticut was silent the following afternoon. The silence was not a comfortable one. Asher kept waiting for Riley to snap and was pleased when she didn't. He felt the pending discussion was an event best saved for the privacy of their apartment.

When they got there, however, it seemed that the *uncomfortable silence* would continue. Riley headed for the bathroom. Asher was about to follow when his phone vibrated. It was Talib, and judging from the sound of his voice, things weren't going altogether smoothly.

"New Jersey's having issues with Vic maintaining his free-agent status in light of the kind of money they're shelling out."

"Why am I not surprised?" Asher's mind was still on his wife, but he shifted gears easily to business. "I'll meet you at your hotel." He headed for the study to grab his briefcase. "We'll strategize and then give a call to Vic to discuss his options."

"What's up?" Talib inquired, sensing the distress coloring his friend's voice.

Asher didn't bother to deny it. "Just trying to understand the mind of a pregnant woman, is all."

Talib whistled across the line. "*That* is harder than negotiating a contract could *ever* be, I'm sure. Good luck, mate."

"Mmm," Asher grunted and closed the phone. He walked in the direction his wife had taken to the bathroom. Along the way, he shed the lightweight jacket he wore over the black shirt, which hung outside his sagging denims.

Having stripped down to a lacy bra and panty set, Riley was

adjusting the water for a bath. She straightened and rolled her eyes away from Asher when she noticed him leaning against the doorjamb.

"You gonna make me guess, Riley?"

"Guess what?" She selected a bath oil from one of the oak cabinets above the toilet and carried the bottle to the tub.

Asher caught her on her way back to the cabinet and trapped her against the marble countertop. "Spill it."

"Oh, come off it." She bristled at his hold. "You know what this is. We've been skirting around it since you came to town."

His light eyes narrowed dangerously. "And you pick now to catch an attitude over it."

"I think an ultimatum like the one you issued is good cause for an attitude." She relaxed a bit, yet her eyes were throwing ice daggers at his.

Asher bowed his head close to her shoulder. "Can't you just forget about it?"

"Why? You haven't."

"What?"

"Not once did you correct your parents about us moving to Phoenix. Why is that?" She waited for him to look at her. "Because you knew I'd go along with it in the end? Or maybe you were just caught up in all that fairy-tale land up there...I don't know...."

"Hell, Riley, I wasn't about to get into that with them when *we* haven't even settled it."

"Your father's hoping the baby will be enough to get you to come home." She smiled when new emotion flickered in his deep-set gaze. "Guess I'm not the *only* one who's wondering why it can't be *you* who does the relocating."

Asher turned and began massaging the back of his neck. "New York's no place to raise a kid," he grumbled.

Riley heard him clearly. "Is that a fact? Well, someone should've told my mom or all the other parents raising all the kids I see running around the city."

"You know what I mean." He pointed an index finger in her direction.

"Actually, I don't." Riley crossed her arms over her chest. "I mean, we've been together all this time, and I still don't know why you hate this city."

Asher's sleek brows rose. "I think a lot of people feel the way I do."

"Yeah, but it's personal for you. More personal than for most."

He let her glimpse his unease before shaking it off. "I can't talk about this now."

Riley waved him off. "Mmm-hmm… What else is new?" She returned the bath oil to the cabinet and went to stand before the long lighted mirror above the sink. "Why'd you want to marry me, Asher?"

He stopped in the doorway. "What did you say?"

Riley combed her fingers through her clipped crop and then removed her bra. "All the time we were together, I lived here, and all the while, things were great. I never pressured you about marriage. So why'd you marry me?" She watched him in the mirror when he walked into her line of sight. "Why? Did you figure it'd be the best way to keep me faithful to you?"

On slow steps, Asher closed the distance between them. Riley swallowed her nerves. She wanted to rouse his temper in hopes of getting him to tell her whatever he was hiding—whatever he was afraid of.

He trailed his fingers along her spine. "Maybe you should ask me why I didn't marry you long before I did."

Riley blinked. "Because I was in New York, and there's something about this place that you won't—"

He was shaking his head. "More than that. A lot more."

The moment of truth was arriving, but Riley's attention was shattering. Asher's touch grew progressively demanding the longer he spoke.

"I never saw you coming," he admitted while driving his thumb into her spine, using delicious massaging strokes. "A man in my profession doesn't have much trouble attracting women, you know?"

Riley's breath stopped in her throat. Asher Hudson's ability to attract women had nothing at all to do with his profession.

"A relationship with a woman in New York has as little chance for survival as one on the moon." He pulled her back against him. "But there you were, and you terrified me."

Her eyes flew to his face in the mirror. "Terrified?"

"I didn't like what you did to me."

Riley thought she understood. "My story could've ruined your agency."

"Perhaps." His lazy grin appeared. "But that wasn't it, either." Again, he began the circular massage to her spine. "The more I had you, the more I wanted you. When you weren't around me, I couldn't focus." He shrugged in spite of himself. "Started to affect my work. Then we started to see more of each other, and it was enough just knowing you were there in some way."

"So what happened?"

"What happened was I loved you too damn much to not want to make you mine in every way."

"Asher." It was a chore to murmur his name. She ached sweetly from head to toe, as his touch had stirred her to a frenzy. By then his fingers were inside her panties. One hand cupped a breast, and his perfect lips started to nibble her earlobe.

The triple caress dissolved any other thoughts or questions. Asher rested his forehead on her shoulder and freed himself from the confines of his jeans. He took her quickly and enthusiastically against the counter. Afterward, he shut off the water and carried her into the bedroom. Once there, he made love to her all over again. When it was over, Riley couldn't keep her eyes open. Asher left her in bed, sleeping like a stone.

Riley added hot water to the tub, which had only been a quarter filled when Asher had shut off the taps before carrying her off to the bedroom earlier. She tried not to think about the fact that they'd made love because he was trying to shut her up. And she'd let him. But as she settled into the fragrant heated water, her thoughts would center around nothing else.

Still, he'd told her much more involving his love for her and their marriage. Yet there was lots more he wasn't saying, and for the life of her, she couldn't imagine why he was keeping his secrets.

Whatever he was hiding, she had little doubt it would encourage him to understand why she wanted to remain in New York. *And he doesn't even know about your new job offer.*

Riley groaned and buried her face in a wet cloth. She had to tell him. He deserved to know that little tidbit as much as he had deserved to know about their child. *Hell, Riley, your job as it stands now is a major factor in why you want to stay!* How deeply into this conversation was she willing to go? She wondered and recalled the talk with her mother.

Was she ready to tell Asher why working meant so much to her? Whatever happened, she needed to tell him and fast. Things would go from tension filled to untenable in the span of ten seconds if he heard it from someone else.

Over a late lunch, Asher and Talib were brainstorming options for their newest client. They worked in silence for a time, each so involved with his individual tasks that they had no idea how closely they were being studied.

"Asher Hudson ain't a media-friendly guy," Diane Sims noted as she watched her friend and colleague hunt for a fresh pad.

Justine Duke offered a simple smile and continued her search. "A grunt from Asher Hudson is like a full-page comment from anyone else of interest in the sports world."

Diane shook her head of kinky twists. "So you just wanna go over there and get shot down?"

"There's always a story surrounding Asher Hudson."

"Well, forget Victor Lyne's rumored signing deal. I'm pretty sure that's gonna be confirmed and handled in-house."

"Agreed." Justine cheered as she located a pad. "But what I'm interested in has little to do with sports and everything to do with entertainment."

Diane was floored and didn't mind letting the amazement show all over her round dark face. "The man is in town to negotiate a surprise multimillion-dollar deal for a walk-on, and you're interested in him for an entertainment angle?"

"You got it." Justine set aside her pad and tote and fixed Diane with a focused baby-blue glare. "Do you know how long I've been in awe of that marriage?"

"Asher Hudson and Riley Stamper."

"They're fascinating public figures who have managed to keep their very unorthodox marriage out of the papers. Doesn't anyone find that unusual?" Justine leaned back and spread her frail-looking hands about her. "All that distance between them and they remain just as in love as ever."

"And this is what you want to ask him about?"

Justine gave a one-shoulder shrug. "I'd work my way up to it."

"He's not a man who enjoys questions about his business. I doubt he'd take ones regarding his personal life too well, either."

"And why is that? A man like that just accepting his wife living in a different time zone…" Justine passed the salt when Diane pointed. "I'm willing to bet that's cause for some very interesting arguments."

"Let it go, girl. You're an editorial assistant. You don't want to mess that up by screwing around, trying to find a story where there isn't one."

Justine smiled yet again. "Oh, there's a story there all right, and I'm gonna break it and get *my* break."

"Get your break is right if Bob and Grady find out you're wasting time on this," said Diane, mentioned their editors.

"Dammit," Justine muttered, noticing that she'd missed her chance to catch Asher for comment. Four other men had approached the table. No worries, she decided, completely oblivious to Diane's words of caution. She'd get a quote; she'd get the dirt. No one's marriage was that happy. If it was, she'd move on. But if this panned out, she'd have one helluva story and the groundwork for one sensational career.

"Crikey, what round is it?" Talib groaned following the departure of the New Jersey team execs.

Asher chuckled and watched his partner massage his neck with both hands. "No one ever said contract negotiating was easy."

Talib reclined in his chair. "You think they'll go for what we've suggested?"

"They will. The kid's too talented and too…upstanding to pass up." Asher smirked, with a confidence he had every right to. "He's well-spoken, educated, interested in the game before stardom. No...they're ready to get him signed, trust me."

Talib did just that, knowing Asher had a sixth sense when it came to reading people. He'd once boasted the same talent himself, before he'd misread someone and it cost him his heart. As if on cue, the person in question was approaching their table just then.

Asher's grin turned into full laughter when he saw Misha. They embraced warmly and exchanged loud kisses on the cheeks.

"So Riley finally ran you out of the house with all that pregnancy angst, huh?" said Misha.

Asher replied to the dig with a playful wince. "Does it show that much?"

Misha smacked his cheek. "You're too gorgeous to let it make you look bad."

"Still good for my ego," said Asher.

She winked and clapped her hands to her sides. "One of my many talents. Seriously, though, congratulations on the baby."

Asher pulled her close again. "Thanks, Misha."

"Talib," Misha greeted in a faint tone once she stepped out of Asher's embrace. She looked back at her best friend's husband before Talib could respond to her greeting—as if she really hadn't expected him to. "So I wanted to talk to you about having a party for Riley."

"Misha, you know how she hates that stuff—especially when it's in her honor."

"That's why I need *you* to get her there."

"Putting me in the line of fire, eh?"

Misha knocked a fist on his shoulder. "I can't think of anyone better."

Asher closed his eyes resignedly and stroked the scar along his cheek. "I'll get her there." He sighed and leaned down so Misha could kiss his cheek.

Her expression dimmed when she looked down at Talib. "You're invited as well," she said, pressing her lips together when he nodded. "I'll see you soon, Asher." She excused herself a second later.

"How long you gonna torture yourself before you go after her?" Asher inquired while reclaiming his seat.

Talib hesitated, his hypnotic browns following Misha and reluctantly appraising her slender frame. The softness in his stare turned sly. "You forget that I've already *gone after* her and got her."

"Trouble is, you want more of her."

"*No*, the trouble is, she's a schemer—a beautiful one, but a schemer just the same."

Asher reached for his water glass. "And you never had a better time in your life, and have you ever thought maybe she wasn't scheming you? Maybe it was a misunderstanding?"

Talib's responding stare was not obliging.

"Misha Bales doesn't look like a schemer. Especially when she looks at you. She looks like she's suffering."

Talib got his things together. "That's because she got caught. They always look like they're suffering when they get caught, mate." He stood and drew a few bills from the back pocket of his khakis. "I pray you never have to see that look on Riley's face." He left Asher, with a grim smile.

Victor Lyne's contract with the New Jersey ball club was secure. The execs accepted Asher's proposal without further objections. Once all the proper paperwork was signed and in-house, it was time for the fun to begin. Victor was busy accepting accolades from his coworkers, being hunted down by every sports broadcaster in the country and preparing for a huge signing party.

Through it all, Asher and Riley thrived in the semblance of normal married life. They each considered it a treat to be living under the same roof, enjoying meals together, debating the latest news topics, debating baby names and whether they wanted to know or be surprised by the baby's gender.

They hadn't revisited the topic of exactly *where* they'd raise the baby, and Riley felt they'd avoided it for far too long. She'd come downstairs one afternoon to broach that very subject, only to discover her husband was nowhere to be found. Moments later, a key scratched the lock, and he walked inside.

"You had a craving that I didn't satisfy last night," he said to answer the question on her face.

Her mind was thoroughly in the gutter. "No, I think you *more* than satisfied my cravings last night."

Grinning, Asher waved a box before her, and Riley uttered a delighted shriek. She opened the package to find it filled with individually wrapped chocolate peanut butter cups.

"Thank you," she breathed, marveling at her favorite candy waiting nice and neat for her to tear into. Forgetting her husband, she focused her attention on the treat.

Asher watched in amazement as his wife devoured four cups in rapid succession. Scratching at the dark waves of his hair, he glanced down at the larger box he carried.

"Guess I should've given you this one first."

"More candy?" Riley guessed, her gaze full of hope and her mouth full of chocolate.

Asher shook his head and then laughed. He led Riley to an armchair and placed the box on her lap. Wetting a napkin, he wiped her fingers and mouth before opening the box for her.

The gorgeous evening gown inside took Riley's mind off the chocolate. Slowly, she pulled it from the wrapping, delighting in the stylish cut of the maternity frock.

"Well, Asher...thank you, but...I can't seem to recall craving a dress."

"Funny." He perched on the arm of the sofa. "It's for the party."

"What party?" Riley's voice was as absent as the expression she wore while studying the dress.

"Victor's." He allowed his hurt to show when she finally looked up, still wearing the absent expression. "Riley..."

"Oh. Damn." She winced. "Baby, I'm sorry." She left her chair and the dress behind and rushed over to console her husband. "Sweetie, I'm sorry. It just slipped my mind for a minute."

"S'all right," he soothed and folded his hand over the small but increasingly noticeable bump in her belly. "You got a lot on your mind, so I understand," he teased and nuzzled his nose against hers. "You think you can make it?"

Riley linked her arms about his neck. "I wouldn't miss it."

"I was hoping you wouldn't have to work."

"Nope. No work."

Her clipped tone intrigued him. "Is everything all right there?"

"Yeah." She rubbed her thumb along his collarbone and debated a second. "There *is* something I need to tell you, though."

"About the job," he guessed, watching her nod. "Spill it."

The phone rang before she could begin. It didn't take long to realize the calls with questions on the deal had begun full force. Asher promised to be only a second, but Riley urged him to bask in the moment. His laughter over the success robbed Riley of her ability to ruin the moment with her job news.

The calls must've lasted into the wee hours, for when Riley next saw her husband, it was the following morning. He stood at the foot of the bed, securing the belt around tanned slacks, while she slumbered, naked, in their bed.

"Mmm…Asher? Handle that, will you?" she grunted and motioned toward the sunlight streaming through the windows.

"Not natural to hate the sun," he scolded while seeing to the blinds.

Riley stretched like a lazy cat. "I don't hate the sun. I hate when the sun streams through my windows at seven o'clock."

Asher rolled his eyes while rushing for his suit coat. "Evil. I hope the kid won't have your outlook."

Mention of the baby made Riley think of how wonderful everything had been and how ugly it was about to become.

"You okay?" His head tilted in concern. "Need anything?" He stepped over to the bed and trailed his fingers across the faint shadows beneath her eyes. "You don't look like you got enough sleep last night."

Riley pulled his hand to her mouth and kissed its center. "Pregnant women don't always look their best."

"To hell with that," he muttered, his gaze turning from concern to adoration. "You could have shadows as deep as moon craters beneath your eyes and still be gorgeous."

"Why, honey, you say the sweetest things," said Riley, pretending to gush.

He curved his hand around her chin. "This is about more than that. Like maybe you're not feeling well, and there's something going on with the baby that you don't want to tell me about."

"No, that's not it, I swear." She squeezed his hand.

Asher had tossed aside his suit coat and taken a seat on the edge of the bed. He toyed with the clipped locks covering her head before his fingers journeyed down to cup and fondle her breast.

Riley moaned and reclined against the padded headboard. She relished the feel of his thumb grazing an achy nipple. When she punctuated her moan with a wince, Asher slowed the caress.

"Am I hurting you?"

"No, no." She shook her head quickly. "Don't stop. This helps... They're just itchy, that's all. It happens some-times...when they grow."

"They grow?" Asher's handsome honey-toned face was alive with fascination.

Riley shivered while the heavenly sensations coursed through her. "Your boobs grow when you're pregnant," she shared.

"More?" he asked, looking every bit the prepubescent boy as he ogled the seductive rise and fall of her bosom. "More than all this?" he breathed.

"Will that be a problem, Mr. Hudson?"

"Don't ask stupid questions."

She pressed a hand to his chest when he leaned close. "What are you doing?"

"Helping." He pressed her down into the covering.

A wavering cry rippled from Riley's throat when his lips covered a puckering nipple. His thumb soothed the other, and she spasmed from delight.

Asher was true to his word. The mind-clouding suckling and nibbling truly soothed the tender buds.

"How's that?" His nose encircled the dark cloud surrounding one nipple.

Riley licked her lips and ground against his thigh. "Don't ask stupid questions."

Seconds turned into climactic minutes as the pleasure mounted. Riley moved to undo Asher's belt while he tugged at his tie. The attention he'd lavished on her breasts traveled onward, as he cherished the rising mound of her belly, and then on to the part of her anatomy he craved like a drug.

His arrogance peaked when she shrieked his name and arched into the torturous attention he paid to the sensitized flesh above her womanhood. When his tongue delved deeply to rotate amidst the heavy moisture filling her sex, Riley was sure she could've melted into the covers.

"I need more than your tongue, Asher." She felt his body shake when he chuckled at her bold request.

Before he could oblige, his cellular pierced the air.

"No please." Riley felt as if her body were sizzling for him. "Asher, please…"

"Shh…"

"Don't answer it. Mmm…" She writhed on the sheets when he dropped soft pecks on her thighs and belly as he rooted around inside his trouser pockets for the phone.

Leaving her with a cool wink, he answered the line. His voice was deep and clear; he was all business.

Somehow, Riley managed to pull herself together and listened as he handled his call. Hearing him speak and watching him across the room, lean and sexy, with one hand pushed into his pocket, head bowed as he conversed, were almost as arousing as having him touch her.

"Yeah…I was on my way out the door." Asher flashed Riley a naughty wink when he looked back at her. "All right. See you in thirty." While pushing the phone back into his pocket, he told her, "Talib says hello. Sorry I can't stay." He cupped her face. "You goin' in?"

"I'd planned to."

"I'll drop in on you later, okay?"

Riley nodded, eagerly accepting his kiss, which ended once she'd sucked every ounce of her taste from his tongue.

Asher debated whether he should go or stay. Responsibility won out, and he straightened, only to have her clutch his hand, as if she wanted to tell him something.

"I'll, um, I'll see you later."

He waged war within himself but held back from making her come clean. "Get some sleep," he whispered and tucked her in before he revisited the bathroom. She was snoring lightly when he left the bedroom.

Riley looked on as her doctor nodded in that patented doctor manner while she studied the long clipboard in her hand. When Dr. Lettia Breene looked over at her patient and smiled, Riley bristled.

"If you're going for soothing, the effect is lost, because I don't like it."

"Well, you should, because everything's lovely." Lettia's round, pretty face was a picture of serenity.

"Everything. I feel far from lovely."

"Well, I've got some concerns, but the baby is lovely."

Content with that news, Riley sighed. "Tell me the rest."

"I'm reading some tension, and I don't like those shadows under your eyes."

Riley massaged the bridge of her nose. "Asher mentioned those, too."

"Any stress with him being back?" Lettia removed her glasses and let a touch of wickedness gloss her eyes. "Course, I don't see how any woman could be stressed with a beautiful thing like that." She cleared her throat. "You didn't even hear me say that."

Riley laughed, as she often did whenever the no-nonsense, full-figured obstetrician lost her cool. "It's all right, and it's not that. There's a conversation I need to have with him, and I've been putting it off."

"Ah…" Lettia perched her gold spectacles back on her nose. "Any thoughts on when you might tell him?"

Recrossing her legs, Riley set her fist on her knee, bared by the slit in the hem of her dress. "I started to this morning, but, well…other things came up."

"Well, you just get it out—whatever it is. The first three months of pregnancy are the most tenuous. Not only should you refrain from lifting heavy items, but you shouldn't allow heavy matters to weigh too long on your mind."

Riley shielded her face in her palms. "That's good in theory. In practice, it's hell."

"Well, *try*." Lettia tapped her pen on the glass top of her desk. "And try to have fun. This is a happy time, remember?"

"Right."

"And you can start by enjoying the party Misha's giving you." Lettia winced when her patient's gaze narrowed. "I was told it wasn't a secret."

"It's fine, but you know parties aren't my thing, and I've got not one, but two, to suffer through."

Lettia tapped her desk again. "Well, I think it's great. If *that* doesn't help you shed some of that tension, nothing will."

Riley tried but couldn't seem to latch onto her doctor's excitement.

After the appointment, Riley went back to her office, where she finished the last of the chocolate peanut butter cups and chased them with two bottles of water. The water, however, was more to make up for gorging on the delicious candy than to quench her thirst. Closing her eyes, she savored the last piece and followed it with more water. She was dumping wrappers into the wastebasket when the office door closed behind her. Glancing across her shoulder, she expected to see anyone other than her husband, who stood leaning against the door, with his arms folded across his shirt.

"How'd it go?" She took note of his sexy, haggard appearance. His tie was loosened, and the shirt hung outside his trousers.

Asher studied his loafer-shod feet, one crossed over the other. "Went great. Guess I could've enjoyed it more if it weren't for other things on my mind."

Riley leaned on the front of her desk. "What other things?"

He didn't see fit to give a verbal reply. Instead, he bounded across the room. His mouth came crashing down upon hers as he pulled her impossibly close.

Her moans were gurgled and faint, yet Riley hungrily encircled her husband's neck with her arms as their tongues fought a lusty battle. She felt his fingers venture beneath the slit hemline of her pin-striped dress.

"Asher—"

"I've been thinking about this all day." His tongue lunged long and deep. "Don't stop me."

"Only going to ask if you locked the door."

"Done."

Riley heard her panties rip and cursed Asher, even as she cheered the forethought to wear stockings instead of hose. She brushed away his hands and handled the job herself.

Asher kissed his way down her body, worked back up and settled for nibbling an earlobe while his fingers worked a nipple. Using his other hand, he freed himself from the confines of trousers and boxers.

"Hush." He spoke the gruff order as he entered her body.

Riley buried her face in the crook of his neck and let her cries settle there as she inhaled the fantastic scent of his cologne. She lost her fingers in the silken beauty of his close-cut waves and accepted all that he gave.

They took each other slowly yet with much enthusiasm. Asher's satisfied grunts were low, tortured sounds while he relished her moisture drenching his length as her walls gripped him like the perfect glove.

A knock sounded on the office door. The phone rang a few times. Both forms of communication were ignored.

Chapter 15

Riley literally floated past her front door that afternoon. The interlude with Asher had ended all too soon, and she could only hope he'd return home early to continue what had been an ongoing love scene.

She grabbed a glass of orange juice from the kitchen, ignored the flashing light on the answering machine and opted for a soothing bath, which she hoped to follow with a hearty dinner and lovemaking with her husband. Not to mention alleviating the source of tension she could no longer tolerate. She planned to tell Asher about the job offer that evening. The only remaining question was, should she tell him before or after they made love?

Riley decided to ponder the question during her bath. It didn't take much time to fill the tub with scented oil and remove her clothes. As she passed before one of the mirrors, she caught sight of her body. A smile of curious wonder tugged at her lips, and she trailed her fingers across the tiny rise of her belly.

A bump. The baby was really there. Closing her eyes, she uttered a tiny prayer that her child would not be disappointed in her, that she'd do right by it. While her own childhood hadn't been a tragedy, she'd ensure her child had a far better one than she'd had.

And doesn't that include having its father in the same house?

Contemplating the question, Riley went to enjoy the hot bath and cold glass of orange juice.

She heard the front door close over the easy listening CD she had playing at low volume in the bathroom. "Asher?" she called and shivered happily when his deep voice responded.

Settling back in the still-warm bath, she'd closed her eyes for only a second when she heard the voice of her publisher, Gloria Reynolds, wafting in the air. Tapping fingers on her forehead then, Riley realized the flashing light on the answering machine was something she should have seen to.

Gloria was speaking of the new publication and saying there was one more meeting with a few people she and Misha hadn't spoken with before.

"...Riley please rest assured that I'm not trying to pressure you here. I know you still need to hash out all the details with your husband. It's just that these folks are eager to speak with you and Misha. They've heard so much about you both and are quite pleased by the possibility of you coming on board."

Gloria apologized for the lengthy message, explaining she hadn't wanted to risk having to leave it on her cell. "We're looking at the middle of next week for a dinner meet, but I'll give you a call with the particulars. Oh! And feel free to bring Asher along. The group would definitely *love* to meet him."

An emptiness filled the loft then. Gloria's bubbly message only accentuated the dread now soaking the air. Riley sat in the middle of the water, which now felt tepid around her. She didn't dare move, especially when she heard Asher's footsteps bringing him closer to the bathroom.

It took only a few seconds for him to arrive. To Riley, it felt like hours. When he leaned against the doorjamb and eased both hands into his pockets, she knew her voice had deserted her before she tried to utter a word.

"So when were you gonna tell me about that?"

"I've been...trying to for weeks. I could never work up the nerve to do it."

The muscle in his jaw flexed wickedly. "Is that because you're going to tell me you're taking the job?"

"Well, I haven't really decided." She stopped talking when his expression told her the answer didn't pass muster.

With slow steps, he entered the bathroom and took a seat on the counter. "I think they'll want an answer soon. Surely you're favoring one decision over another?" He felt his heart lurch at the guilt he saw in her eyes and knew she'd probably made her decision the very first day.

Riley ran a shaky hand through her hair. "It's hard to make a decision like this, Asher. I can't—"

"Damn, stop lying to me, Ri!" He stopped and forced a measure of calm to his voice. "This isn't a hard choice to make. It's our marriage or your job."

"You're wrong! There's a lot more!"

"What more?" His gaze took on a curious gleam that seemed harsh. "Is there another reason why you're so reluctant to leave New York?"

Riley didn't need further clarification. "Jackass. Don't do that. You know I'd never—"

"Do I, Ri? Do I really know that? Hell, you can't decide between me and our child and some job writing for a paper. What the hell do you expect me to think!"

Her temper flaring, Riley commanded her tears to stay hidden. "Why can't *you* come back?" She pinned him with a glare of her own. "Why don't you tell me the secret *you're* keeping, Asher? Admit it, there's a lot more to you not wanting to be here with me and the baby than you're letting on."

He smirked knowingly. "So you *have* made your decision, huh?"

"Don't turn this around on me."

"It already *is* on you." He aimed an index finger in her direction. "You're the one with a decision to make."

"Snake." She pounded a wet fist on the edge of the tub. "You can work just as easily here as you can in Phoenix. You *are* the boss, Asher."

He was pacing the dark tiled floor. "I told you New York is no place to raise a child."

She rolled her eyes. "Jeez, not this again."

Turning the tables, he stormed to the tub and leaned down to cup her chin. "New York is no place to raise *my* child."

"Damn you, Asher." Riley blinked the tears from her lashes. "I don't want to fight about this anymore."

His smile was grim. "Then thank them for the offer and turn

it down." With those words, he smacked a hand against the surface of the chilled bathwater and walked out of the door.

Riley lifted her head quickly and then dropped it back to the pillow when she realized she wasn't late. She'd taken the day off to rest and be refreshed for Victor Lyne's signing party. Groaning into the pillow, she wondered if she shouldn't just go on into work.

Asher probably wouldn't want her at the party, anyway. She smoothed a hand across the mattress, feeling the coolness of the sheets. He hadn't come to bed last night, and she'd bet good money he was nowhere inside the loft. Rarely had she seen him lose his temper—not even when she'd written that story that prompted their meeting and refused to give up her source.

"Mmm…hungry, baby?" she inquired when her stomach growled. "Me too." She moved to leave the bed but found she had no strength to push back the covers.

"In a little while, baby," she whispered seconds before falling back into a dead sleep.

Asher hadn't left the loft. He'd wanted to, but something wouldn't let him walk out the door. He wouldn't lose her over this. They'd been through too much. She was his, and his she would remain. But he had to tell her. He had to tell her the truth about why living in New York wasn't an option for him.

She already knew he was keeping something from her, and she was too sharp to let it slide much longer. Soon she would begin to dig and gather the facts on her own. He stood in the bedroom doorway and watched her sleep. Admitting he was afraid wasn't a thing he was finding it easy to tell her. He'd dealt with it long enough before hightailing it to Phoenix all those years ago. Then Riley came into his life, and she was an NYC girl through and through. Then he fell in love with her, and slowly the fear began to root itself in his soul once more.

When she told him about the baby, he was a hair's breath away from hustling her out of New York, by force if he had to. He strolled over to take a seat on the bed. He smiled at the haphazard hairstyle that flattered her lovely dark face. Idly, he toyed with the clipped locks while she dozed. He wouldn't lose her, but he couldn't move back. Stalling or sharing the reasons why would only add more damage to the situation. That wasn't fair to her, and it couldn't be good for the baby.

He felt a vibration in his pocket and pulled out his Black-Berry. Pressing a kiss to Riley's temple, he left the room to take the call.

"Oooh, Justine, he's so…lovely. I don't think I'd want a man like that pissed at me," Diane Sims noted as she watched Asher greet his lunch partner across the dining room.

Justine Duke rolled her baby-blue gaze and checked that her recorder was filled with a fresh cassette. "I'm not trying to sleep with him. I only want a story."

Diane shrugged and spared her friend a fleeting glance. "Sleeping with him might just be the way."

"Please. Everyone knows the man's obsessed with his wife."

"True." Diane sighed, a smidgen of envy in her eyes. "Riley Stamper is definitely a goddess." She grimaced and turned to face her friend more fully. "Are you really sure about this?"

"I have to be if I expect to get my story."

"But are you really sure there *is* a story? Like you said, the man is obsessed with his wife."

"There's a story there. I know it." Justine placed a perfect French-manicured fingertip on the table. "No way is all that distance *not* an issue between them."

"Justine…sweetie, every couple is different. Asher and Riley are a high-powered couple. Maybe it works for them."

"Bull."

"And you just expect him to admit that?"

Justine winked. "No, but I'm a good enough reporter to squeeze out at least one comment that'll tell me if I'm on the right track."

"And if you're not and Bob and Grady find out?"

Justine was on the verge of laughter. "Then *they'll* know there's a story there, too, and I'm all set."

Asher and Talib chuckled heartily over the joke made by their lunch partner—reporter Hayes Ortiz.

"Seriously, though, guys, congrats on Victor Lyne's signing. That was a matchup no one saw coming. Any comment?"

Asher and Talib exchanged glances. They generally shied away from the spotlight, preferring to leave that domain to their clients. Hayes was a friend who usually got first dibs on the goings-on at Hud-Mason.

Talib nudged his partner's elbow. "Is he fishing for a story or an apology?"

Hayes laughed. "Only a story. I swear." His dark eyes sparkled as brightly as his smile. "No one's surprised Bastian Grovers got the exclusive. After all, the kid worked at his paper and on Riley's team, no less. I'm sure the lovely Mrs. Hudson looks out for her own contacts before her husband's."

"Damn right." Asher tilted back a bit of his gin. "Word to the wise, though, Hay. If Riley hears you call her Mrs. Hudson, she'll break your jaw."

The resulting laughter from the male trio only roused further interest from the restaurant's female diners.

Talib and Hayes left shortly after Asher offered to pick up the check. He stood next to the table, signing the receipt and adding a hefty tip for their server.

"Mr. Hudson?"

Asher turned, offering a soft smile to the attractive brunette who'd called his name.

"Justine Duke." She offered her hand. "The *First Beacon*."

Asher's smile began to fade into a grim line. "I leave all media comments to my clients, Ms. Duke."

"I understand, Mr. Hudson, but my interest isn't in your clients, but you."

Asher bowed his head at the obvious manner in which she batted her lashes. "Ms. Duke, I'm a married man. I'm sure you know that." He studied the keys in his palm as he spoke.

Justine nodded. "I do. You and Riley are one of New York's dream couples."

Asher eased the keys into the pocket of his dark trousers.

"Then you know I love my wife, and the thought of doing anything to hurt her nauseates me."

Again, Justine nodded, but she raised her hand defensively. "If I could just clarify, Mr. Hudson." Her gaze softened a bit more. "While any woman in her right mind would adore a moment of your time that way, my *interest* is actually in the *dream couple* status that you and Ms. Stamper enjoy."

Curious, Asher remained silent.

"It's interesting that you've maintained such a great relationship when there's such distance between you." A wave of excitement shook her voice when she noticed a flicker of emotion in the man's bright, alluring stare.

"It's incredible that it hasn't upset things overly much. Or has it?" She went on, glimpsing the muscle jumping along his jaw, in addition to the emotion now blazing in his eyes.

Asher scanned the dining room before stepping close to Justine. "I don't give comments about my business, Ms. Duke. Acquiring one about my marriage is even less of a possibility. Good day," he said and brushed past her.

Justine fought to keep her smile from broadening. "Just as I thought." She clicked off her recorder.

Riley cast a resentful look at the peach frock hanging from the back of her washroom door. The party for Victor Lyne's signing was not an event she was looking forward to attending.

She put down the lipstick tube and braced both hands around the basin of the sink. Lately, keeping her eyes open was about as difficult as staying on her feet. She needed a vacation. No, that wasn't it… She needed her husband to meet her halfway. Actually, she needed her husband to meet her in New York.

They'd barely spoken since the bathroom blowup a few days earlier. She'd always known Asher to be a reasonable man. She'd assumed it was one of the greatest keys to his success, and it was one of the many things she loved about him. Now, he was like a man she didn't know—stubborn, close minded, argumentative….

Of course, the issue of his child's upbringing was the topic now.

But there was more. It was time for Asher to be a little forthcoming about why he was really so against relocating to New York.

Pushing herself away from the sink, Riley made it over to her desk and began a search of the newspaper archives. She did a search on Asher's name, and for the next thirty-five minutes, she read what she already knew: how a black kid from Connecticut graduated with honors from Rutgers and went on to make a great name for himself in pro basketball.

It was a pretty good life until he walked into a convenience store around ten one evening and found himself in the middle of a holdup. Instead of doing what the gunman said, Asher played hero, suffering a gash along the cheek and a bullet wound to the knee, which ended his young career.

When asked if he'd do it again, Asher said, "In a heartbeat." The store owner, along with a mother and her two kids, never stopped singing his praises. Riley read on until she got to the rather sensationalized coverage of their relationship. She then conducted an extensive search, which uncovered pretty much the same documents. There were always ways to go deeper, but Riley decided it would just be a waste of her time. She asked if it was really something she wanted to know. *Want,* however, had nothing to do with it. Whatever *it* was, *it* was starting to unravel her marriage and to destroy her child's home before he or she even entered the world.

"Twice in one week! I don't know whether to be honored or suspicious!"

Hayes Ortiz only managed a brief smile at Talib's quip and stepped inside the suite. "Sorry for dropping by unannounced, man."

Talib waved him forward. "Not a problem."

"I didn't want to sit on this for long. I've probably waited too long as it is."

"Can I get you a drink?" Talib tried to lighten the mood, not caring for Hayes's foreboding tone.

"Whatever you're havin'."

"Spill it," Talib urged while preparing two Scotch and waters.

"Some, uh…some pics came through the lab yesterday." Hayes cleared his throat. "We got a lot of photographers on staff who take on freelance projects."

Talib passed Hayes a glass and sipped from his drink while waiting.

"Um…a lot of the photographers come across interesting pieces and usually try to sell them to reporters on staff for a hefty sum and a photo cred."

Talib noticed the man slapping a wide manila envelope against his thigh.

"These photos weren't sold in-house. Probably because I'm on staff." Hayes lost his taste for the drink and set the glass on the nearest table. "I got a few photographers down there who look out for me when the juicy stuff comes through. Guess I found out about this because I'm friends with Asher."

Talib's glass stopped midway to his mouth. "Hayes, why don't you get to the point? What's this all about?"

Wasting no more time with words, Hayes passed the envelope. Talib finished his drink and tore into the envelope. His frown vanished as he shuffled through shots of Riley and Bastian Grovers.

"So?" He shrugged and looked up at Hayes.

"You don't think those could be misconstrued?"

"How?" Talib waved the photos slightly. "His hand on her cheek, sitting next to her on the back of a car? Hardly a hotel-room romp here, Hay."

Hayes reached for his glass and motioned toward the pictures with it. "What about the hug and kiss? Two of 'em."

"Could be anything." Talib scanned the shots again.

Hayes considered Talib's disinterest and shrugged. "Guess you're right. But would you believe that if you were a husband living over halfway across the country, with a wife living here in New York and looking like that?" He smirked and tilted back a bit of his drink. "I haven't met a man yet who doesn't envy Ashe for snagging her."

Talib stroked his jaw. "She loves him. She wouldn't betray him that way. I know women who pull this crap on the regular." His dark gaze took on a cooler tint. "Riley Stamper's not one of 'em."

"Hey, man, I know Riley, and I believe that, too, but if these pics run in place with some screwball story, then it won't matter if they were discussing an article on the garden club." Hayes set down the glass again. "You may want to let Ashe know these are out there. He may want to bite the bullet before it's loaded in the gun."

Hayes left the suite while Talib studied the photos again.

"When I asked you to relieve your tension, I didn't expect you to get your blood pressure up over it."

Riley moved to the edge of the chair and watched her doctor behind the desk. "Is that why I've been so tired?"

Lettia nodded. "That's part of it." She studied Riley over the top of her gold glasses. "Fatigue goes hand in hand with pregnancy sometimes, and the high blood pressure doesn't help."

Riley's smoky stare widened. "The baby?"

"Fine. Fine. It's fine, but that could change if we don't get the pressure down." She began to scribble on a pad. "I want you to go home and sleep. Stay in bed, and keep the cabinets stocked with the herbal tea I've got on the list. What?" she asked, looking up to see Riley shaking her head.

"Like I've been telling you, it's easier said than done."

"I'm losing my patience with you, Riley." Lettia removed her glasses. "I'm moments away from putting you on strict bed rest. For someone as active as you, that'd be like a death sentence. But I'll do it if it's the only way to keep you and the baby healthy."

"I want to rest." Riley focused on the pointed toe of her burgundy pump tapping one leg of the desk. "The signing party for Victor Lyne is tonight, and I have to be there. Asher's counting on me, and things are bad enough between us without me backing out of this."

"I want to see you again next week." Lettia went back to scribbling on her pad. "If the pressure is still up, then it's bed rest for you. No questions."

Riley swallowed with effort before nodding her agreement.

Misha flipped through the pages of the folder she was studying on the way to her office. She did a double take and stumbled on her four-inch heels when she saw Talib Mason enjoying the view from her office windows. For several moments, she enjoyed the sight of him. Though his days as a linebacker were far behind him, he remained a prime specimen. With effort, she shook herself back to reality before she began to swoon right there.

"Surprise, surprise," she sang while strolling into her office.

Talib turned slowly from the view and indulged in a brief appraisal of her pencil-slim yet sultry form. He noticed her tilting stare narrow and turned away before his expression grew too telling.

"So to what do I owe the honor?" Misha waltzed toward her desk, determined to keep her demeanor light.

Instead of responding, Talib tossed a legal-size envelope on the desk. Misha opened it and scanned the photos inside. Finding nothing torrid, she looked up at him.

"Riley and Bastian Grovers? Bastian's our—"

"I know him."

"And you're showing me this because?"

Talib's pointed expression roused a hearty laugh from Misha. "Are you serious? Riley'd never do a thing like that."

Talib agreed but wanted to play devil's advocate a little longer. "Phoenix is a long way from New York, Misha."

She slammed down the photos, her onyx stare ablaze. "Isn't it, though? I wonder what Riley might find out if she asked how Asher spends those long, lonely nights out West."

Talib appeared unaffected. "Who knows why people do what they do."

Misha accepted the blow. "Riley wouldn't."

"I agree." He focused on tugging at the cuff of his shirt. "She's not that type of woman, and Lord knows, I've got experience enough to know the difference."

Misha accepted blow number two and decided that was enough. Gathering the photos, she slammed them to Talib's broad chest and went to stand at her open door. "Get out."

Talib hesitated, in that moment, truly sorry for what he'd said. He did as she asked, wincing when the door slammed behind his back.

* * *

Applause rang out following a toast from one of Victor's new teammates. Laughter mingled with hand claps throughout the upscale dining hall located on the top floor of a Manhattan skyscraper.

Asher's hearty chuckle resounded as loudly as anyone else's. That is, until he caught sight of his wife in a daring peach gown that gloved her curves and showed a hint of the telltale bulge in her belly. He blinked, watching her with a look that was a mix of desire and helplessness.

Victor called out to his agent twice before grabbing his attention. "Rory here is interested in talking to you about representation," he said, gesturing toward one of his newest teammates.

Asher shrugged and spread his hands wide. "Grab me now. I'm on a roll!" he boasted playfully, his response generating swells of laughter. His mind was still on Riley, but when he looked around, she was gone.

Riley met up with several colleagues and felt even more at ease when Bastian Grovers nudged her elbow.

"How'd *you* get past security?" she teased.

"You're forgetting my exclusive on Victor." Bastian winked. "Thank you again." He kissed her cheek. "Dance?"

Riley glanced around for Asher, then told herself he probably wouldn't want to talk to her, anyway. With a smile in place, she accepted the arm Bastian offered, and they laughed all the way to the dance floor.

Asher had already caught sight of the laughing couple on the dance floor. He was heading over to claim his wife when he was cornered by Justine Duke.

"My, my, you *do* keep turning up," Asher murmured.

Justine shrugged. "Guess I'm just your average bad penny."

"May I quote you on that?"

"Actually, it's *your* quote I'm interested in." She waited a beat and then glanced across one shoulder, left bare by her backless frock. "Riley's positively radiant. But then again, she's always glowing." She smiled up at Asher. "Many are commenting on that stunning gown of hers and the fact that it's doing nothing to hide that bulge in her tummy. Will you two be making an announcement of the baby sort anytime soon?"

Asher simply nodded. "Good evening, Ms. Duke."

She moved into his path before he could walk by her. "A baby might make the distance in your relationship quite difficult. But then…" Her expression was as coy as her tone of voice. "I'm sure a woman like Riley Stamper wouldn't have a problem finding someone to *look out* for her if her husband—"

Asher took a sudden step forward, and Justine took an instinctive step back.

"You can quote me on this." His voice was low, monotone and deadly in its intensity. "If I get one whiff about any unsubstantiated stories carrying your byline, you won't even be able to get a job scrubbing toilets for a tabloid when I'm done with you."

When he walked away, Justine closed her eyes and took several deep breaths to calm herself. Steadier then, she managed a refreshing smile. "Unsubstantiated, huh? Not by a long shot, Mr. Hudson."

Chapter 16

Riley and Bastian were still laughing and enjoying their dance when Bastian's smile broadened.

"Well, hey, hey! The man of the hour!" The sports editor greeted Asher warmly.

"Grovers," Asher said, then acknowledged the greeting with a stiff nod.

"Congratulations, man. Seriously." Bastian offered his hand. "Quite a coup. Glad I was part of it in some way."

"Thanks, man."

Settling Riley's hand in her husband's, Bastian left the couple with a good-night nod.

The easiness of the moment left with her colleague. Riley took note of the tightness in Asher's jaw the second he pulled her close.

"What's wrong?" she murmured, praying it had to do with something other than them.

No such luck.

"Have you told them you're not taking the job?" His voice was as hard as his expression.

Whatever lightness Riley felt vanished like mist. She looked round to see if they were being observed and then rolled her eyes back to Asher. "Let's not do this here."

Asher, unfortunately, was itching for a fight. "Do what?" The words shot out through his clenched teeth. "Ask my wife to put our life before her career?"

Her fist curled against the front lapel of his suit coat. "I will not have this same tired argument with you, and *here* of all places." She moved to walk away, but he held her fast.

"I'm losing it with you, Ri."

She laughed. "Then you're late, baby, since I lost it with you a long time ago. Let go of me."

"No."

"Excuse me? Mr. Hudson? Ms. Stamper?"

The couple stopped snarling at each other long enough to be informed that they were wanted for a photo op.

"This won't take long," Asher was saying once they were alone. Riley's dark face was aglow with amazement. "You don't really expect me to smile with you for a camera?"

He didn't bother to spare her a glance. "And make it good." He took her upper arm in a firm hold. For good measure, he drew her into a thorough and lengthy kiss. As usual, the long, deep thrusts of his tongue made her forget everything except becoming an eager participant in the act. By the time he pulled back, her calm intermingled with her rage.

Riley stormed her way into the loft, stripped out of the daring gown and went to the bathroom, where she splashed cold water over her face. From there, it was back to the kitchen, where she raided the fridge for a quart of fudge ripple ice cream and whipped topping. She gorged on the sinful treats as if they were the last things she'd ever eat. She was sitting on the kitchen floor, near the fridge, when her husband came home.

"Riley," he called, a clear apology on his lips when he found her.

"Jackass," she greeted.

He nodded, his handsome face soft with regret as he moved farther into the kitchen. "I deserved that."

"Nooo." Riley knocked the back of her head against a cabinet. "No, *horse's* ass. That's it." She spooned a mound of fudge ripple into her mouth. "That one fits you better."

"Will you let me apologize?"

"I don't want to hear it." She moved to get up from the floor and pushed Asher away when he tried to help her.

"Everyone was saying how you were glowing and noticing that little rise in your stomach and asking if a baby might be on the way…" he shared while leaning against the counter. "Guess it all just got to me."

"Damn dress," Riley hissed and tossed her spoon into the sink. "Haven't worn it since I bought it last summer. I'm not big enough to wear the one you bought me, so I figured I'd go put that one on." She shrugged. "Tonight was probably my last chance to wear it before the baby."

"I'm sorry."

She pinned him with her smoky browns and shook her head. "Don't apologize unless you didn't mean what you said." His expression told her that wasn't the case. She shoved the treats back in the refrigerator and left the kitchen.

He caught her before she cleared the living room. Pulling her back against him, he pressed his face into the nape of her neck.

"I have a life here," she whispered. "I have a career I love. Why can't you accept how hard it is for me to let go of all that?"

Instead of answering, Asher began to ply her skin with kisses while massaging the dull achiness from her breasts.

"This won't save what's wrong between us," she warned, wanting to melt against him.

"Doesn't have to." His free hand dipped into her panties.

Riley whimpered.

When Asher felt the abundance of moisture coating his fingers, his legs went watery beneath him. Effortlessly, he hoisted Riley into his arms and carried her to their bedroom. The minutes passed in a dull haze of desire and possession as Asher made love to her with his hands and mouth before losing his clothes and taking her completely.

Riley's laughter held only the faintest trace of humor as she sipped tea and scanned the entertainment section of the newspaper the following morning.

"What's up?" Asher left the eggs he'd been scrambling to peer over her shoulder.

"My colleagues didn't waste a minute." Riley folded the paper into a smaller section and recited the quote that had sparked her laughter. "'Asher Hudson and Riley Stamper—

gorgeous as usual—with the lovely Riley sporting a mysterious bulge.'" She read the caption below the picture they'd posed for at the signing party. "'Could the gorgeous Mr. Hudson be bringing on a new player?'"

Asher grinned and waved a hand as a request for the paper. He continued to read from the story accompanying the photo. "'The question now is how long will the respected columnist remain a resident of our fair city?'"

Losing her taste for the tea, Riley dumped the remnants into the sink and took longer than necessary to rinse her mug.

"Guess that's the question of the year." Asher's observation was void of amusement. He tossed the paper on the dining table. "Maybe they'll be able to get an answer out of you."

"Asher…"

"God knows I can't."

Riley slammed the orange ceramic mug into the dish rack. "Do you have any idea what you're putting me through with this?"

"Putting *you* through?"

"Yes, Asher, *me*. Remember me?" Her thumbnail poked her chest. "The woman who's pregnant with your child. Sorry to break this to you, but it's not about you. It's about me and the baby and what's best for us!"

Asher stepped back, as though she'd hit him. "Us? Don't I fit into that group, Riley?"

She knew she'd hurt him, even though he chose to hide the emotion by turning away. She wouldn't apologize. She was hurting, too, and it was time he understood how much.

"This is not a difficult decision to make." Asher tugged on the drawstring of his sleep pants, desperate to soothe the rage he'd managed to quell as they'd loved each other the previous night. "Forgive me if I sound cold about your column, but you really can work on it from anywhere. As for this position of yours—" he let her see his face then "—I know it's a chance of a lifetime, but so is our child coming into the world." He moved toward her, softness taking root in his expression and voice. "I can give you anything you want. You could do whatever your heart desires in Phoenix."

"Except work doing something I love and make it my own."

"Dammit, Ri, you're my wife! Making it on your own isn't a thing you have to worry about!"

"Until I find myself alone, with a child to raise!" she blurted, closing her eyes as she whirled away from him.

Asher froze. Other than the fire stirring in his provocative stare, he was like stone.

"Is that what you think I'd do to you?" His voice was half groan, half whisper.

"It's what my father did," she mumbled.

Asher came up behind her and made her turn to face him. "Is that what you think *I'd* do?"

Riley couldn't make herself take it back. "I believe...here now you'd never leave or never abandon us...never find someone else to love." She rubbed clammy hands across the seat of her shorts. "My mother believed the same thing, but that didn't stop it from happening." She met his gaze with her own stony one. "I know you're not my father, but things change. People change. Things they think they want... change."

He seemed to wilt. "Have you always felt this way?"

"Yes." She owed him her honesty. "I tried to tell you that marriage wasn't for me, but you didn't seem to want it any other way." Tears sprinkled her cheeks suddenly. "And...and I love you so much."

"You *love* me?" The admission only set Asher further on edge. "Is that what you said? Seconds ago you're telling me you think one day I'll walk out on you and my child, that you've always felt this way, and now you expect me to believe you love me?"

Riley could hardly decipher his image through the tears blurring her eyes. "Asher." She reached out to him, her heart lurching when he wrenched back from her touch.

"I need to go." He looked everywhere but her face.

"Wait—"

"It's best that I leave." He looked over at the eggs he'd scrambled. "I'll grab somethin' while I'm out."

"Asher, please..."

He squeezed his eyes shut, surprised to find wetness spiking his lashes. Riley called his name as he left the kitchen, but he didn't look back.

Talib had barely pulled the door open halfway when Asher stormed through it.

"Well, good morning!" When his cheery greeting was met by a stony glare, Talib rubbed his hands, his expression a mix of humor and curiosity. "Now this I can't figure!" The Manchester, England, in his voice gave his amused bellow a regal undertone. "Are you forgetting last night being a total success? That we may be snagging a few new clients? Blokes who are a bit disillusioned with their present representation?"

"Riley never wanted to marry me."

"Get out."

"It's true." Asher's sullen grimace was unmistakably honest.

Talib felt his excitement over the previous evening's success begin to fade. "Well…" He glanced down at his glass of cranberry juice and decided it could stand a bit of hardening. "You gotta know this isn't true, Ashe." He splashed a bit of gin onto the burgundy juice. "The two of you are a unit. You're made for each other."

Asher smoothed one hand across the dull ache in the center of his chest. "She practically told me so. I don't know why I'm surprised. Hell, I practically bullied her into marrying me, anyway."

"Sit, mate." Talib pressed a drink into his friend's hand, then took note of the time on his wristwatch. "Have you eaten?"

"I left before…. We started fighting over a newspaper story about the party."

"Well, that's just foolish." Talib took the armchair across from Asher. "They were all raving accounts."

Asher sampled the drink. Savoring the burn, he tossed back a bit more. "One of 'em speculated on how long she'd stay in New York if a baby was really in the picture."

"Ah." Talib finished his drink in one gulp. "And I guess the answer she gave wasn't the reply you wanted."

"Tal, the answer she gave…I never saw it comin'." Asher

recapped the argument with his wife while Talib listened intently. "What?" Asher asked, not liking the look on his friend's face.

"You won't like it," Talib said.

"Do I ever?" He tapped his glass on a jean-clad knee.

"She's got a valid argument. It's probably unfair to you, but based on the kind of life she's had… All of us weren't as lucky in our childhoods as you were."

"So I should feel guilty about that?" Asher stood. "She should be thrilled that I know what a stable home is. That's part of the reason a lot of men walk away. They've got no experience like that to draw from." He sat back down. "They don't know how important it is to stick around and give it their all."

"You're right, man." Talib leaned forward. "But in Riley's defense and speaking as a kid from a one-parent home…I know what it's like to have your father walk out for good, and I know what it's like to *not* know if there's gonna be anything on the table for dinner, if there'll be lights on to see how to eat or if there's gonna be a *place* for the lights to burn."

"Jesus…" Asher dropped his face in his hands.

"She probably never really had to face how all the fear and unease of that time affected her." Talib leaned back. "Now she's married and about to start her own family. She's in the same position her mother was in." He smiled when Asher's jaw clenched. "She's not in *that* position literally. But still, it's got to be dealt with."

"She doesn't trust me. She doesn't have trust in us—in me." The anger was gone from his voice. In its place was the unmistakable tinge of hurt. "I thought I knew her—everything about her. All the times we talked, talked about things we wanted, and she never shared what was most important."

"And have you shared everything with her, mate?"

Asher's mouth tightened to a thin line. He wanted to argue that it wasn't the same, but that would've been a lie. Perhaps it was time to move beyond his fears. Perhaps it was the only way to save his marriage.

Talib could see that Asher was thinking hard. Maybe admitting to himself that this entire situation had gone too far and for too long. Deciding they could both use breakfast, Talib rubbed a hand across his jeans and stood to dial room service.

Leaving his armchair as well, Asher began strolling around the living area of the suite as he contemplated.

"Yeah, yeah, a double order of coffee, orange juice, double order of eggs. Scrambled?" Talib voiced the question for Asher, who responded with a thumbs-up. "Scrambled eggs, steak strips…"

Asher continued to pace while Talib finished placing the order. Talking with his partner had relieved mounds of his stress and allowed him to think more clearly about the issue at hand. The issue at hand, and everything else for that matter, fled from his mind when he spied what lay on the edge of a table in the far corner of the room.

Talib was still on the phone when Asher helped himself to a lengthy perusal of the black-and-white photos. Photos featuring his wife and her colleague Bastian Grovers.

The ache of hurt feelings that he'd toted around since arguing with Riley merged with feelings of rage and disbelief. Smoothing a hand across his jaw, Asher forced himself to review every shot. He was finishing up with the last one when Talib ended the call and announced breakfast was on its way.

"There's nothing to it, man," Talib explained when Asher turned, with a photo clutched in a fist.

"Would you believe that?" Asher's calm was frightening.

Talib shrugged. "I probably wouldn't, since this is Riley, and she's stupid in love with you. She'd never—"

"Would you believe that? Huh, mate?" Asher mocked his friend's accent as a look of crazed anger drifted into his light eyes. "*Did* you believe that when you first saw them?" Talib's expression told Asher all he needed to know, and he broke for the front door.

Talib didn't bother to call for him to stop. Instead, he massaged his nose and muttered a vicious oath.

"What the hell did you do, Talib? Letting your own hurt feelings get in the way of common sense. Riley'd never—"

"Dammit, Misha, this isn't about us. I didn't tell Asher a thing. He came over here after he and Riley argued. He saw the photos…I didn't have a chance to put them away."

Misha rolled her eyes. She could hear the anxiety and remorse in his voice and knew he was telling the truth. Too bad he couldn't believe in her as easily, she mused.

"What do you expect me to do?" she asked after shaking herself free of memories of an unfortunate past.

"I just want you to get Riley to leave the office and go home."

"Oh please. Asher wouldn't—"

"That's not what I'm thinking, but he doesn't need to see her now." Talib paced around the suite, with quick barefoot steps. "He needs to cool off and realize that what he's thinking is stupid."

"I agree with you on that." Misha was in her office and pacing as well. "All right. Um, I'll talk to Riley. She looked like hell when she got here, so it shouldn't be too hard to convince her to go. So is that it, Talib? Anything else?"

"That's it. Thanks."

Misha cursed when the buzz sounded to signal that he'd ended the connection. She cursed a second time when she felt tears at the back of her eyes.

"Get it together, Mish." She rounded her desk, intending to find Riley. Screams mingled with thunderous bumping sounds, and everything else fled from her mind.

Praying she wouldn't take a tumble in her black heels, Misha quickened her steps en route to Riley's office. The scene meeting her eyes was chaotic at best when she peered around the corner. The bulk of the chaos, however, was not centered around Riley's door, but around Bastian Grovers's.

Misha said a quick prayer and made her way toward the melee. There, she found several men pulling Asher Hudson off Bastian, who sat cupping a hand to a busted lip as his swollen left eye began to darken.

"Get him out of here—as quietly as possible," Misha ordered the men gripping Asher. "Laylee? You and Rita get some help for Bastian."

* * *

Riley had heard the noise and had left her office to investigate as well. Nothing prepared her to see her husband being led away by force.

"Asher," she called, and the look he slanted stopped her heart. It was possibly not the best time for inquiries, she decided and was about to follow the men carting Asher away when Misha addressed her.

"That's a bad idea, Rile."

"What's going on?" Riley switched directions and went to stand before Misha.

Sighing, Misha pulled a hand from her trouser pocket and waved Riley toward her office door. She gave her friend an abbreviated but no less shocking account of recent events. Riley's legs weakened, and she was barely sitting on the edge of her seat before Misha was even halfway through the story.

"The only time I've seen Bastian alone is here, and he's *never* kissed me." She recalled the day outside the Shell. "Dammit…" She had her face in her hands and inhaled. "He was asking about getting the exclusive on Vic's story. I was supposed to meet him at the Shell for lunch. I was late because of an appointment with Lettia. He asked me to walk out with him…God…he was so upbeat about it, he hugged me." She shrugged. "Kissed me a few times as well, and we laughed about it. But it was all innocent, Misha, I swear."

"Everybody already knows that, honey." Misha stooped to pat Riley's knee. "But you know how the game is played, girl. An innocent picture can turn into scandal easy. Hey? Why don't you just take off for the day?" she suggested when Riley groaned again.

Riley slumped back against the chair and toyed with the row of buttons on her coffee-colored blouse. "I don't want to go home. The place is starting to close in on me." She nodded at Misha's surprised look. "It's true. I've even been looking through real estate pubs."

"Moving?" Misha folded her arms across her suit coat.

"Just need more space, I guess. But it's on the back burner just now. Lots more I need to get done first." She started to push herself out of the chair. "There's that meeting next week with Gloria and the execs."

"Precisely why you need to sit out today. Unwind from all this drama."

"And waste an entire day? No, Misha, I don't think—"

"I could always call Lett, see what she thinks about it."

Threatened that her doctor would be brought into the situation, Riley stood and fixed Misha with a resigned smile. "Guess I should go talk to Bastian first, try to explain, apologize. Hope he doesn't press charges against my baby's daddy."

Misha smirked. "Forget it. I'll look in on him and see what's up. *You* go get your stuff together. When you're done, we're out of here."

Asher drove around for about forty minutes. Surprisingly, the rage had left the second he stumbled, er, was pushed, out onto the pavement outside the paper. He'd called himself stupid about ten times and then got the hell out of there before someone called the cops. He didn't know what led him to Virginia Stamper's gorgeous penthouse condo but celebrated the workings of his subconscious. He could certainly use a wiser ear to vent to just then.

He pressed his forehead against the steering wheel and squeezed his eyes shut tight. All he could see was Riley. The way she'd looked at him as her colleagues *ushered* him off the premises. She'd watched as though he were a stranger—some fool who'd bounded in to bring harm to the innocent souls inside.

God, what was happening to him? he asked himself. Quick, sharp laughter livened the interior of the SUV then. He knew it was the dramatic episode from his past that was coming back to haunt him. He also knew he needed to share it with his wife. But would sharing it cause him to think or feel differently? What was the answer here? He'd give anything to find someone who could tell him how to handle this. Looking up at the skyscraper he'd parked next to, he prayed he'd find that someone inside.

Virginia Stamper had been toiling away in her rooftop garden, as usual. She did a double take when she noticed her son-in-law knocking on the glass door of the enclosed rooftop entrance.

Without hesitation, she set aside her pruning shears and went to let him in.

Asher marveled in silence as his mother-in-law drew closer. He was awed by the way a woman dressed in oversize gardening clothes, a hat and gloves, all powdered with dirt, could look so lovely. Shrugging, he accepted the fact that the effect was just one of the many things he'd come to adore about his wife's mother.

"Look at you!" Virginia raved, reaching out to pull him close and then changing her mind. "I don't want to get you all dusty," she explained.

"Please." Asher rolled his eyes and tugged her close. "No way am I missing out on a hug from a beauty like you."

Virginia's melodic laughter filled the glass greenhouse, and thoroughly charmed, she hugged Asher tight. When they pulled apart, it didn't take long for Virginia to surmise that there was something wrong. Still, she decided to approach questioning her son-in-law very carefully.

"Can I get you a drink?" she offered while removing her hat and gloves. "How's that daughter of mine? I haven't seen her in a week or two." Virginia reached into the mini-fridge, which claimed the far corner of the greenhouse. She grabbed two bottles of chilled orange juice. "Tell me, love, how's a concerned mother supposed to assist a daughter as independent as my Riley?"

Asher took the juice and grinned. "I think she'll be happy with whatever you do, Miss Ginny."

"Lord," Virginia breathed, her features contorted into an expression of horror and curiosity. She'd glimpsed the vicious bruises on Asher's knuckles when she handed him the juice. "What's happened?" She wasted no time questioning him then. Pushing him onto the wrought-iron lawn chair, she listened intently while he explained the scene that had just transpired.

"I suppose I don't have to tell you that you behaved like an idiot." Virginia leaned back and sipped her juice.

Asher followed suit. "I've been telling myself that since they threw me off the premises."

"How's Riley?"

Asher grimaced and smoothed the back of his unbruised hand across the scar he carried. "The way she looked at me...I know she's as disappointed in me as I am in myself."

Virginia set aside her juice and then leaned forward to brace her elbows on her knees. "How'd all this happen, honey?"

"Well, the pictures—"

"No, this isn't just about that. Whatever's going on started way before that." She looked back at him. "How much of this has to do with that ultimatum of yours?"

Asher grinned in spite of himself. "Stupidest thing I've ever done. We had an argument about it, and then...she tells me that she could've done without being married, but *I* wanted it so...." He drank deeply of the juice in an attempt to scorch the heat rising at his neck. "Miss Ginny, she told me she didn't think I'd stick around."

Virginia clutched his forearm, bared by the rolled sleeve of his shirt. "Did she really say that, Asher?"

He was already nodding. "Close enough to it. I don't think she knew what hearing that did to me." He met Virginia's probing gaze for barely a moment. "I know she had a rough childhood, and that messed with her head as an adult, but I at least thought she trusted me."

"She does." Virginia gave his arm a reassuring squeeze. "She trusts in you and your love for her, but probably...not in all the unforeseen elements that can bring havoc to any marriage."

"What the hell does that mean?" Asher closed his eyes. "Sorry, Miss Ginny."

She rubbed his back in understanding. "Try to envision your own childhood, and then picture it the exact opposite of that. *That* was your wife's childhood, and I..." A look of weariness settled on her usually glowing face. "I'm afraid I didn't handle it well, either. I think she's afraid she may put her own child through the same thing."

Asher's expression brought a lost quality to his handsome face. "How do I fight that?"

"You can't, baby. Not now, anyway. You and Riley have to

realize that it's not about the two of you anymore. It's about that life inside her, and it's about doing what's necessary to ensure that it enters the world healthy." Virginia stood and relieved Asher of his empty bottle. "The two of you are at odds over the past, your fears, her anxieties… You have to set that all in the back of the bus now."

"You're right. God, you're right." Asher spoke as though he was just grasping something that had been staring him in the face all along.

"This is a happy time." Virginia studied him from the make-shift kitchenette in the greenhouse. "It should be a happy time for many reasons, but most importantly, because it's good for the baby. Riley needs to be as relaxed as possible. She needs to put the unrest between you aside for now, and that's where *you* come in." She watched Asher staring off into the distance, as though he was weighing her arguments. Satisfied that she'd given him enough to think on, she clapped her hands suddenly. "Can I interest you in a salad, courtesy of my garden?"

In spite of his woes, Asher had a bright smile when he stood.

"So are you sure he won't press charges?"

"Mmm-hmm…" Misha's tone was absent while she deleted messages from her i-Phone. "Once I explained why Asher went off, he was cool. Well…" She smirked. "About as cool as you can be with a black eye and busted lip."

"Damn." Riley grumbled the curse while tossing her house keys on the message table.

Misha followed, kicking the front door shut and locking it behind her.

"I should thank him."

"Send him an e-mail." Misha's stare was locked on her phone again. "We don't need you two getting caught on camera again."

Again, Riley cursed and dragged a hand through her hair in silent rage over everything that had happened.

"Why don't you just calm down?" Misha set aside the phone and then ushered her friend into the bedroom. "Get out of that suit while I fix us some snacks."

Riley tugged on the cuff of Misha's suit coat. "Thanks, girl."

Misha replied with a wave. "You just grab me a T-shirt and some shorts to change into."

"You don't have to babysit me." Riley bristled.

"Well, I'm figuring Asher's gonna want to stay as far away from here as possible tonight, and you don't need to be alone. Besides, I figure I'm due for babysitting practice. Gotta be ready for my nephew."

"And just how do you know it's a boy?"

Tapping a finger on the baby hair on her temple, Misha winked. "Men are drawn to me, so it's inevitable. Now get comfortable. That's an order."

While Riley did as she was told, Misha kicked off her pumps and headed for the kitchen to prepare much-needed snacks for a girls' night in. Her head was in the fridge when she heard the vibration of her phone against the counter.

"What the hell?" She spotted Talib's name on the faceplate. After a moment's hesitation, she answered. "How the hell did you get my number?"

"My secret."

"Talib—"

"I want to apologize."

"Well?" Misha prompted once silence had ensued for many moments.

Talib's laughter was brief, but it was there. "In person, Misha."

"Why?"

"Humor me."

"I only humor friends."

"Of which you have many."

She clenched her teeth. "Goodbye, Talib."

"Tomorrow. I'll meet you at your office around lunchtime."

"Talib—"

"Tomorrow."

"Humph," she sniffed when the call ended. "I just won't be there when you come by." She spoke into the dead line, knowing all the while that she'd be there and counting the hours till he arrived. Would she ever stop being a fool for that man?

Casting Talib Mason's arousing image from her mind, Misha concentrated on preparing a platter of fruits, cheese, veggies, crackers and spread.

"Hey, Riley, what do you want to drink?" she called when she ran out into the hall. "Riley!" She moved farther down the hall. When her third call went unanswered, she went to the bedroom and called out again.

Riley wasn't in the bedroom, and for good measure, Misha took a quick look inside the adjoining bath. Nothing prepared her for the sight of her best friend passed out on the floor.

Chapter 17

Confusion replaced the sleep in Riley's eyes when she woke later that evening to find herself tucked into bed.

"Me and Dr. Lett got your butt in bed after you passed out in the bathroom." Misha's face loomed above Riley as she sat on the edge of the bed and explained.

"Passed out?"

"Mmm…"

Riley winced and ran a hand down the side of her face. "Dr. Lett?"

"Mmm…"

"Hell, Misha, why'd you call her?"

"Hey, I see my best friend, who's pregnant with my nephew, passed out on the floor. Who'd you think I'd call? The cable guy?"

"Now she's probably gonna want to put me on bed rest." Riley rolled her head across the pillow.

"No *probably* about it, sista. This bed is gonna be your new best friend for the next several weeks."

Riley's resulting groan was drowned by Lettia walking into the room and ordering her to hush.

Riley sighed. "Lett—"

"My mind's made, so don't even *try* to change it," replied Lettia.

"Since when do you make house calls?" asked Riley.

Lettia's sour expression did nothing to mar her lovely features. "It's a service I provide to my most hardheaded patients. Putting the fear of God in them usually does the trick."

"Lett—"

"*Riley,* do you understand that the first few months of pregnancy are the most delicate? Are you trying to lose this baby, hon?"

"What's wrong, Lett?" Riley's eyes were wide with concern then.

"Shh. The baby's fine." Lettia leaned over the foot of the bed and squeezed Riley's foot. "Mommy's blood pressure, however, is *way* up, and with stress and work, that's a bad combination, hon."

Riley remained quiet as she considered her doctor's words.

"Now, I've been on the phone with Ms. Virginia." Lett raised a hand when Riley sat up straight. "I can't think of a better person to make sure you follow orders."

Misha's expression was alive with humor as she struggled not to laugh over Riley's reaction. "Girl, you're lucky your mom's around and a retired nurse. Besides, who can cook her butt off like Ms. V?" She slapped hands with Lettia, who'd sampled Virginia Stamper's cooking and fully agreed.

"So that's it, Riley. You can either stay here or go to your mom's place. Of course, there's always the hospital." Lettia tacked that on when Riley's expression showed no signs of brightening.

"You don't have to decide right away." Misha reached out to fluff the pillows behind Riley's back. "I'll be staying the night with you."

"But I want you in my office as soon as you're on your feet tomorrow. I want to run a few tests to make sure my diagnosis is correct."

"But you're sure the baby's all right?" asked Riley.

Lettia took pity and pulled Riley into a hug. "My nephew is fine." Riley gasped. "Nephew? We haven't even done an ultrasound yet."

Lettia shrugged and exchanged a wink with Misha. "Just a feeling," she sang and left the room.

Misha was up bright and early the next morning to get the paper and prepare breakfast. She celebrated Riley's penchant for subscribing to the competition but could've done without the nifty little exposé in the entertainment section of the *First Beacon*. She admitted those pictures did look far from innocent when run next to the damaging words in the article they accompanied.

Misha took note of the byline, Justine Duke. Her eyes narrowed as the realization that this was her former colleague dawned. "Second time you've hurt someone I care about, bitch. I think it's time for a reunion."

A key scratched the lock, and Misha held the paper against the front of the T-shirt she'd borrowed from Riley.

Asher made his way inside. His weary expression took on a humble sheen when he spotted Misha in the kitchen doorway.

She held up the paper. "Are you here about this?"

He smirked. "Saw it. Not interested." He tossed his keys on the message table. "Here to talk, and not about that."

Satisfied, Misha tossed aside the paper and returned to her kitchen duties.

Asher entered the bedroom slowly and smiled, watching his wife in bed as she studied a book while glancing infrequently at the TV. He knocked once.

"Good morning," he greeted when she fixed him with a stunned expression. "Do you mind?"

Riley shook her head toward the remote he held with the intention of lowering the television's volume. Coolly, she turned over the book she'd been studying and watched him sit on the edge of the bed.

Cupping her neck in one hand, he squeezed gently and pressed his forehead to hers. "I'm sorry."

"Asher, those pictures were—"

"Don't, don't," he soothed, massaging her neck then. "You don't need to explain. I know what a fool I was." He grimaced while gnawing the inside of his cheek. "Guess I should apologize to Grovers."

Riley seemed to shudder. "Send him an e-mail."

They laughed for a while, and then Asher leaned over, as though the weariness had reclaimed him. He sat bracing his elbows on his knees.

"I spent last night doing a lot of thinking." Straightening, he turned back to her, then trailed his hand down her chest, stopping to cup a breast and then her belly. "I can't let anything go wrong here. A wise person informed me that it's not about us anymore. Our fears and hang-ups need to sit on simmer for a while. What's been going on between us can't be good for the baby."

Riley looked away. She didn't want to be reminded of the fear she felt when Lettia walked into her bedroom the previous evening.

"We both need to focus on the baby," he was saying, rubbing the hem of her T-shirt between his fingers. "You've got a tougher job to handle than me, I know, but it's up to me to get out of the way so you can handle it."

Riley frowned at his word choice. His handsome features revealed nothing, so she waited.

"I'm gonna move over to the hotel where Talib is." He cleared his throat uncertainly but then continued. "We've been getting tons of calls—new business after the deal we scored for Vic." He tugged at the rolled cuffs of his wrinkled shirt. "We need to get some things in place before it's time to leave."

"You won't be here?" That was the only fact from Asher's speech that Riley locked on.

His first response was a crooked grin. "I know my timing's poor, based on what you already suspect I'm about."

"Asher—"

"Hey, shh…" He leaned in to murmur against her mouth. "We can't argue about this. My being here is doing you more harm than good."

"Is this the only way?" Her voice was heavy with emotion.

"It's the best way. We're constantly at it, and I don't like it. Do you?"

"No." She couldn't look at him. When his mouth brushed her cheek and stilled there for a time, she shut her eyes to ward off tears.

"I'm gonna grab a few things. I'll be back later for the rest."

Riley watched him push off the bed and clenched a fist to keep from pulling him back. She glanced at the book she'd been studying and shook her head, as if changing her mind. She withdrew into herself while Asher made quick work of collecting a few of his belongings. She heard him calling her name and managed to free herself from the haze to concentrate on his words.

"Misha's preparing quite a feast in there, so I want you to eat up, all right?" He kissed her forehead and once again pressed his against hers.

"I love you," he whispered.

Alone, Riley hugged herself and cried.

Misha felt more like stopping by the paper once she'd showered, changed and accompanied Riley to her doctor's appointment. Everything looked fine as far as the baby was concerned. She took Riley home and then went into the office. An hour later, she was hard at work.

"This looks good, Rob, and have Jerry send those photos to my desktop by two!" Misha roared the order seconds before entering her office, where she found Talib Mason conducting business at her desk. She banged a fist against the leg of her trousers when he waved her forward, as though giving her permission to enter her own domain. Grimacing, she obliged while waiting for him to finish the call.

"You have the nicest assistant." Talib put his phone in the inside pocket of his slate-gray suit coat. "She told me I could wait here as long as I liked."

Misha curved her hands over the back of the chair she stood behind. "Yeah, she's a sucker for a handsome face. Guess we have that in common."

Talib's caramel-toned face was tinged with unmistakable regret. "I'm sorry for the things I said—the things I implied."

Misha refused to give in to the giddy fluttering of her heart. She narrowed her gaze, hoping he bought her cool display. "You know, the drama between us is too great and too varied to even bother with apologies, so let's not, hmm? I think it's way too late for that."

Talib watched her closely for a moment, and then he stood. "I hope it's never too late for apologies."

Misha forbade herself to soften. "What do you want?" Her teeth clenched on the question. "What, Talib? For me to accept? All right then. I accept your apology, okay? Now you can go back to Phoenix guilt free. Have a good trip."

"Misha—"

"Dammit, Talib!" She dropped the facade and let him glimpse

the wetness in her eyes. "I've finally gotten used to the idea that I disgust you, so you'll just have to excuse me if your sudden kindness scares the hell out of me." Breathing deeply, as though the admission had drained her, she stepped back from the chair. "I've, um, I've got to check on some things…I hope you'll be gone by the time I get back." Without another word or glimpse, she left him alone in the office.

After two weeks, Lettia rescinded her staunch orders to keep Riley in bed for an additional three. She did, however, insist that Nurse Stamper remain on call. Of course, the grandmother-to-be was more than pleased to do so.

"And you're sure this is the right move?" Misha was asking Riley for what had to be the twentieth time as they waited on their lunch partners.

Riley shared a playful wink. "What do you expect me to do? I have to support your nephew, you know?"

"I'm serious, Ri." Misha leaned closer to the square table. "I thought with Asher gone, it'd give you time to think about what you could lose if you take this job."

Riley folded her arms over the cobalt knit top and scanned the dining room. "Unlike my marriage, my job's the one thing I can control," she muttered.

Misha resituated her silverware. "Love and passion rarely go hand in hand with things you can control."

Before Riley could question her friend's melancholy reply, she saw Asher being led to a table in the far corner of the room. Her heart lurched, as it usually did whenever she saw him or knew he was near.

Misha was so very wrong, she thought. Her job *did* inspire love and passion, but the emotions didn't hold a candle to what she felt for her husband. Riley noticed a few people joining him, and she was glad, because it stopped her from rushing over and begging him to come home. Asher was right, after all; the tension between them was too great now. It was time for them to put their child above it all. Mature thinking. If only she could stop herself from wanting her husband so.

Riley felt it was perfect timing when her own lunch partners appeared at the table. Gloria Reynolds arrived with Beka Sherwood and Drake Gray in tow. The upper-level execs were from the publisher's wing of Cache Media.

"So is it safe to inquire whether we're all on board with this project?" Gloria was asking once the introductions were out of the way.

Riley cast a meaningful look at Misha and then nodded. "Yes, we're all on board."

Asher had already noticed his wife across the dining room. He had a feeling that there was an official tone to the lunch and guessed she was moving forward in accepting the job offer.

It was for the best, he knew, and he pressed his lips together while frowning over the documents he held. The waiter arrived shortly to take orders, and the conversation swelled over lunch requests.

"Why don't you go have a chat with you wife, eh?" Talib was studying his menu as he spoke. "This moving out thing is crazy—especially now."

"It's because it's *especially now* that I have to stay away." Asher's light eyes strayed toward Riley again. "I couldn't survive if something happened to the baby or her because of the stress I'm causing in her."

As much as he wanted to, Talib couldn't argue overmuch with his friend's reasoning.

The lengthy yet productive meeting with Gloria Reynolds and her staff was reaching its end. Riley had taken her third and, hopefully, final trip to the bathroom. She'd heard frequent toilet trips were a side effect of pregnancy, but she was barely showing. She was eager to see how many trips she'd graduate to when a weighty baby was resting on her bladder.

Smiling, she gave herself the once-over in the wide lighted mirror above the row of sinks. Satisfied by how the chestnut-brown, Empire-waisted top hung past the waistband of her fitted cream pants, she headed out of the bathroom and right into Asher, gasping when they collided.

He appeared as subdued as she once they'd both whispered hushed apologies. Silence hung for a time as they hungrily absorbed one another with meaningful looks. Asher was the first to break the spell.

"I waited to stop and speak. Your, uh, lunch partners looked official."

"It's about the job." She wanted to swoon as the crisp scent of his cologne drifted past her nostrils.

Asher nodded while bowing his head. "They looked happy. I guess you decided to take the job."

"Yeah." Her gaze faltered.

"Congratulations."

His mouth was crushing hers in a thorough kiss before she could even think to utter the words *thank you*. Riley melted onto him, grateful for the power in his hold as he cupped her bottom neatly in his palms.

The kiss was just as powerful, with Asher's tongue exploring and caressing every dark cavern of her mouth. Seconds into that, he taunted her tongue into a sensual duel with his own. Riley didn't need much taunting. She was desperate for him and gasped her need without shame. The kiss deepened until he'd crowded her into the most remote corner of the hallway and helped himself to the feel of her lush curves.

"Asher, please." She raked her fingertips through the dark waves of his hair. "Please come home. I miss you."

He winced, deepening the kiss once more as her words skewered his heart. "It's best this way." He nuzzled the hollow beneath her ear, growing intoxicated by the light floral scent clinging to her skin.

"Asher—"

"I don't want to do anything to hurt you."

"But you *are* hurting me." Her moan bordered on a sob. "I need you." Boldly, she cupped the stiff arousal that strained his zipper.

Asher hissed a curse, weakened by the desire to give in and fueled by the need to do what was best. He broke the kiss and pressed his forehead to hers.

"I'll be over soon."

Riley's smoky stare brightened. "Asher—"

"It'll be to get the rest of my stuff."

She seemed to deflate, using the wall for support when he kissed her cheek and walked away.

A smiling Victor Lyne stood at the head of a long, elegantly designed table at dinner as host of a weekend retreat at his house in the Hamptons. He talked of dreams deferred and how fear of failure had kept him from going after his dream of playing pro ball.

"I felt it was too much of a long shot," he said, smiling crookedly while easing a hand into the pocket of the crisp khakis he wore. "I was also scared that even if I *did* grab the dream, I'd get caught up in some stupid lifestyle that would bring me down faster than any injury ever could." He rubbed his hands together and shook his head. "So I did the responsible thing and finished my education, got a good job, met good people. You know, it's funny how a dream deferred can turn into a dream revisited."

"Riley…" He smiled and raised his glass her way. "Working with you has been more than work. It's been a learning experience about everything from politics to sports." He paused when laughter rose from the guests filling the table. "And then I met your husband." He raised his glass again, to Asher that time. "You're all here this weekend because you all played a huge role in my life *before* I got a million-dollar contract."

"*Multimillion*-dollar contract," Talib corrected to a swarm of laughter.

Vic raised his hand as if he were about to testify. "Million-dollar or one-dollar, I consider you all the best people, and I expect you guys to keep my feet on the ground and tell me when I'm acting like a jackass."

"Count on it!" Asher bellowed amid a round of applause.

"I'm happy you decided to come out," Asher was saying as he hugged Misha.

She shrugged and tugged on the cuff of the black cashmere wrap dress she wore. "It's easy to accept invites for free food and drinks. Besides, I'd never forgive myself if I missed out on a chance to spend the night in Vic's plush new digs."

Soft chuckles rumbled between them until Misha saw Talib approaching. "I'll see you later, Asher," She whispered and hurried away.

Asher patted Talib's chest and leaned his head close. "How long will it be before you do something about this?"

Misha took several deep breaths and enjoyed the view of the river. She went to toss back more of her wine and cursed when she discovered her glass was empty. Torn between wanting more wine and not wanting to run into Talib, she stood there debating, with her head bowed.

"Can I get you another?" Talib asked, having watched her with the empty glass for a few moments.

Misha squeezed her eyes shut. "Talib, go. Please leave me alone." There was no response, and eventually Misha turned. "Would you just go?"

Talib moved with an unexpected quickness. Moments later, he was kissing Misha with a sensual desperation that had her clutching the front of his denim shirt. When she began to thrust her tongue against his, he stopped and cupped her chin.

"I'm sorry, love. You wouldn't let me apologize before." With those words, he walked away.

Riley knocked on Asher's door and waited for his call to enter before she did so. He was half dressed, wearing the jeans he'd worn to the dinner party. He was still holding a pair of rolled socks in his hands and listening to a commentary on ESPN. She'd already closed the distance between them and was sauntering around his chair before he had time to stand.

"Did you ask Vic to put us in separate rooms?"

Asher hesitated. His attention was fixated on the transparent thigh-high negligee she wore beneath an unassuming gray terry robe. "I, um…figured it'd be best, considering…"

"We can't get along in an entire apartment, let alone a single room?" she finished, trailing her fingers through his close-cropped hair.

"Riley…" He closed his eyes as the fragrance of her perfume enticed his nostrils.

Asher was about to stand, but Riley stopped him and straddled his lap instead. It was then that he discovered she wore no panties beneath the thin gown. With great effort, he swallowed past the need lodged in his throat.

"Rile—" His speech was thoroughly silenced when she kissed him. Thrusting her tongue madly, she took the remote and clicked off the TV.

Asher was instantly at her mercy and let her maintain control. Riley wasn't interested in sweet words and grinding then. She made quick work of his jeans fastening, freed him and settled herself onto him. Tossing back her head, she closed her eyes and used him as a tool for her pleasure. Asher didn't mind at all and bit his lip while savoring every lift and rotation of her hips. When they were spent, she withdrew and closed her robe on his vibrant gaze. He reached for her when she stood, but Riley simply passed him the remote.

"Good night," she mouthed, waved and left the room.

Victor was determined to show his guests a fine time, and the ten couples on hand woke up to the smells of what promised to be a grand breakfast. There were omelets made especially to order, toast, bagels and an array of breakfast meats, coffees, teas and juices. Of course, Riley's tummy called out louder than anyone else's and she was the first to the table that morning. Dressed comfortably yet stylishly in flare-legged jeans, a chic T-shirt emblazoned with the words New Mommy Here! Riley filled her plate to overflowing and was having a fine time of it when her husband walked into the dining room.

Asher pressed his lips together as an uneasy expression came to his face. He noticed that he and his wife were as yet the only two people in the room. Before Riley noticed him, he took the time to indulge in a moment of sightseeing and watched his wife at the buffet. The T-shirt she sported easily called his attention to her *growing* bosom, and the jeans emphasized the round firmness of her bottom. Before his daydreaming got the better of him, Asher cleared his throat to call attention to his presence.

He searched for a topic of conversation to start their day, figuring that Riley certainly wouldn't want to discuss the events from their previous evening. The previous evening, however, was exactly what she wanted to discuss.

"Did you sleep well after I left?" she asked, politely enough, but the naughtiness was written all over her face. Then she smiled and nodded. "Of course you did. You always sleep well after we...well, you know?" she teased, being intentionally vague and loving the reaction she roused from her husband.

Asher was actually behaving as though he was a bit embarrassed by the whole thing and cleared his throat a bit more than necessary. "Shouldn't you be taking it easy?" he asked while heading over to sample the buffet. "You are pregnant, you know?" he coolly reminded her and settled for a glass of juice first.

"Ah." Riley nodded as though he'd given her something to think about. "And pregnant women can't screw their husbands too enthusiastically, is that it?" When Asher almost choked on his juice, she nodded again and strolled to the table, satisfied that she'd gotten a proper response.

It took Asher several moments to fill his plate, while Riley wolfed down her food in record time. She was actually getting up for a second helping of some items when he was just sitting down for his first. Soon, they were joined by one of the other couples invited to Victor's weekend event.

Jasper and Molly Fasion were old friends of Riley's who worked in Cache Media's marketing department. Asher became fast friends with the native Californians shortly after he and Riley had become an item.

Molly was congratulating them again, while Jasper and Asher shook hands near the table.

"I was just saying to Jas last night that it'd be nice if we could have a little get-together to celebrate the new addition. We hardly get together anymore, and this would be the perfect excuse."

In spite of her earlier outrageousness, Riley wasn't much feeling a party just then and said so.

Molly didn't agree, in spite of her husband's attempts to ask her to let the matter rest. "You guys are New York's premier couple," she boasted, her light brown eyes twinkling with decision. "You've gotta show everyone else how to do it right."

Molly's words roused much-needed laughter from both Riley *and* Asher.

"You may be overstating things a bit, Mol," Asher said through his laughter.

"I don't think so, and I even think it'd be a better idea to make it a real couples weekend—something like what Vic's done here with this little get-together of his."

"Hmm…a couples weekend, huh?" Riley began to warm up to the idea when she heard the suggestion.

Asher shook his head and focused on sweetening his coffee. "I still think it's a little much, guys."

"I actually think it's not a bad idea." Riley put in her two cents and trailed her finger along Asher's jaw when she left the buffet and passed his chair on her way back to the table. "Don't worry, guys. I'm sure I can get him to warm up to the idea."

Asher pushed aside his coffee, losing his taste for anything heated going into his already *overheated* system. By the time the other guests arrived, the conversation had moved on to sports and Vic's signing.

Misha was on her way downstairs for breakfast. She had her room door open and was slipping into a pair of ankle boots when a knock sounded.

"I'm on my way, Riley. Give me a sec, will you?"

There was no response, and she glanced up to see that it was Talib filling her doorway. Straightening slowly, she moved far from the bed and waited.

"Are you going down for breakfast?" he asked.

Misha frowned at the question but managed a nod. "Going down now and running a bit late, I'm afraid, so…" She moved to brush past him and stiffened when he blocked her path through the door.

"Are you okay?" His dark eyes searched every inch of her face as he looked down at her.

Misha let a short laugh lilt from her throat. "What does it matter? You never cared before."

Talib took a deep breath, and a muscle flexed in his square jaw. "We need to talk, love."

"Why are you doing this?" she snapped, banging a fist on her beige carpenter's pants. She cursed herself for feeling tears fill her eyes. She turned back into the bedroom, and Talib followed.

"I'm sorry for upsetting you."

Whirling around, she slammed her hands against his chest. "It's too late for your apologies, dammit, and it's not nearly enough."

"Will you at least give me the chance to talk to you?"

"About what, Tali?" She winced as the sound of his nickname left her mouth. "Will you just go?" She bowed her head.

"I've done enough of that, and I'm sick of it." He gripped her arm. "I want to make things right, Misha."

"Why? It's too late—much too late—and I don't want to go back…rehashing all the ugliness that made up our relationship. I'm done with you, and anything I felt for you has been dead a long time."

"I don't believe you."

"Why?!" She wrenched against his hold on her arm.

He tugged her back easily. "Because when I kissed you last night, I remembered what I lost when I walked away." With those words, he left her alone.

Vic had shared the fact that he'd always wanted a ranch and said that buying the elaborate spread in the Hamptons would be his only vice. Of course, no one believed him, but they appreciated his "non-bling" frame of mind.

Today horseback riding was the order of the day. Talib and Asher drove out to the stables together, and it didn't take much for Talib to latch on to the fact that something had his partner quite preoccupied.

"Good day for a ride…" Talib tried to start a semblance of a conversation.

Asher kept his gaze averted, out the passenger window. "Mmm…"

Enough small talk, Talib decided. "So let's have it then.

What's going on?" he said. "That bad, huh?" he added when almost a full minute passed with no response.

Asher shook his head, as if in a daze. "It's gonna be harder than I thought to stick to my decision not to move back into the apartment for a while. Riley's…getting very aggressive," he shared and wasn't happy to hear Talib's resulting laughter.

"Sorry, mate. I just can't help but recall that it was *you* who toyed with the idea of seducing her into going back to Phoenix with you. Now she's turning the tables."

Asher grimaced. "Boy, is she turning the tables…," he agreed, and his expression grew murderous at Talib's humorous reaction. "So how'd it go last night with Misha?" he asked, deciding to turn the conversation in another direction.

It worked, and Talib was immediately on edge. "What's that supposed to mean?"

Asher shrugged, loving the turnabout. "Both of you were real quiet this morning…."

Talib grunted and dropped the hard act. "I don't know what the hell's happening," he admitted.

"You want her back."

"Every day."

Asher grinned. "So what's stopping you?"

"Misha. She doesn't believe. She doesn't trust me." He rolled his eyes away from the stunning view beyond the windows. "Bloody hell, I can't blame her…."

"So are you gonna let it go at that?"

"I can't." Talib flexed his hand around the steering wheel. "I never should've kissed her."

This time it was Asher's laughter that filled the SUV. "Well, well, and what brought that on?"

"I don't know why…"

"You want her back, remember? And now the hard part is making her believe in you again."

Talib smirked. "I couldn't have said it better myself."

Riley and Misha were driving toward the stables just then as well. "I've come all the way out here, and now I can't even go horseback riding. I never should've called Lett." Riley referred to her doctor, who had forbidden her to even look at a horse.

"It's for your own good." Misha's voice was as absent as the look on her face.

Riley noticed right away. "Honey, are you okay?"

Silence.

"Please don't make me beg. Is this about Talib?" she asked when Misha offered no information.

"Yes."

Riley nodded at the uncharacteristically lost tone in her friend's voice. "You wanna talk about it?"

Misha waved off the suggestion. "Talking about it just makes it real, and this is just Talib being…I don't know…"

"Don't you think he's serious?"

"He's not."

"But how—"

"He's not, Riley, all right!" She bit out the words.

Riley drove in silence for a while. "Maybe he's regretting the way he handled things before."

"He's not. He doesn't know what he's saying."

"I remember when I used to say that about Asher."

Misha rolled her eyes. "Whatever you do, please don't sit there and try to compare Talib and me to you and Asher."

Riley shook her head. "All I'm saying is maybe you should hear him out."

"No."

"Why?"

"Riley…"

"Hey?" She pulled over and stopped the SUV. "Talk to me."

Misha fought an inner battle with herself. Years of playing the cool, hard role warred with her desire to share. Finally, she began to speak. "I went down an ugly road when things fizzled with me and Talib. It was a scary road, and I…I almost didn't come back from it, Ri."

"Misha…" Riley sighed, understanding the full scope of what her best friend was confiding.

"I can't let him back in, Riley." She bristled and focused

straight ahead. "If that means letting him think I'm the worst type of woman, then so be it. So be it."

"It's all right…" Riley soothed and pulled Misha into a hug as she sobbed.

"You really didn't have to stay, Asher."

"When you have the baby, we can ask Vic to have us out here again. We'll do it up right, horseback riding and all," he promised.

The couple sat perched on the hood of one of the SUVs and watched the dust kicking up in the wake of the horseback riders as they set off for the day.

A chill shimmied up Riley's spine, and she hugged herself.

"What?" Asher propped his chin on his fist.

"We're about to be parents," Riley whispered in disbelief.

He hooked a hand beneath her knee and pulled her close. "We're gonna do fine."

"Promise?" Riley spoke into his denim-clad shoulder.

He chuckled. "Sure. Don't you know we're New York's premier couple?"

She laughed then, too. "We've made a mess of things, haven't we?"

He pressed a hard kiss to her head. "We have at that, darlin'."

"I'm scared, Asher."

"Me, too, love."

They sat, embracing and silent, for the longest time.

Chapter 18

Over breakfast one morning, Virginia Stamper made the decision that she'd stirred her coffee long enough. The time had come to either drink it down or spit out the question that had been gnawing its way up her throat.

"Are you really sure about this, girl? You've lived in New York all your life." Realizing her coffee had gone cold amid all the stirring, Virginia left the table. "I've known people who moved to the burbs after living in the city all their lives and went crazy." She dumped the coffee and refilled her mug with a fresh serving. "It's true," she said, with a wink, while pouring.

Riley burst into laughter.

"What's so funny?" She sipped the dark brew, adding cream and sugar until the taste was acceptable to her. "I'm a nurse. I know these things."

Riley used the sleeve of her lavender chenille robe to wipe tears of laughter from her eyes. "I'm certain about this, Ma." Her demeanor began to sober. "I'm also uncertain. Does that make any sense at all?"

"Yes and no."

"Ma…"

"Now, now, I'm not trying to be funny." Virginia gave the marble countertop a quick wipe down and returned to the table. "What you've said is very easy to understand. Your emotions are all over the place, baby. The decisions you have to make aren't easy ones." She pursed her lips and blew at the surface of the coffee. "I *am* curious, though, about what's got you browsing real estate catalogs. Asher's…ultimatum stipulated that you move back to Phoenix, not just relocate outside the city."

"I know." Riley pushed away the plate, which had been loaded with fluffy scrambled eggs, turkey bacon and toast. "Even though he said he was wrong to give that ultimatum, I know he wants me and the baby in Phoenix with him. He's not asking for the utterly impossible, Ma. He just wants his family together."

Virginia kept her almond-shaped stare on her coffee. "So what will you do?"

"Regardless of how *noble* Asher's motives are, this is where I want to be." She shrugged. "I'm just not sure I want my child slam in the middle of it. Asher's right. The city is not a prime place to raise a child if you can give it more. That's what I want to do." She stood and selected one of the realty brochures from the counter.

Riley went on. "That's why I started looking at these things. We're going to outgrow this before the baby outgrows its diapers. Ma?" Riley noticed Virginia wiping from her cheek what looked suspiciously like a tear. "Are you all right?" She knelt beside her mother's chair.

"My baby's gonna be a mama." She sighed and put a smile in place. "More importantly, she's beginning to sound like one."

Riley laughed. Bubbling through her were the twin emotions of love for her mother and exuberance over the fact that the woman was truly proud of her. Mother and daughter laughed and cried while sharing a tight hug.

While Riley spoke to her mother regarding her real estate choices, Asher was standing smack-dab in the middle of his own real estate dilemma.

Talib whistled while scoping out the view from the gargantuan penthouse office.

"Does that mean you approve?"

Talib shook his head. "It's worth it for the view."

Asher eased both his hands inside olive-green trouser pockets and waited for a more substantial reply.

Talib massaged the back of his neck and turned his back on the Manhattan view. "Without question, we can fill the whole damn skyscraper with bodies and make tons of money. But can you take being back here on the regular, mate?"

Asher nodded, having expected that very question. Talib probably knew him better than his wife did.

"That's why I've yet to sign on the dotted line." Asher began to stroll the perimeter of the office.

Talib chose his spot along a wide window ledge. "You're still hoping she'll change her mind?"

Asher grunted a laugh. "I know that won't happen. I don't want it to, not because of some ultimatum I've issued."

"So what is it, then?" Talib tossed his eggshell suit coat on the ledge.

Asher stopped his strolling. "I want to be where my child is. I want to be where Riley is, and I can do that from here and still make tons of money."

"Except?"

"*Except* I need to come clean with her before we make this thing concrete."

"Ah." Talib's handsome face was alive with sudden delight. "So you'll finally tell her what happened that night?"

"I've waited long enough, right?"

"Amen."

Asher studied the tip of his tie. "You think I made too much of it, don't you?"

"Things got way out of hand that night, and I believe you have beaten yourself up over it for way too long."

"If I hadn't froze up that night—"

"You'd probably be just as dead as that son of a bitch who busted up that store. Telling Riley's the thing to do, but unless *you* get past it, it'll haunt you and your actions forever."

"And just how do I *get past* it?" In spite of a quick laugh, there was still a noticeable bite to his tone.

Talib shrugged. "It'll take time, I know. But you're makin' a big step by facing your fears now." He grabbed his suit coat and clapped Asher's shoulder on the way out of the office.

Alone, Asher admitted that he hadn't come close to facing his fears. Not when his biggest fear was talking to his wife.

* * *

"What the hell are you doing!" Misha was fit to be tied when she found Riley in the kitchen, getting napkins from a cabinet. "You *are* the guest of honor *and* pregnant, you know? You should be off your feet and enjoying being spoiled, because once the baby comes, all this will be over, sista."

Riley's laughter came in uncontrollable waves. "It's only napkins—not that thousand-pound cake you're about to heft out of here."

Misha tapped a nail on her chin. "If I didn't know you better, I'd swear you were happy about this party."

Riley winked. "Well, I am. Besides, I needed to blow off some steam. I would've never expected a baby shower to do that. But here we are." She slapped her hands on the sides of her denim capris.

Misha nodded, understanding all too well. "So I guess turning this thing into a girls-only mommy-to-be event was all right?" she asked.

Riley drew her friend into a hug. "It was *very* all right."

"So what's the haps on the house?" Misha asked when they drew apart. "You haven't said much about the place since we went to take a look with Miss V a few days ago."

In response, Riley puffed out her cheeks and went to lean against the counter.

"I know you must've loved it. *I* loved it." Misha pressed a hand to her chest and pretended to swoon. "So you've just got to buy it because I really need a place like that to kick back in after a hard workweek."

Riley laughed, but the humor didn't quite reach her eyes. "It just, um…put a bad taste in my mouth, that's all."

Misha concentrated. "Could've been morning sickness, you know?"

Riley managed a smirk for good measure. "It was a beautiful place, Mish. Incredible but…"

"If Asher's not there, then incredible might be too strong a phrase?" Misha nodded when Riley smiled her agreement.

"What can I say, Misha? I want the job, the house, the baby

and the man. I want it all. Why's that proving to be so impossible to have?"

"Best things in life are usually the most difficult to acquire." Misha turned to pull the cover off the cake.

"Amen." Riley sighed.

Silence hung between the two, until their friends began to call out from the living room. Misha nudged Riley's shoulder then. "You get the napkins. I'll grab the cake."

"Scandalous wenches…" Riley whispered two hours later as she tried on the third of five pieces of baby-doll lingerie her guests had presented her with.

According to the group of women who'd attended the party, there'd be cause for two showers. The first was for baby, of course, and the second was for mommy. And they had taken that quite seriously, having plied the mom-to-be with everything from sparkling grape juices and bath oils to her favorite chocolates and dirty movies.

Riley stood admiring herself in the full-length mirror just outside the walk-in closet. She smiled happily at the ever-rounder protrusion at her waist.

"Good thing I tried these on now, huh, kid?" Riley helped herself to a piece of chocolate and then flopped on the bed, where she shuffled through a few of the movies while glancing at the one presently playing on the television screen. Eventually, her glances grew lengthier, and soon she was wholly focused on the screen while absently nibbling the chocolate.

She was still entranced when her husband strolled into the bedroom. Asher's mouth fell open at the sight of his wife, looking every bit the sinful dark treat atop a cake. As he leaned against the doorjamb, his handsome honey-toned face was a picture of stunned delight. Then he took note of the TV, and a smile tugged at the curve of his mouth.

"This any good?"

Surprised to find him there, Riley maintained her cool and offered a shrug with her guilty smile. "It was a gift from friends."

Asher whistled. "Wanna trade friends?"

"My *baby* shower was actually a mommy shower." Riley helped herself to another peanut butter cup.

"Ah…" Asher brushed the back of his hand against his scar. "Misha's idea," he guessed.

Riley snapped her fingers. "Give the man a cigar."

Asher's striking light browns narrowed at her attire once more. "I'll have to remember to thank her." He pushed off the doorjamb to ease out of the jacket, which was suddenly stifling him.

Riley pressed her lips together when a heavy silence touched the room. "So are you here for more of your stuff?" She felt desperate to make conversation.

Asher was checking his jacket pocket. "I have a present for you, too." He pulled out a square velvet box.

Riley took it in both hands when he came to the bed. She lifted the box and smiled. "Guess it's not another dress?"

"Open it."

His serious tone caused her to clear her throat. She did as he asked, gasping when she saw the solid gold frame with their picture on one side. The other side was empty.

"'My love, our life, my love.'" She looked up after reading the inscription.

Asher took his place on the edge of the bed. "For the baby's ultrasound photo, when we have it." His index finger tapped the empty side of the frame.

"Asher…"

Across the frame he leaned, cupping her neck and nuzzling her nose with his. "I love you…and I *do* miss you."

"Come home…."

He pleasured her with a thorough kiss as opposed to giving her an answer. The coral and lavender baby-doll teddy had teased him for far too long. He set about helping himself to what lay beneath. Gently and with unwavering intent, he moved closer in a silent demand that she lie back.

"I love you…."

"Come home," she begged, her hands venturing beneath the hem of his jersey to stroke the array of muscles lining his abdomen. "Asher, please, I—" Her words ended on another gasp when he suckled her earlobe while his fingers delved into the crotchless bikinis and inside her body.

Biting her lip, Riley arched into the touch. She rode his fingers with abandon, having missed his touch so much more than she'd realized.

Asher pulled back only a tad, to pleasure himself by the look of sheer bliss on her lovely face. Still fondling her, he bowed his head, his perfect teeth untying the singular fastening of the lingerie.

Riley was lost in a myriad of sensations as his nose trailed along her collarbone and down and around the curve of her breast and the valley between. When his tongue outlined her nipple, she whimpered. When he suckled so lightly she could scarcely feel it, she sobbed. Desperately, she arched more of herself against his mouth as a silent invite that he take more—much more. She curved her hand about the back of his neck to make him obey, but he had other intentions.

Turning the tables, Asher captured her wrists in his free hand and held them above her head. All the while, he tortured her with the scandalous finger thrusts and the light suckling of her nipple.

"Mmm…Asher, please…please stop playing around."

He chuckled. "Stop playing around? But you're my favorite toy."

"At least take off your clothes…"

Asher knew if he did that, the moment could be done with all too soon. Just then his wife's satisfaction was his only agenda. Riley's toes flexed into his thighs as her desire mounted when he finally suckled her nipples fully. When he alternated between them, her delighted laughter filled the room.

"That's it…." Her moan was throaty and uninhibited. She began to strain against his hold on her wrists, but he held her fast. Adding another finger to the caress, Asher grunted when the creamy moisture drenched his skin.

Riley felt him release her wrists, and she celebrated her freedom. She went back to pulling the jersey from his back, but Asher moved before she could finish the chore. Kissing his way down her body, he stopped to nuzzle his face against the soft swell of her belly.

He encircled the area with his nose and then showered it with the most tender kisses. Those kisses adopted a new fire as he journeyed downward, across the smattering of hair dusting the triangle above her womanhood. His mouth brushed the sensitive flesh of her sex just before his tongue tasted the damp brought on by his generous affection.

The intimate kiss was thoroughly probing. Instead of thrusting, his tongue delved farther and farther, as if he were testing the depth of a well. Again, Riley tugged her lip between her teeth while rotating herself into his delicious exploration of her body.

Asher set his hands beneath her, and the penetration increased tenfold. Once more, Riley sobbed from the pleasure. When she began to tremble uncontrollably, he showed mercy, brushing kisses across her inner thighs as the orgasm ripped through her.

When Riley felt him next to her, he was as naked as she. Linking her arms about him, she worshiped his jaw with wet kisses as he claimed her. The second orgasm built just as deliciously as the first. Riley's whimpers took on urgency as she sought to take all that Asher had to give.

Chapter 19

Riley woke, still surrounded by all her sexy presents, but there was no sign of her sexy husband. A stab of disappointment turned her satisfied smile into a momentary pout. But then memories of the night before emerged to stir a dull ache at the heart of her. With great effort, she cast aside the sweet images and prayed Asher would stay closer to her now.

One of the X-rated flicks Misha had bought was lying on Asher's pillow. Riley noticed a sticky note on its cover, which read, *This is a good one!* and was scribbled in Asher's distinct handwriting.

Riley's laughter filled the room then. With a sudden burst of energy claiming her, not to mention the urge to pee, she whipped back the covers. She noticed the frame on the nightstand and recalled that she'd given Asher every clue to make him aware of how much she wanted him home.

In the end, however, it was always Asher's way or no way. Unfair? Certainly. Still, Riley was fast approaching the point where she didn't care. She wanted her husband. She wanted to raise her child with its father. She knew then that she'd sacrifice anything else to have that.

"When exactly do you plan to talk to your wife about all this?" Talib was asking as he topped off his coffee that morning.

Asher didn't raise his gaze from the building contract. "Soon. Guess I better before Hayes runs that story, huh?" He referred to their sports reporter friend Hayes Ortiz.

"There's also a lot of talent out there wanting to switch to

Hud-Mason," Talib noted, without sounding at all cocky. "Lot of talk out there that'll probably beat Hayes's story to the punch."

"Doubt she'll be upset by it."

Talib's brown eyes twinkled. "Yet you're still dragging your feet by not telling her?"

Asher rapped his knuckles against the contract. "We ready to sign here?"

"Ready as we'll ever be."

"What else is on the schedule for today?"

"Got a meet with Rake Crawford's physician at one. Why? You in a rush?"

Asher clapped Talib's shoulder and stood. "Seems I need to have a serious and lengthy chat with my wife, mate."

Gloria Reynolds smoothed both hands across her sheer hose while recrossing her legs. "Are you really sure about this, Riley? You've waited for a chance like this for as long as I've known you." Her surprise was what would be expected in light of the decision her brightest writer had come to share.

Riley's expression relayed just as much surprise, yet it also conveyed delight. "I never thought I'd want a chance to be a mom, either." She shrugged. "I can't think of a better use of my life than this."

"But to quit the paper, Riley?" Gloria leaned forward, her firm voice hushed with disbelief. "Many women manage to balance work and motherhood, you know? You certainly don't have to quit your job."

"I do if I want my husband." Riley raised her hands to ward off Gloria's rebuttal. "I know, I know... It pisses me off, too. But he wants his wife and child where he is. How can I condemn him for that?"

Gloria's expression softened, and she tucked an auburn lock behind her ear. "I realize his organization is a multibillion-dollar outfit. Guess I'd expect it to be easier for him to be where *you* are."

"Yeah...I thought so, too." Riley set the teacup and saucer she held on the small round table between her and Gloria's chairs. "It's just that I'm at the point where I'm not willing to risk my marriage and family by playing the holdout game." Absently, she fidgeted with the hem of the hunter-green swing dress she wore. "I do plan to find out about his aversion to being here in New York, but I guess I'll just have to do that in Phoenix."

"I rest my case." Gloria rubbed her hands across the carved arms of her chair. "But I have to tell you, I've got a feeling that you're underestimating your husband here. Some men rise to a higher level when they become fathers. I wouldn't be surprised if he changes his mind about demanding you go out there. He wouldn't be the first man to have a baby turn him into a soft-hearted sap." She leaned over to pat Riley's knee. "You'll understand if I don't take your name out of the loop just yet?"

Riley's laughter filled the office. "Whatever makes you feel better." She glanced at her watch and cursed. "I'm gonna be late for my doctor's appointment." She leaned over to kiss Gloria's cheek and then hurried out.

Asher was making a notation in his PDA when Talib stepped into the hallway outside the doctor's office.

"Crawford's doc says his decision on whether he'll be cleared for next season depends on how well the ankle surgery goes next month. All the other diagnoses we discussed in there look promising, but there will be another check following the surgery."

"Mmm…" Asher continued making notes in the BlackBerry handheld. "Any specific date on that?"

Talib provided the info while he and Asher strolled toward the elevator bay, discussing the particulars. Asher was slipping the BlackBerry handheld into his coat when his bright eyes locked on his wife exiting one of the elevator cars at the far end of the corridor.

"See you later, Tal." Asher walked in the direction she'd taken.

Riley was easing her keys into her purse when she felt her arm being clutched. "Hey!" she gasped, whirling around to see that it was Asher who'd caught her.

"Hey," he responded in kind and followed the greeting with a throaty kiss, in which she eagerly participated.

Asher dropped his forehead to her shoulder. "What are you doing here?"

"Doctor's appointment." She tried to catch her breath. "And you?"

"Same. For a potential client." He raised his head and smiled down at her. "You want company?"

She nodded quickly as a rush of happiness filled her chest. Arm in arm, they strolled to Lettia's office.

"We need to talk," Riley said.

Asher nudged her shoulder with his. "Damn right."

They stepped into the office and were greeted promptly. Riley was right on time for the appointment, so they didn't have to wait to be shown to an examining room.

Silently, they removed their coats. The hungry look in Asher's eyes as they raked the cashmere swing dress she sported gave Riley pause.

"You okay?" she asked when his stare took on a deeper intensity.

"I miss you."

His simple response almost stopped her heart, yet she gave him a playful smile. "You saw me just this morning, remember?"

Asher ran the back of his hand across his scar. "Perhaps you could remind me…but Dr. Lett's gonna walk in on more than she bargains for."

The electric tension in the room was somewhat doused, however, by the time the good doctor entered the examining room.

"Asher Hudson! Fine and scrumptious as always!" Lettia boasted and greeted the man with a hug and kiss.

"Lett! You always make a man feel welcomed." He savored the hug and kept hold of Lettia's hand as they crossed the room.

They discussed things in an idle, cursory fashion at first. Lettia directed the majority of her comments to Asher, knowing he'd be curious. This was the first appointment he'd made it to with his wife. She explained what the exam would consist of: checking Riley's blood pressure, the baby's heart rate, vitals, etcetera. Then she looked over at her patient and winked.

"Let's see if that bed rest I prescribed has done any good."

Neither Riley nor Lettia noticed Asher's reaction to the piece of news he'd had no clue about.

After performing and reviewing the tests, Lettia's lovely round face was an image of satisfaction. Everything, including Riley's stress levels, appeared very much improved.

"I'll see you in two weeks, hon," Lettia said as she made a few notations on her pad and then eased her pen into a pocket on her coat. She fixed Asher with a dazzling smile. "Good to see you, sweetie." She hugged and kissed his cheek again. "Don't make this your last visit, okay?"

He winked and cupped her chin. "Don't worry."

Lettia headed out to her next appointment, leaving the couple alone. Riley grabbed her bag and was preparing to leave as well.

"Bed rest. Why didn't you tell me?" asked Asher.

"What difference does it make?" Riley shrugged slowly; it was clear that she had no clue how upset he was. "Everything's fine now." She glanced up and noticed his rising temper. Unconsciously, she retreated as he moved toward her.

"Fine *now*, but not then, right?"

Riley dropped her bag and swallowed around the ball of emotion wedged in her throat. Every bit of his anger clung to the words he spoke.

"Why the hell didn't you tell me, Ri?"

"I didn't. So what happens now? I've rattled your cage once again. So what's the penalty?" Her own temper was loosed, and it felt so good to show him how angry she was, too. "What's the penalty, Asher? Serve me with divorce papers, go back to Phoenix and wait me out? What's the ultimatum now?"

Asher only rolled his eyes and put space between them.

"We were going through enough, Asher." She sighed, massaging her neck as she turned away as well. "Hell, you were moving out. Telling you that Lett put me on bed rest wouldn't have done a damn thing except upset an already upsetting situation. We didn't need that. *I* didn't need that. *I'm* the one carrying the baby, remember?"

"I remember." His voice was soft—too soft. She was right, of course; he admitted it and wanted to kick himself for once again playing the selfish jerk. "I'm sorry, Riley. For everything. If…if it weren't for my ultimatums and other bullshit, you might never have been confined to a bed."

Riley felt a pang of regret then as well. She wouldn't let him take all the blame. "I've got a very hectic lifestyle, you know?" She spread her hands about her. "In a city like this, I can understand why you were so hung up on my leaving."

"Riley, please." He rubbed the side of his nose in a show of sudden weariness.

"It's understandable, Asher. You just care, and I gave you such a hard time—"

"Riley, *please*." He waited for her to take heed to his tone that time. "My *hang-ups* about New York began way before I ever set eyes on you."

Silent, Riley leaned back on the desk and prayed he'd continue. She prayed he'd *finally* continue.

Asher flipped his coat across a chair. "Do you remember my knee injury?"

She nodded. "You were shot. A convenience store robbery you walked in on."

Asher nodded then, too, while raking a hand through the dark waves covering his head.

"There was more to the story, wasn't there?" she asked.

He wouldn't look her way, preferring instead to go stare out of the examining room windows.

"I remember the mom… She was so grateful to you, and you were being called a hero." She focused on her hands and realized she'd been wringing them. "You never told me all that went on there. I always figured there was a lot more."

Asher chuckled briefly, his gaze still focused on the street below. Pulling a hand from his trouser pocket, he stroked his jaw. "Yeah, there was a whole helluva lot more."

"I remember it was all over the news for weeks. I remember them talking to you, and I couldn't help but wonder what it must've been like inside that store—the pro baller stumbling into a robbery and saving a mom and her kids from a madman."

Asher had turned from the windows and was watching his wife, with a look mixed with surprise and curiosity. "You saw me on TV?"

Riley laughed. "At first, I was just interested in the story because you were so damned good to look at…." She shook her head at the memory. "Then I started to really listen to your story. There was something in your eyes…I don't know… It was like what you were saying was a gloss. Not all the story, you know?"

He smirked. "I see why you're so good at your job." His easy expression faded into something haunted. "The media never uncovered the connection between the gunman and the woman. They were too dazzled by my involvement. They'd lived together several years. The kids were his, too. He'd been abusing her, and then he did her a favor and walked out on 'em. She got it together on her own. She was very…independent." He sent Riley a knowing look. "Anyway, he decided he wanted back in, started following her. She went into the store that night for cold medicine, and he came in, with the gun, to *persuade* her. He shot the clerk on sight."

Asher began to walk the examining room as memories returned. "I walked in while they were arguing." He shook his head. "I'm no hero, Riley. The guy freaked the minute he saw me. Shot me. I never knew what hit me. Fell. Cut my face." He waved toward the scar. "He was satisfied I was down…shot out the tape system and camera for good measure. Then he turned to yell at the woman some more. It got uglier and uglier. It all happened like that." He snapped his fingers. "He hit her, and she pushed him, caught him off guard. He fell into a display, dropped the gun." Asher seemed to shudder then and took a moment to breathe deep into his hands. "When he went to look for it, he found it in the hands of his eight-year-old son. The kid shot him…point-blank, all on target, all through the heart."

Riley covered her mouth. Her eyes were wide.

"She thought fast." Asher remembered, spilling the story as though he were pouring water from a pitcher. "She took the gun, wiped it down, tossed it…She begged me not to tell anyone what had really happened. Cops showed up. They just assumed…the guy had a record as long as my arm. Clerk was unconscious during the whole thing but stated it was the guy who shot him. It was October, so everyone had gloves. There was no question about prints on the gun. Everybody assumed I just walked in, surprised the guy and wrestled him for the gun. They all figured I got one to the knee for my trouble before putting half a clip in the fool's chest. We never changed the story."

"What happened to the mother and her kids?"

For the first time, Asher's expression seemed to brighten. "Most of her family was in Puerto Rico. She moved back there."

Riley was seated in a chair before the desk by then. Her arms wrapped tight about her, she shook her head out of sheer awe.

"I loved you so much," he said. "I wanted you—all of you." He moved closer to where she sat. "Didn't matter where you were or about the distance…at first." He reached out to rub a silky lock of her clipped hair between his fingers. "Then the excitement of having an unorthodox marriage wore off, and I just wanted us to be like everyone else—under the same roof, in the same bed, preferably mine." He sighed and slipped a hand inside his suit coat to massage his heart. "I negotiate million-dollar deals without breaking a sweat and was arrogant enough to think wearing you down would be a cakewalk." He knelt before her then. "You told me you were pregnant, and…it took me right back to that night in the store, watching that kid kill his father. No love in his eyes, no recognition… All the boy saw was a stranger." His lashes fluttered and closed over his eyes. "I don't want my child to see me like that."

"Asher." Riley pulled him into a desperate hug. "It won't. I swear it won't."

"How can you say that?" He pulled back, searching her gaze with the same desperation that fueled their embrace. "I'm in Phoenix. *Phoenix*, Riley. And what happens when the kid starts school? How often will I get to see him or her? How often will I get to see you?" He buried his face in his hands and groaned. "I been goin' out of my mind thinking about this. I know it's all in the future."

Riley squeezed his hands in hers. "Obsessing about the future is a necessary side effect of parenthood, I think. I'm afraid you're stuck with it. So am I, for that matter." Smiling then, she grabbed her bag from the floor and withdrew a photo of the home she'd been considering. "City's a great place. Many wonderful kids are raised here, with great lives, but if given a chance, I think many parents would opt for a house and backyard for their child to mill around in."

Asher took the photo.

"It's a really nice place in Bedford," she explained while Asher studied the photo. "It'll be easy for my mom and your parents to drive in to see their only grandchild. My mom's already seen it. She loves it."

"Do *you* love it?" Asher continued to scan the snapshot.

She nodded quickly. "I love it."

"Then so do I." He raised a hand when she started to speak. "I want to be where *you* are." He curved a hand around her belly. "Where you both are. Doesn't matter where—either a small, cramped apartment in NYC or a flashy house in the burbs. I love you."

"I love you," Riley breathed and plied him with a sweet kiss. Cupping his face in her hands, she pulled back, wearing a coy smile. "I want to be where you are, too, but a big, flashy house may be a bit hard to pull off since I just quit my job."

"You quit? You're serious?"

"We need you," she swore, her heart soaring when she saw the light spark in his eyes. "Can you support us, Mr. Hudson?" She linked her arms about his neck.

He shrugged, nuzzling her ear with his nose. "I can probably keep us comfy, in baby food and diapers for a few months, but then you're gonna have to go and ask Gloria for your job back. If I gotta work, so do you." He sobered a bit then. "If that's what you want. If you're okay with stayin' home and raising my babies, then I'm good with that, too."

Riley laughed. "I really love you." She kissed him slow. Then she pulled back again, as if troubled. "What about Talib? How's he gonna feel about this?"

"He'll like it just fine." Asher rested his head on her thigh and delighted himself with rubbing the back of her knee. "He's always wanted to be the lone dog out in Phoenix. Doesn't think I know it." He looked up and graced her with a sly wink. "If I can tear myself away from you guys, I'm gonna have to try filling this building we just bought with bodies to assist all these new East Coast clients we've got."

Riley's head was spinning. "New—new building? East Coast clients?"

"We decided to establish another office here. It would be more convenient for our clients in this part of the country and Vic's deal brought in even more."

"Asher… Are you *really* sure about this? Really? This is all wonderful, but I was prepared to go back with you to Phoenix."

His smile was serene. "I don't want you to do that, because you don't want to do that. I love you. Once I reminded myself how much, all the other decisions were easy."

"Asher…"

"Now can we get past all this and focus on the fun stuff?"

"Oh, Daddy." Riley moved her forehead against his. "That's the best thing you've said all day." She watched him press a kiss to their baby, still slumbering in her belly, before he favored her mouth with the same attention.

Epilogue

Seven months later…

Mother's Day in the maternity ward at St. Joseph's was usually quite an eventful time, but everyone acknowledged that this particular day was even more eventful.

The news had quickly spread that super couple Asher Hudson and Riley Stamper had given birth to a healthy baby boy. The new mom couldn't help but wonder if Misha had done something to ensure those results, as she'd been so certain Riley would provide her with a little nephew. Of course, Riley didn't have time to dwell on the matter for long, since her attention was completely centered on the tiny, beautiful man in her arms.

Still, a small portion of the new mom's attention was given to the tiny man's father. Asher rested his chin on her shoulder while staring down, totally absorbed with his son.

"Thank you, thank you…" His tone was soft, almost reverent.

She brushed her mouth across his jaw. "Thank *you*."

"So does anyone know about all of us yet?"

"Well, Misha ran out with her phone," Riley said when Asher laughed. "I'm sure all of New York'll be in here before the day is out."

"And have we decided on this guy's name?"

Riley gasped. "I've only been calling him 'my little angel' for the past seven months," she said and drew the baby close to nuzzle a satiny caramel-toned cheek.

Asher pressed a kiss to his son's palm. "I've been callin' him 'big guy'…guess they won't let us put either of those on the birth certificate, huh?"

"I don't think so."

The parents contemplated in silence, agreeing that the baby should have its own identity. Riley noted that she wouldn't mind the two most important men in her life having names beginning with *A*. After little debate, they settled on the name Ahmad.

"You think he'll like it?" Riley whispered.

The parents' contemplation was interrupted by the almost inaudible sound of their son's yawn. Riley's eyes filled with tears, and Asher clenched his jaw when his heart lurched in response to the sound.

"I think he likes it." Asher gave a soft tug on the blue blanket swaddling the child. "I like it, too, but I think this man wants to sleep on it a while." He nuzzled Riley's ear with the tip of his nose. "Personally, I can't think of a better time for a nap. What do you say, Mom?"

She showered his jaw with kisses. "Daddy, didn't you know that *sleep* is a new mommy's favorite word?"

Asher and Riley shared a chuckle before sharing a lengthy kiss. Moments later, the new family drifted off into a delightful nap.

When you can't trust anyone, the only thing
you can do is trust your heart....

Essence Bestselling Author

GWYNNE FORSTER

PRIVATE LIVES

Following a bitter divorce, Allison Sawyer seeks seclusion at
a rustic mountain retreat. Though attracted to her neighbor,
Brock Lightner, she's wary and keeps her distance. Intrigued
by Allison, Brock wonders who she's running from—and how
he can convince her he'll do anything to protect her.

"A delightful book romance lovers will enjoy."
—*Romantic Times BOOKreviews*
on *Love Me or Leave Me*

*Coming the first week of March 2009
wherever books are sold.*

KIMANI™
ROMANCE

www.kimanipress.com
www.myspace.com/kimanipress   KPGFI040309

Are they ready for their close-up?

Essence **Bestselling Author**

LINDA HUDSON-SMITH

Romancing THE RUNWAY

It seems as if supermodels Kennedy and Xavier have it all—hot careers and each other. But crazed schedules, constant media attention and unruly paparazzi threaten their fragile new relationship. Can their searing physical attraction and soul-deep connection be enough to guarantee a picture-perfect ending?

Coming the first week of March 2009
wherever books are sold.

KIMANI™
ROMANCE

www.kimanipress.com
www.myspace.com/kimanipress

Welcome to Temptation Island...

Fan Favorite Author

Michelle Monkou

Only in PARADISE

For teacher Athena Crawford, the career opportunity of a
lifetime is set on an idyllic Caribbean island. But then she
and her project's administrator, Collin Winslow, start locking
horns—and sharing kisses. Can their delicate relationship
weather the storms about to break?

Coming the first week of March 2009 wherever books are sold.

KIMANI™
ROMANCE

REQUEST YOUR FREE BOOKS!

2 FREE NOVELS
PLUS 2 *FREE GIFTS!*

Love's ultimate destination!

National bestselling author

ROCHELLE ALERS

Naughty

Parties, paparazzi, red-carpet catfights…

Wild child Breanna Parker's antics have
always been a ploy to gain attention from
her diva mother and record-producer father.
As her marriage implodes, Bree moves to
Rome. There she meets charismatic Reuben,
who becomes both her romantic and business
partner. But just as she's enjoying her
successful new life, Bree is confronted
with a devastating scandal that threatens
everything she's worked so hard for.…

*Coming the first week of March 2009
wherever books are sold.*

KIMANI PRESS™

**www.kimanipress.com
www.myspace.com/kimanipress**

KPRA1280309

New York Times

BRENDA
JACKSON

invites you to continue your journey
with the always sexy and always satisfying
Madaris family novels....

FIRE AND DESIRE
January 2009

SECRET LOVE
February 2009

TRUE LOVE
March 2009

SURRENDER
April 2009

ARABESQUE®

www.kimanipress.com
www.myspace.com/kimanipress   KPBJREISSUES09